HOW TO KISS YOUR GRUMPY BOSS

HOW TO KISS YOUR GRUMPY BOSS

JENNY PROCTOR

Srishti
PUBLISHERS & DISTRIBUTORS

Srishti Publishers & Distributors
A unit of AJR Publishing LLP
212A, Peacock Lane
Shahpur Jat, New Delhi – 110 049

editorial@srishtipublishers.com

First published in India by
Srishti Publishers & Distributors in 2024

First Published by Jenny Proctor Creative in 2022

10 9 8 7 6 5 4 3 2 1

Printed and bound in India

For Lucy
Wait for it. I promise.

Chapter One

Perry

I DON'T HAVE A lot of experience sweet talking pigs.

Which is unfortunate, because I'm face-to-face with a three-hundred-pound behemoth armed with nothing but my charm, a bag of apples, and opposable thumbs.

Trouble is, I've never been very charming, and this pig might actually be smarter than I am. It's the only way to explain how she got out of her fully secure enclosure where there is no sign of escape. If she left through the gate, she closed it on her way out. And she *doesn't* have opposable thumbs.

Pig, one. Perry, zero.

"It's just you and me, Buttercup," I say, rolling an apple toward her snout. She looks up, one ear twitching. The look in her eye says I'm not nearly as interesting as the cabbage she's eating out of my brother's garden. "Come on. Apples are better than cabbage. Any fool knows that."

She snuffles and finally shifts toward the apple, and I wince at the snap and crackle of the crushed leaves and broken stems she's leaving in her wake.

It's a good thing Lennox is out of town. Though truthfully, I'd endure his scolding if it meant having his help. Or anyone's help. For being a commercial farm and event center, my family's business enterprise, Stonebrook Farm, is unusually quiet. Well, this half of Stonebrook is quiet. There's a wedding reception just getting started over in the pavilion. All the more reason for me to corral Buttercup before she makes a break for it.

Forget Lennox's cabbages. A pig crashing a wedding reception will do permanent damage to our five-star Google review reputation.

Buttercup inches toward me, and I roll her another apple. I know from experience she'll bolt if I get too close. I also know she'll never wander back to her pen on her own, which means, at some point, the slip lead in my hand needs to make it around her neck. "I'm feeling pretty hungry, Buttercup." I crouch low and inch forward. "You know what sounds good right now? Bacon. Fresh, crispy, melt-in-your-mouth bacon."

My sister, Olivia, would be horrified if she could hear me right now. Buttercup is *her* pig, adopted a few months ago from a family who thought they were purchasing a miniature pig but got the exact opposite. When Buttercup outgrew their backyard, they reached out to see if we had a place for her on the farm. I wanted to say no, but Olivia's the softer side of our two-person executive team. We run the family business together. There's a lot of crossover, but generally, I handle the numbers. She handles the people. And the pigs, apparently. She immediately caved, promising the kids they could come and visit Buttercup whenever they wanted.

Which is part of the problem. Buttercup loves people. She hates that she lives outside like a normal farm animal with only the other pigs and—horror of all horrors—the chickens for company. She'd much rather chill on the back porch like she's the family pet.

Unless I'm on the porch.

She dislikes me just as much as I dislike her.

The fact that I keep threatening to turn her into pork chops might have something to do with it.

If Olivia were here, she'd call Buttercup's name, snap her fingers, and the stupid pig would probably trot right toward her with a smile on her face, carefully tiptoeing over the cabbages as she goes.

Unfortunately for me, my sister has a week-old newborn. I'm not mean enough to expect her to come corral a pig *now.*

I'd call someone else, but there *is* no one else.

Lennox is out of town.

My parents are at some school awards thing with Brody, my second younger brother, where he's being honored as teacher of the year at the high school where he teaches.

Our farm manager, Kelly, is on her honeymoon.

The farm hands are enjoying a rare night off.

I'm the only one standing between three-hundred pounds of portentous pork and a four-tiered wedding cake.

I take another step. "But you don't want to be bacon, do you, Buttercup? You're a good girl."

A chorus of laughter and applause drifts across the evening air, and my eyes dart toward the sound. I can't see the pavilion from here. The way the farm is nestled into the rolling hills at the foot of the Appalachian Mountains, you generally can't see more than a few hundred yards before a rising hillside or a stretch of forest obscures your view. But it isn't that far. If I cut through the pasture where Mom grazes her goats, I could be there in a matter of minutes.

So could Buttercup.

Another cheer sounds, this one louder than the first, and Buttercup's ears perk up.

"Don't even think about it," I say, inching closer. "There's nothing for you over there. You know all about the little piggy that went to market, right? I'm just saying. He wasn't there to do the shopping."

Buttercup stares, her porcine eyes looking alarmingly human, grunts as she swallows the last of the apple she finally took interest in, then bolts.

I lunge after her, my hands raking over her enormous hide before she slips away and disappears into the shallow stretch of trees that line the garden. I belly flop onto the dirt with a thud, but quick as lightning, I'm back on my feet and racing after a pig that should not, by all logic, be able to run as fast as she's running.

I cut through the trees, heart pounding, and make it to the road in time to see Buttercup tearing down the hill . . . heading straight for the pavilion.

No. No, no, no, no, NO.

I filter through my very sparse list of options for rerouting a charging pig away from a pavilion full of fancily dressed wedding guests.

One: Outrun. Body slam. Slip lead. Grunt and beat my chest in victory.

Two:

...

...

...

I've got nothing. I'm doing this thing WWE style or I'm not doing it at all.

I've only made it a few yards when the sound of a Gator, one of the four-by-four utility vehicles we use to get around the farm, draws my attention. I don't have time to slow down, but when Brody appears at the top of the hill, a surge of relief pushes through me. I point toward the pavilion. "Pig!" I yell as I point. "Go cut her off."

Brody looks down the hill and races after Buttercup while I cut across the pasture, channeling my high school hurdling days and jumping the fence in a move I wish someone could have caught on camera. I watch as Brody veers in front of Buttercup just before she turns into the field that holds the pavilion. Instead, she turns the opposite direction, heading straight toward me. There's one more fence between us, and I barely clear this one, clipping my shin on the board and sending a shooting pain up my leg.

But when I launch onto Buttercup, my arms wrapping around her middle as I roll us into the irrigation ditch beside the road, I'm not thinking about my shin. I'm thinking that of all the ways to die, this might be the most embarrassing one.

I can see the headlines now. *Man Crushed by Giant Pig. Saves Wedding as Final Act.*

Because that's what's going to happen. This pig is going to land on top of me and crush my lungs. I'm a decent-sized guy. A little over six feet. Two hundred pounds. Not as ripped as any of my brothers but cut enough not to be embarrassed when I'm standing next to them.

But Buttercup is massive. *Monstrous.*

The air whooshes out of my lungs when I hit the ground, and Buttercup squeals, feet flailing. The ditch is barely wide enough for both of us, and I use that to my advantage, pressing my back against the banked dirt and using it to brace myself while I pin the lower half of Buttercup's body with my legs.

The pig huffs and struggles, but that only makes me tighten my grip. After fifteen seconds or so, she finally stills, but the grunts she's making don't sound like she's very happy about it.

Yeah, me neither, pig. Me freaking neither.

"How're you doing down there?" Brody asks from the road, laughter in his tone. "That was a real . . . *ham*bush."

"You did not just say that," I manage on a grunt. My lungs don't feel fully functional yet.

"Do you need me to call you a . . . *ham*bulance?"

"Brody. Slip lead. Do you see it on the ground anywhere?" I know I had it when I took off across the pasture, but the only thing I'm holding now is pig.

"Got it," he says. He steps to the edge of the ditch and slips the lead over Buttercup's head. Once the lead is secure, I shift again, rotating the pig enough for her to gain her footing. I follow, scrambling to my feet, only now realizing that the two inches of muddy water in the bottom of the ditch have soaked into my shirt.

Buttercup stands placidly next to Brody like this is all perfectly normal. Like we're out for an evening stroll and didn't just have a life-threatening wrestling match.

Brody eyes my muddy clothes and presses his lips together. "She was running pretty fast," he says, barely containing his laughter. "We should enter her in the Olym—"

"Stop." I hold up my hand. "Don't say it."

He grins. "Olym . . . pigs."

"I hate you so much right now."

I ride in the Gator next to Brody, holding onto Buttercup's lead while she trots slowly beside us. Now that she's had her adventure, she almost seems anxious to return home. "What are you doing here anyway?" I ask Brody. "I thought you had your thing at the school."

"I did." He reaches up and loosens his tie. "It didn't last long. I got a parking spot. And free coffee from the corner bakery for a year."

"And bragging rights."

He shrugs. "Those too, I guess."

"You here alone? Where's Kate?" It's unusual to see him without his wife. They're still disgustingly newlywed. Attached at the hip if not the lips.

"At Olivia's with Mom and Dad. She wanted to go see Asher."

"You didn't?"

He eyes me before slowing the Gator to a stop outside Buttercup's pen. "No, I did. I just . . . felt like coming to see you, so I headed home to grab the Gator. Mom will drop Kate off later."

It's almost fully dark now, but not so dark that I can't pick up on the guilt in Brody's expression. Understanding dawns. "Olivia sent you here."

Brody holds my gaze. "So what if she did? She's worried about you."

I roll my eyes and climb out, tugging Buttercup behind me and toward the gate of her enclosure. Half a dozen other pigs snort and snuffle in what sounds like a 'welcome home' greeting, and Buttercup squeals in response. "I'm sure you'll tell them all about it," I say, rubbing at my ribs as the pig lumbers inside. I latch the gate behind her. "I'll be sore tomorrow, thanks to you."

Brody steps up beside me. "How did she get out?"

"Beats me. This is the second time it's happened."

He crouches down and studies the latch on the gate. "Could she be lifting this, you think? She's tall enough to reach it with her snout."

"And thoughtful enough to close it behind her on her way out?"

"I'll come by and take a look after school tomorrow. Move the latch, maybe. I'll figure something out."

It's a classic Brody response. He's always been a problem solver. And a middle-child peacemaker—there are five of us, and he's dead center—which is probably why Olivia sent him over. She has an idea she wants to spring on me and thinks it will come better from Brody.

We walk back to the Gator, and Brody drives us toward the farmhouse. Behind it, there's a wide trail that cuts across the west side of Stonebrook Farm property, then winds through public land until it connects to the road where he and Kate live now, in the house Kate grew up in. Childhood best friends. And now they're married.

A sharp pain shoots through my chest, this one not caused by lung-crushing pig wrestling.

I'm happy to see my siblings happy. Getting married. Having kids. But I'm the oldest. I always thought I'd be the first to start a family.

I managed the getting-married part well enough.

Then limped through a divorce. We lasted long enough to at least think about having kids, but the way things ended with Jocelyn, I'm glad it never felt like the right choice.

Brody stops behind the farmhouse that doubles as Stonebrook's offices and overnight accommodations for wedding parties and other event guests. Once upon a time, it was the Hawthorne family residence, but as the farm grew, our parents decided to build something on a more secluded corner of the farm.

"Want to go inside?" Brody asks. "Or we could head down to the kitchen and see if catering has any wedding food left over."

I look toward my truck. What I really want is to go home and shower off the pig smell still clinging to my clothes. "Or we could skip all the chit-chat, and you could tell me what Olivia wants you to tell me."

"I always forget what a great conversationalist you are."

"Why? Because I haven't been this way my entire life?" I *have* always been this way. But the past few years since the divorce, it's possible I've gotten worse, settling firmly into grumpy (not quite) old man territory. I can't even bring myself to care.

"Fair point." Brody takes a deep breath and cuts the engine of the Gator. "She wants to hire you an assistant."

"No," I say, not even hesitating. "I don't need an assistant."

I know how assistants work. I was a corporate consultant not so long ago, and I *had* an assistant. There are ten different ways that work relationship turned sour, which was part of the appeal of coming home. I could lose the assistant and work alone. Work outside. Manage my time how I want to manage it. This is a *farm*. It shouldn't be as demanding as the corporate world.

Somewhere in the back of my mind, I recognize that, by definition, Stonebrook *is* a corporation. And a multifaceted one. There's a farm store, the event center and catering kitchen, and now Lennox's farm-to-table restaurant that should open—despite numerous delays—by the end of next month, just before the start of the holiday season. Not to mention the hundreds and hundreds of acres of apple orchards that gave my parents their start when they bought the place thirty years ago. We're now the second-largest apple wholesaler in the state of North

Carolina and employ more than seventy-five full-time and seasonal staff.

"Perry. Stonebrook is growing," Brody says, echoing my thoughts. "You can't do this by yourself. Not with Olivia on maternity leave and Mom and Dad stepping back like they are. You need help."

"Then I'll hire more help," I grumble. "But I don't need an assistant."

"Olivia guessed you'd say that."

Of course she did. "And how did she tell you to respond?"

He clears his throat and tosses his voice up a couple of octaves in a surprisingly accurate imitation of our little sister. "Perry, the *farm* doesn't need more help, you do. It's your schedule that's a mess. Your calendar. Your inbox. Hiring an extra farmhand won't solve those problems."

"But it might solve the Buttercup problem."

"I'll solve the Buttercup problem tomorrow. I just need to modify the latch." He slaps me on the back. "Think about it, all right? That's all I'm saying."

I shoot him a look, and he grins.

"That's all Olivia is saying," he amends. "But I agree with her. You could use some help."

I climb out of the Gator and push my hands into my pockets. "Hey, how's the baby?" I went to see Olivia and her husband Tyler in the hospital when Asher was born, but I haven't been by since.

Brody's expression softens. "He's great. Perfect."

I shift my weight from one foot to the other. "Does it . . . make you want one?"

"What, a kid?"

I nod.

He shrugs. "Sure. I mean, I did before. But yeah. It makes me a little more excited about kids. Not yet though. You?"

I wave a hand dismissively, a little too quickly judging by Brody's expression. "Nah. You know me. I'm fine being the grouchy uncle."

Brody raises an eyebrow, but he doesn't contradict me.

I must be worse off than I thought.

"Maybe you wouldn't be so grouchy if you weren't so busy," Brody says. "If you had someone to help organize your life. It's a shame they don't have people who do that sort of thing."

I turn and walk toward my truck. "No assistants," I yell over my shoulder. "End of discussion."

It's possible I'm being unreasonable, but even just having the conversation feels like picking at a scab. If I don't have to open this wound, I'd rather not.

"Not every assistant will be like Ryan," Brody calls after me.

I stop in my tracks, my jaw clenching no matter the years it's been since the only assistant I've ever had ruined my marriage *and* my business all at once.

Fine. I'm being dramatic. He didn't *personally* ruin my business or my marriage. But he *facilitated.* Chose sides. Betrayed my trust.

I turn around. It's brave of Brody to bring him up. My family has gotten pretty good at pretending the *dark year,* as I like to call it, when my life imploded and I came limping home, didn't happen. Mostly because whenever they bring it up, I tend to bark and growl and behave like an imbecile.

Grouchy uncle. Yep. That's me.

"But that's the trouble," I say. "It doesn't matter if *all* assistants aren't like Ryan. It would only take *one*. And with people like that, you never know until it's too late."

Brody drops the subject, probably because he'd rather drive home to his wife than sit around and listen to me grumble. But I know better than to think this argument is over. If I know my sister, she'll hit me with round two before the end of the week.

Though, if I can battle it out with Buttercup and come out unscathed, surely I can fend off Olivia's attempts to meddle.

An early fall breeze stirs the first of the fallen leaves at my feet and presses my still-damp shirt closer to my skin. I shiver, wincing away from the chill, then wince again when a shot of pain radiates out from my ribs.

Maybe I'm not *completely* unscathed.

But Olivia isn't going to win this fight. I can manage my life—my business—without anyone else trying to tell me where I need to be and what I need to be doing.

My nosy sister can live her life and let me live mine.

Chapter Two

Lila

So help me, if my child doesn't get his hind end into the car right this minute, I am legitimately going to lose my ever-lovin' mind. I pinch the bridge of my nose and force a deep breath. You'd think the child has rocks in his shoes for how slow he moves. So far, we've been late more than we've been on time. It's hard to be annoyed by it. He's so perfectly precious with his giant backpack and his fierce determination to do everything himself. But if I get one more patronizing smile from the lady at the desk while she hands him yet another tardy slip . . .

"Jackson!" I yell one more time. "We've got to go!"

My adorable five-year-old comes strolling into the living room like he's got all the time in the world. He's only wearing one sock, his hair is sticking up in the back, and he's got two different shoes in his hands. "I was looking for my library book," he says. He plops down on the couch and collapses onto the back cushions with a sigh. "I can't find it *anywhere.*"

My mom senses start tingling. I know that voice. He's trying to convince me of something, which means he probably hid his library book and is only pretending he can't find it.

I drop my purse by the door and walk over, grabbing the missing sneaker from under the ottoman and swapping it for the loafer I suppose he thought he'd wear in its absence. I put on his shoes, tying them myself despite the mom guilt telling me that if I don't let *him* tie his shoes, he'll never learn how to do it.

"I guess you'll have to tell the librarian it's missing," I say.

"But then she won't let me get a new book," Jack says.

I nod. "Yeah. That's too bad. You sure you don't know where it is?"

His eyes get all shifty, and my heart squeezes. It'd be easier to stay mad over all his stalling tactics if he weren't so cute.

"What if I stay home with you?" he says, his voice a little smaller than it was before.

I expected my generally sunshiny outgoing kid to like school, but for whatever reason, he's having some separation anxiety. Maybe because as long as he can remember, it's mostly been the two of us. We've left the tears behind, and we're to the point now where he only needs a little encouragement to go. But he's a master negotiator. If he thinks there's a way out of kindergarten, he'll do his best to find it.

I finish tying his shoes and scoot onto the couch next to him, pulling him into my arms. "We've been over this, Jack. You gotta go to school. But I'll be here waiting for you when you get off the bus. I promise. If you're good, we can walk over to McFarlan's and get a cinnamon roll."

If we're embracing the mom guilt today, I might as well go all in. I've already got a truant child who can't tie his own shoes. What's a little bribery going to hurt?

Jack breathes out a weary sigh that makes him sound fifty instead of five. "Okay." He scoots off my lap and takes off down the hallway. "I'll be right back."

That child might look like his daddy, but he's all me on the inside.

There's nothing I won't do for a cinnamon roll either.

Plus, Jack is generally sweet like me. Optimistic. As tender-hearted as they come.

On the other hand, his dad was . . . well, he was . . . this part is always tough.

My Southern upbringing taught me not to speak ill of the dead, a rule doubly true when the dead in question was a fighter pilot in the Navy and died serving his country. Nobody speaks poorly of a military hero, especially not his widow, so I can't ever talk about the way things really were at home. But maybe that's better. I feel guilty enough even just thinking these thoughts, let alone saying them out loud.

We pull up to the drop-off forty-five seconds after the teachers close down the car-rider line. I jump out, waving at the gym teacher who is ushering the last kids through the big double doors that lead into the cafeteria. I gesture and point at Jack, hoping he'll come and open the gate for me so I won't have to walk him into the office, but he frowns and points at his watch.

"It's not even 8:01!" I call. "We're still on time!"

Jack tugs on my hand. "We could just go get that cinnamon roll now."

"Nice try, kiddo," I say with a sigh. "Come on. I'll drive around to the front and walk you in."

The front desk lady buzzes us through the door, then stares, her face set in a perpetual frown as I use a fancy touch pad to sign Jack in. I don't know why the woman and her judgy expression even need to be here. The computer's doing all the work. I offer a polite smile while the tiny printer next to the touch pad spits out a tardy slip with Jack's name on it.

The woman's frown only deepens. So much for being friendly. I want to tell her she ought to be careful. The older she gets, the more those frown lines are going to make her look like she has jowls, but I bite the comment back. Jack is too perceptive for me to fully unleash my snark in his presence. The child repeats everything I say. He's already smart enough without my sassiness added into the mix.

I hand the tardy slip to Jack and kiss him on the head. "Have a good day, okay?"

He nods and shuffles down the hallway. He only has to go a few doors down to get to his classroom, so I watch him the whole way, knowing he'll turn and smile before he pushes through the door. I hate that I know this. That we've been late enough times that *this* has become the routine.

"You know," the admin lady says to me through pursed lips, "it really does impact the functionality of the classroom when kids are continually late. And it diminishes the importance of promptness to our children when we allow tardiness to become the norm."

I know all this. *Of course* I do. But I'm doing the best I can, and I'm doing it alone. Putting on a brave face for my kid. Pushing through the never-ending exhaustion because I don't have another person to help balance the load. It's just me.

"Have you thought about putting Jack on the bus in the morning?" the woman continues.

Ha. That's a funny suggestion. Our house falls at the beginning of the bus route. We tried it a few times at the beginning of the school year, but Jack had to be at the bus stop by seven-fifteen. Which, if we can barely handle eight o'clock, we for sure aren't ready for seven-fifteen.

I force a smile. "The bus comes pretty early to our house. And things have been pretty tough since Jack's dad died."

The woman's expression shifts, the stony edges and stark lines of her features softening the slightest bit. "Well. Yes, I'm . . . I'm sure." She presses a hand against her chest.

It's a common response. That hand right up against the sternum. Like people are trying to anchor their bodies to the earth.

I smile, this time a little more sincerely.

She'll be nicer to me now.

I give her a little wave on my way out. "Have a nice day."

It maybe wasn't completely fair. I mean, it has been hard since Trevor died. It's also been three years, and my feelings surrounding the loss are more complicated than most. It's hard without Trevor. It was also hard . . . *with* Trevor.

But no matter that, or how long ago it was, or whether the sharpness of loss has started to dim, I'm still alone. Parenting alone, trying to make ends meet alone. Sending my only child off to school alone.

We *should* get to school on time.

But if showing my hand earns us a little grace, I'll take it wherever I can get it. Lord knows I need it.

Back at home, I settle at my desk with an enormous coffee and two slices of thick, buttered toast and log in to the software that connects me with my clients. I only have two, and so far, their needs have been pretty low key, but I like to log in early anyway. It's only been a couple of months since I completed my training as a virtual assistant, but Marley, my trainer and the liaison who helps me find my clients, says we're being paid to be available as much as we're being paid to do the actual work. If we're inside our hours of availability, our clients should never have to wait more than a few minutes for a response.

Fortunately, my hours of availability are only during Jack's school hours. I'm lucky I can get by working fewer hours than a typical nine to five. My schedule is more like nine to two. Trevor's military benefits and insurance policies fill in the gaps, but I'd rather save the majority of that money for Jack.

A familiar twinge of guilt rises up like bile in the back of my throat, but I swallow it down. Jack deserves everything. Even if I'm not so sure that I do.

Either way, I like working. I don't necessarily like *the work,* but it feels good to be doing something to contribute toward Jack's wellbeing.

Maybe one day I'll figure out how to make work something I truly love.

In my wildest dreams, I'm teaching piano and voice lessons out of an at-home music studio. But I know better than to give that dream roots. I'm hardly qualified, no matter how much I like to sing. And truly, answering emails and managing calendars from the comfort of my own home isn't a half-bad gig.

My inbox and task list are still empty, so I kill time by fiddling on my iPad, using a drawing program to finish the avatar I've been working on. The program Marley uses to connect us with clients has a "personal bio" section that contains a little information about me and has a place for a photo. When I first started, I put up a fairly recent photo and called it good. But after the experience I had with my first client—a fancy pants CEO who took less than a week to ask me if he could fly me to

Chicago and pay me a thousand dollars a night for escort services—I pulled the photo down and haven't replaced it. Marley suggested I create a cartoon avatar, something that still looks like a representation of me but is a little less personal.

"You're young, Lila. And beautiful," Marley told me. "And most of your clients are going to be men twice your age. Unfortunately, the more distance you keep between them and your personal life, the easier this job is going to be." I'm not sure if I believe the beautiful part, but for Jack's sake, I'm on board with keeping things impersonal, even if it goes against my natural inclination.

I'm not a great artist by any stretch, but I still think my avatar is pretty cute. Her hair is up in a ponytail and is the same deep brown that Jackson and I share. She's featureless, but the way she's tilting her head makes her seem friendly. Approachable. But she also seems . . . *young*. Maybe it's the ponytail? Struck with a sudden wave of inspiration, I make a few tweaks, changing the hairstyle and adjusting a few colors.

There. Now she's perfect. Gray hair. Glasses. Pearls and a dowdy sweater set. Not anything like me. But does she really need to be? These men I'm working for will never meet me in person. It's the magic of a virtual job. It really is all virtual.

I've just finished uploading my new and improved avatar when my phone rings and Marley's face fills the screen.

"Hey, Marley."

"Hey! I'm glad I caught you. I have news. Or, a job, really. Kind of a big one."

"Excellent. I definitely have room for a third client."

"Actually, this would be a solo gig. This client is okay with your shorter hours of availability, but they think they have enough to keep you busy and would like to pay for exclusivity."

"So they'd be my only client?"

"That's right. I'll shift the two you currently have to someone else."

I don't love the idea of losing the clients I currently have. There was a learning curve when I started working with both of them, and I'm finally starting to feel like I've figured out how each client wants me to do things. "Why me?"

"A few reasons. One, exclusivity pays a little higher, so that will be a nice boost for you. It's a higher rate, plus, instead of only getting paid for the hours you work, you get paid the same hours every day regardless of whether they have anything for you to do. Second, I actually know these people. Well, sort of. My cousin Rosie—have I told you about her? She's married to the famous YouTuber."

"Right. *Random I.* You've mentioned her."

"Yes! So, I guess *Random I*—his name is Isaac—is best friends with a guy who married into the family that owns this farm down in Silver Creek. That's close to where you are, right?"

"Yeah. About twenty minutes down the mountain."

"So that's another perk. It's almost local for you. Not that I anticipate them needing you in person. I reiterated that you are a *virtual* assistant, and they get that, but they did like that your proximity to them gives you a working knowledge of the area. I guess they do a lot of wholesale with local retailers, and they have this festival coming up—"

"Wait, what kind of business is this? You said it's a farm?"

"Oh, right. Stonebrook Farm and Event Center. So, a lot more than just a farm. Have you heard of it?"

"Shut. Up. Are you talking about the Hawthornes?"

"You know them?" Marley says.

"I know *of* them. But everyone around here does. They're like North Carolina royalty. You know Flint Hawthorne? The actor? That's his family."

"Oh, that's right! I remember Rosie telling me that."

"They hold this enormous harvest festival every fall. It's huge. Almost like another county fair. Though, I think half the people who go are mostly just hoping they'll catch a glimpse of Flint."

A memory pops into my mind. The last time I went to Stonebrook's harvest festival, Jack and I had just moved home. Trevor hadn't been dead more than a month, but I hadn't seen my little boy smile in too many days. We needed to do something normal. Something to make him happy. I walked around the festival with a hollow chest, but Jack loved it.

"Olivia actually mentioned the harvest festival specifically," Marley says. "I guess they're way behind on the planning and are hoping you can step in and—"

"Olivia? Is she a Hawthorne?"

"Oh, right. Yes. And she's the one married to Isaac's best friend. But the most important thing for you to know is that Olivia and her brother run the farm together, and since she's out on maternity leave, she wants to hire him an assistant."

It's not lost on me that Marley is saying *Olivia* is the one who wants to hire me. Which leaves me to wonder how the actual brother feels about me working for him.

"I don't suppose Flint is the brother who's running the farm now, is he? Good grief, can you imagine?"

Even just thinking about working for Flint's *brother* feels crazy.

Flint Hawthorne is huge.

So famous.

Maybe not Tom Hanks or Tom Cruise famous, but definitely Chris Hemsworth famous.

"Not Flint. His name is Perry. Olivia didn't tell me much about him, but I get the sense they're all really good people. Genuine. Honest. I think this will be a good fit for you, Lila."

"Maybe, but I'm still concerned about the hours. With Jack, will they give me the flexibility I need?"

Truth is, even living in the town where I grew up, I don't have much of a support network. I live right down the street from my grandparents, who raised me, but for lack of a better way to say it, they're *old.* They live in one of those assisted living neighborhoods where, even though they're technically on their own, there are people on standby to help with the basics. Grocery shopping, doctor's appointments. Neither of them drives, and they aren't quite mobile enough to keep up with Jack, so even though we visit a lot, I can't rely on them to help babysit or pick up the slack when I fall short.

I really *am* on my own.

"They'll be fine with that," Marley says. "I promise. I told Olivia about Jack, and she says it won't be a problem. Family comes first."

I take a deep breath. "Well, okay then. I guess I'm in."

Marley says goodbye, promising to send over the digital agreement for my new client/assistant relationship. When it appears in my inbox minutes later, I read it over, my eyes catching on the name of the man I'll be assisting. *Perry Hawthorne.*

I have so many questions. Does he look like his famous brother? Is he older? Younger? If he's even half as handsome, I might have a hard time forming sentences around the man. Except, I won't really *be* around him, will I? Email. Direct messages.

Maybe a phone call every once in a while, depending on what he prefers.

My fingers itch to google him, but Marley's counsel echoes in my mind. Keep things strictly professional. No social media stalking. No deep-diving into decades-old MySpace photos. "*The less you know about things that do not pertain to your work, the easier it will be to do your job in a professional, unbiased way.*"

But it's not every day you get a client who is related to one of Hollywood's biggest stars.

Finally caving to the impulse, I pull up a new window on my computer and run a search.

Flint Hawthorne brothers.

And there they are. In all their FREAKING UNBELIEVABLE glory.

"You have got to be kidding me," I say out loud as I magnify the picture. Four men stand together, arms wrapped around each other, in attendance at what looks to be some kind of fancy, black-tie event.

Flint is in the middle, his brothers standing on either side. And they're clearly brothers. There's a common thread that runs through all of them. An incredibly handsome common thread. I mean, talk about winning the genetic lottery. These men are *transcendent.* Their collective handsomeness is almost blinding. They should all be in the movies. Or at least decorating billboards modeling Calvin Klein underwear. I think I'd buy anything these men were trying to sell. Lightbulbs? *Why yes, yes I do think I need a year's supply, thank you.*

There's no caption with the picture, so I can't know which brother is which, but my eyes are drawn to the one on the end. His hair is a little longer, he's the only one with a beard, and he's not quite smiling. There's a seriousness about him that's different from the other three.

That's Perry, I think to myself, though maybe it's just that I want him to be Perry. Why, I can't say, but the impression is crystal clear.

It only takes one more search query to confirm my hunch. *Perry Hawthorne Stonebrook Farm.*

The image that pops up first is definitely the unsmiling man from the end. He isn't smiling in this photo either, but he's no less handsome. He's sitting on the steps of a white house—probably the big farmhouse at Stonebrook—his arms propped on his knees, his expression serious.

He is . . . I let out a little groan. Five minutes ago, I wouldn't have thought it possible, but I think he's actually more handsome than Flint.

I don't know why I feel so out of sorts. I'm a *virtual* assistant. This will be a *virtual* relationship just like the ones I've had with my previous clients. There isn't a single reason for me to feel so much trepidation. But my hands are shaking right now. Like, actual, visible, shaking.

I force a deep breath. I'm being ridiculous. The guy is probably married anyway.

I lean forward and squint at the picture. His ring finger is bare, but that doesn't necessarily mean anything. Trevor hardly ever wore his wedding band.

I swallow away the discomfort that thought brings and focus on the picture. "Good morning, Mr. Hawthorne," I say out loud, in my best assistant voice. "Ready for your morning update?"

I flop back into my chair. *Ugh. I am going to mess this up.*

I sit up again and tuck a strand of hair behind my ear. "Here are the files you asked for, Mr. Hawthorne," I say in a syrupy sweet voice. "Can I get you anything else? A candlelit dinner for two? A moonlit stroll?"

Oh good grief. Definitely not that.

I clear my throat. "Hey. Hawthorne," I say, my voice unnaturally deep. "Here are your files. If you need me, just light the bat signal."

If Jack were here, he'd be rolling on the floor laughing at my Batman voice, and that thought is enough to bring me back to earth and ground me in reality.

Jack is my priority.

This is just a job.

Perry will just be a boss. It doesn't matter that Marley knows his family personally or that he's only twenty minutes down the road. It doesn't even matter that I've been going to Stonebrook's harvest festival since I was a kid. This will not be a personal relationship.

And good thing too, because I wouldn't have the first clue how to have one of those.

I've been on exactly zero dates since becoming a widow. And since I met Trevor right after high school and married him when I was too young and much too stupid, I can't even rely on past dating experience to help me muddle through. I need Ryan Gosling's character in *Crazy, Stupid, Love* to come and teach me how to date. (Or maybe I just need Ryan Gosling?) Except the PG version where all he teaches me is how to have a conversation without using my Batman voice to break the ice.

I fidget my way through the rest of my shift, doing my best to keep my mind *away* from my new and exciting, one-degree-away-from-a-celebrity, very attractive client. But no matter how much I tell my brain this is NO BIG DEAL, the rest of me seems to be operating with some secret insider knowledge, because I keep waffling between feeling flushed with heat and prickled with goose bumps, like a cool breeze just blew across my skin.

I don't know what's going on, but I know I don't like it.

Chapter Three

Lila

My inbox pings with a notification the minute Perry Hawthorne signs his paperwork. I swear, it almost feels like something pings inside of me at the same time, waking up a flurry of nerves and excitement.

It's possible anticipation has made my reaction larger than it should be. I've been waiting three days for Perry to make our working relationship official.

Marley already shifted my previous clients to other assistants, so I've just been killing time. Granted, two of those three days, Jack was home with a fever (real, not faked, though I did question at first) so I was grateful for the time off.

But Jack's back in school today, so I'm ready to get back to work. And now I finally have a boss who needs me.

My fingers are only a tiny bit shaky as I key a "nice to virtually meet you" message into the chat box part of the integration software Marley uses, but why am I nervous? I shouldn't be nervous. He's just a client. Albeit a super-hot brother-of-a-movie-star client, but STILL. I'm not the fangirly type. I'm a dorky mom who mostly works in yoga pants and stretchy denim and makes her kid laugh by imitating superheroes.

I hit send, then copy and paste instructions that will walk Perry through giving me access to his email and calendar and give *him* access to my task list.

A solid hour passes before the chat box pings with a return message. Not like I'm counting or anything. (I'm totally counting. It's been sixty-two minutes.)

Perry: I'd like to keep our interactions as brief as possible. I've put together a list below of some tasks I need completed ASAP, as well as parameters for how I'd like you to handle my email. Let me know if you have any questions.

My chest deflates the tiniest bit at the chilliness of his tone. But that's stupid. Can direct messages really have a tone? Just because I read it one way doesn't mean that's how Perry would say it were he speaking to me in person. Then again, is there really a warm way to say *I'd like to keep our interactions as brief as possible?*

I clear my throat and sit up a little straighter.

Lila: Understood. Brief interactions. Like phone calls with the mother-in-law.

I wait for Perry to respond with a laughing emoji or even just a thumbs up. Brief doesn't have to be *boring,* does it? My hope surges when the dots at the bottom of the chat window flash for a moment or two, but then they disappear, and the green light indicating that Perry is online switches to an offline red.

I immediately second guess the joke, even if it was relatively harmless. Yes, Marley has told me to keep things professional, and I do. But I can be professional and *not a robot* at the same time. It only feels right to remind my clients there's a person behind my avatar.

But then, maybe the joke didn't land because Perry has a wonderful mother-in-law whom he talks to every Sunday afternoon.

Or maybe Perry is the actual robot.

For the rest of the week and all of the next one, I work every hour of Jack's school day, slowly plowing my way through Perry's never-ending task list. It's easy work, but only because Perry is so thorough (and unrelentingly impersonal) in his requirements. A few things are so simple, I wonder if it took him as long to type out the instructions as it does for me to complete the tasks.

I feel guilty about those things. Does he really need to pay me to track down a missing invoice he could have found with a simple file search? But then I'll spend four hours chasing after the still-unsigned vendor contracts from the food trucks who want to be present at Stonebrook's harvest festival, and I don't feel guilty anymore.

Through it all, Perry is responsive to my questions and detailed in his replies.

He is also colder than a giant block of ice.

At first, I was intimidated. But now, it's become a bit of a game for me. A special challenge to see if I can get him to crack.

Lila: I've gathered the quotes you requested for the apple bushel boxes. Sending them in an email attachment now. It took some hard *core* negotiating, but I got every supplier to drop their quotes by fifteen percent.

Perry: Good work. Thanks.

Lila: All food truck and food stall vendors have confirmed and paid their fee for the harvest festival. I've staggered their arrival times to avoid congestion. I really had to *peel* back the layers to make it work, but they'll all be set up when gates open at eleven a.m.

Perry: Excellent.

Lila: I really apple-lied myself this afternoon, and now all the vendor bills from the Hamilton/Smith wedding are paid and filed appropriately.

Perry: Thanks.

Just when I think I need to abandon the puns and revert back to boring professionalism, a personal email shows up in Perry's inbox. I immediately wonder if this is the moment I've been waiting for. I finally have an in. A reason to make an actual phone call.

But then, by the time I've read the email, I'm not so sure. If I'm going to have a "first" conversation with my boss, I don't think I want it to be about whatever drama is behind this message.

The email is brief, and though it's clearly addressed to Perry's work email, it is *not* work related.

Perry— I'm still awaiting your RSVP to the reunion. I hope we can be mature about this. Just because I'm in charge doesn't mean you shouldn't come. Have you blocked my messages from your personal account? They keep getting returned, which is why

I'm emailing you here. I've attached the official reunion invite in case you haven't gotten it. Please RSVP. And please come. -JH

My fingers hover over the chat box. When clients set up the parameters of their email accounts, they can specify a list of senders or even entire domains to filter into a private inbox that I can't see. Most prefer that all return emails go directly to them, or anything from existing contacts, leaving only new or general inquiries going to the VA. If anything slips through that looks like something the client should handle on their own, I can move it into their private inbox.

That's probably what I should do now. But if someone has been hounding Perry's personal email accounts, maybe he'd prefer I handle this for him, keep some level of distance between him and whoever this person is.

Perry is online and logged into the VA software, so I type him a quick message.

Lila: Good *apple*noon, Mr. Hawthorne . . .

Oh good grief.

My brain is working against me now. I delete and try again. There's a time to be punny and a time to not, and I sense that this is definitely a time to not.

Lila: Good afternoon, Mr. Hawthorne. I've just received an email from someone regarding some sort of reunion for you. I don't want to overstep, but the email feels a little . . . pushy? I'm happy to reply if you'd prefer not to hear from them again.

To my (too much) delight, he replies immediately.

Perry: Pushy? In what way?

Rather than move the email into his private inbox, which would cut off my access to the message, I go old school and simply forward it to him so that I can still reply should he need me to.

Lila: Just forwarded the email.

I drum my fingers against my desk, waiting for him to respond.

When five minutes go by with no new messages, I pull up Perry's calendar and check the date, referring back to the invitation attached to the email. "The Grove Park Inn," I say out loud. "Fancy."

I skim the remaining details. It's for Perry's high school graduating class. Fifteen years, which means he's only four years older than I am. *Interesting.* I'd always imagined him slightly older. The fact that he isn't sends a tiny thrill shooting through me. Four years isn't a very big age gap. If that sort of thing mattered, which, because Perry is my boss and also might be very married, it does *not.*

The reunion is an overnight event, which feels kinda swanky, but then, I don't really have anything to compare it to. My ten-year reunion was last year, and I skipped it. The idea of trying to find my place among the happily married couples and the still-single-and-living-it-up crowd sounded much too stressful. Plus, my senior class created a new senior superlative just for me: Most Likely to Be on *American Idol*. The fact that I didn't make it to Nashville to pursue a singing career like I hoped did a good job of dampening my desire to go and reconnect with old classmates.

There's nothing on Perry's calendar that conflicts with the reunion. It's before both the harvest festival and the restaurant opening, so there's no reason Perry can't go. Though, based on the tone of the email, I'm guessing he probably doesn't want to. The message doesn't read like a "first contact" email; it reads more like a "you still haven't responded" email.

When another five minutes go by, I begin to think I should have just forwarded the message and kept myself out of it. But I already started the conversation. I type out one more message. If he doesn't engage after this one, I'll leave it alone.

Lila: Fifteen years! That's a big one. Would you like me to send in your RSVP? I checked your calendar, and it's clear on the dates of the reunion.

Perry's reply comes through almost immediately.

Perry: I'll take care of the email. Thanks for forwarding.

And . . . our conversation is over.

When the three dots appear indicating that Perry is typing again, a surge of hope pulses through me.

Perry: I'm heading out early today, so you're welcome to do the same.

I breathe out a sigh. It was almost a conversation. But not really.

Perry: And Lila? I *apple-laud* your efforts this week.

I nearly gasp when I read his message.

He's alive! A living, thinking human! And he's noticed my attempts to add a bit of levity to his day.

Still, I sense a need to manage my expectations.

One pun does not a friendship make. In fact, "friendly banter" is written nowhere in my job description. Marley would even discourage me from engaging in such a thing, though she's reiterated multiple times it's up to me to set boundaries according to my own comfort level. And my comfort level is a lot closer to "friends with everyone" than "professional and impersonal."

I stand up and stretch, happy to be out of my chair after so many hours in it.

I look around my cluttered living room. I probably ought to spend a few hours cleaning the house once I get Jack from the bus, especially since he's got soccer practice tonight, and there won't be time later.

Our place has more than enough space for the two of us, but by general standards, it's tiny—tiny enough that it ought to be easier to keep clean. But cleaning is one of those things that used to feel simple but now seems like an enormously complicated task.

The list of those things was a lot longer at first. Getting out of bed. Doing basic things like brushing my teeth or making myself a cup of coffee. Forget showering or going to the grocery store. I honestly don't even know how we ate the first few months right after Trevor died.

Things are easier now. *Most* things, anyway. But it's also been long enough that I'm finally sorting through the layers of complicated emotions I still haul around with me every day. Things like how much Trevor cared about the house (and Jack and me) always looking neat and tidy and at "our best."

I never slacked off before. I half wonder if that's why I'm more lenient about things now.

Because I can be.

Guilt, sharp and familiar, wells up, pushing against my lungs, making my chest feel tight. Trevor's gone, and I'm relieved I don't have to keep the house as clean?

I brush the thought into the corner with the dust bunnies and look for my shoes. It's nearly time to walk to the bus stop to meet Jack. I'd rather do that than sweep the floors anyway.

Jack is all smiles and sticky hands when he climbs off the bus. He's holding a giant sheet of posterboard in one hand and a ring pop in the other, the sticky juices dripping down his hand

and staining his skin blue. His lips have the same blue tint. Somehow, it only makes him cuter.

"Ughh, Mom. You're squeezing me too tight," he says when I scoop him into my arms.

I drop him back to the sidewalk and tug on his backpack until it slips from his shoulders. It's only a hundred yards or so to the house, but the thing almost weighs as much as he does. I throw it over my shoulder and nudge Jack toward home.

"What's on the poster?" I ask, and he unfolds it to show me as we walk.

"Our family," he says. He points to the figure on the far left. "That's you. And this is me beside you."

"It looks so great, Jack. What's that up there?" I point to an airplane-looking thing above the trees.

"That's Daddy. He's in his jet. Watching us from heaven."

My heart squeezes. (*Will it ever stop?*) Jack was too little to remember his dad, but he's heard the story enough times to know how he died. And that he was heroically serving his country when he did.

"So, if that's Daddy up in the jet, who is this down here?" I point to the other figure standing on the opposite side of Jack.

"That's my new dad."

Oh. Oh wow.

I clear my throat. "Your new dad, huh?"

"Yeah. My friend Chloe at school says her parents got a divorce, and her mom moved out, but then her dad brought home a new mom. Now she has two. Her real mom and then another kind. A stairmom."

I press my lips together to stifle a giggle. "I think you mean stepmom, baby."

"Oh, right. Stepmom. Am I getting one though? A new dad? Would he be my stairdad? I mean, stepdad?"

We reach our tiny front porch, and I turn and sit on the step. Jack moves to the front yard and starts combing a patch of grass for four-leaf clovers. It's late enough in the season I don't think he's going to find any. The grass has mostly stopped growing—I doubt we'll even need to cut it again before spring—but I'm grateful he's occupied anyway so I can have a minute to gather my thoughts.

"Chloe said her dad found her stepmom at the bar," Jack says. He's stretched out on his belly, his legs kicked out behind him, his face close to the browning grass. "What's a bar? Is it like a people store?"

Oh my heart. This child. "It's a little more complicated than that," I say. "A bar is a place where grownups go to get fancy adult drinks. Sometimes they meet other people while they're there. But it's not like shopping. It's more like making friends. Deciding who you like and who you might want to spend more time with."

He looks up and studies me. "So if you went to a bar, would you meet a stepdad?"

I shrug. "Maybe. But I could also meet someone anywhere. It doesn't have to be at a bar."

He stands up and brushes off his shirt. "Should we go look?"

I narrow my gaze. "For a stepdad?"

He nods, his expression so earnest, it nearly kills me. "What's going on here, Jack?" I tug him forward and pull him onto my lap. "It's been just the two of us for a while now. Why the sudden desire to have a stepdad?"

He sniffs and picks at a scab on his elbow, his eyes down. His shoulder lifts in the tiniest of shrugs. "I don't know."

"Jack," I say softly. "You can tell me anything, you know that, right?"

He huffs. "I don't want to. Because you'll just tell me *you* can come with me, but that won't be the same."

"Come with you to what?"

He's fidgety now, squirming like he wants to get away from me. I loosen my hold, knowing him well enough to give him the space he wants when he wants it. He heaves out a sigh. "The father-son breakfast."

When I was little, I used to think heartbreak was only something you could experience one time. Once your heart broke, that was it. It was *broken.* But I know better now. Because in the past three years, my heart has broken a million different times.

Make that a million and one.

Just as I expected him to, Jack wiggles out of my arms and goes back to the yard.

"Would it be so bad if I came to the breakfast with you? I'm sure you aren't the only one who doesn't have a dad around."

"Ms. Kennedy says grandpas can go. Or uncles or big brothers." Jack looks at me now, hope in his eyes. "Could Grandpa Jamison go?"

"I don't think he's strong enough to leave the house, sweetie. But we can maybe see if your Grandpa Templeton can come up and take you."

Trevor's parents live two hours south in Columbia and are always asking me to bring Jack down to visit. Truly, if they had their way, I'd do more than visit. I'd move in and turn over Jack's parenting to them. We're talking private kindergarten for thirty grand a year, private tennis lessons at the country club, after-school tutors for Latin and elocution. All of it.

It isn't that Trevor's parents are unkind. I appreciate how much they care about Jack. But I'm not sure their life is the life I want for him. And as much as I want Jack to have every good and nice thing, I don't think I'd be capable of living a life where, every day, I'd have to pretend Trevor was as perfect as his parents still believe he was.

Jack shrugs and sighs, clearly underwhelmed by the idea. "Yeah. Maybe."

I stand up, recognizing that sometimes the only way to beat the melancholy is to distract yourself out of it. "Come on. Let's get inside. If you can help me get the living room clean, we can have an early dinner, then pop some popcorn and watch a movie."

Jack follows me inside where I clean up his sticky hands and face. Then we crank up the music, cleaning and dancing until the sparkle is back in his eyes. But hours later, after I finally tuck him into bed, I sit at the kitchen counter and stare at his poster, my eyes drifting from Trevor's scribbled form floating high in the sky to the man drawn right next to Jack.

Logically, I've always expected that at some point far down the road, I'd meet someone. Fall in love. Get married again. But I don't even know how I'd go about starting the process. How do you date when you also have a five-year-old? If Marley was concerned about me getting personal with business associates, how much more caution should I have when it comes to my personal life? Because it isn't just *me* I have to consider. There's Jack, too.

And that complicates everything.

I trace my fingers over the dark hair Jack scribbled onto the mystery man in his drawing. For the briefest moment, I imagine my overly professional, dark-haired boss.

The thought is completely laughable. Absurd to the billionth degree.

Me and Perry Hawthorne?

Me and *any* Hawthorne?

I should know better than to even consider it.

But that doesn't stop me from going to sleep imagining Perry Hawthorne's dark hair and the way he *apple-lauded* my efforts.

Chapter Four

Perry

Preston Whitaker walks me back to my truck, carrying a bushel basket of apples like it's full of gold instead of fruit. I offered to carry it—Mr. Whitaker has to be pushing eighty—but he insisted, and I know better than to wound the old man's pride.

When we reach the truck, I take the basket and place it gently in the passenger seat. "Thanks, Preston. I'll make sure Dad gets them."

"Don't you tell him though," he says in his gruff voice. "This is a blind taste test."

I nod along as he speaks. "Understood. I won't tell him. And I'll call you the minute he's tried one to let you know what he thinks."

Preston is an old friend of my dad's. His orchard isn't big enough to be commercial; he makes a few trips to the farmers market every fall to sell his harvest, but it's more a hobby than it is a business. His real passion is apple pomology—cultivating new varieties of apples more resistant to disease or improved for taste or texture.

This new variety is supposed to be the perfect combination of crispness and tart sweetness. At least, that's how Preston described it. And dad has a reputation in the apple-growing community. He's got a nose—or maybe a taste bud?—for the most marketable varieties of apples, and when he calls something a winner, he's pretty much always right.

Preston practically giggled when he called and invited me out to pick up a bushel of the hybrid fruit he's been working on for the past three years.

I climb into my truck and roll the window down. Preston moves up, leaning his arms on the driver's side door. "Tell him I still need a name," he says, nodding toward the apples. "And if you're interested in growing it out at Stonebrook, well, we can talk about that too."

"I'll tell him."

He pats my arm. "It's good to see you, Perry. I was surprised you came so quickly, as busy as you are."

"There's always time for you, Mr. Whitaker."

He offers one final wave as I pull down the gravel drive of his small farm. The Whitaker farm is one county over, near Hendersonville, but still ten miles outside of anything that resembles a town. This far out, it's just winding roads and trees in every direction. I wind my window down and breathe in the crisp, clean fall air. A row of sugar maples along the road blazes yellow, their leaves dancing in the afternoon breeze. It's the perfect kind of afternoon for a drive, and I have Lila to thank for the opportunity. If not for her efforts the past two weeks, I wouldn't have had the time to make the trip.

The thing is, I'm generally very organized.

On top of my life.

In control.

I actually pride myself on that control. On getting things done in a proper, orderly fashion. Some say it makes me grumpy, to be so . . . *specific* about things. I say it makes me effective. Reliable. Efficient.

At least, I thought so before my run-in with Buttercup.

I haven't found the connection yet, but I'm convinced that stupid pig is directly responsible for the disintegration of my organizational skills. Or maybe she was just the catalyst? Either way, that night marked the beginning of my decline into desperation. Things quickly went from bad to worse, so much so that I've started using Buttercup's name as a favorite swear word. Forgotten meetings. Missed opportunities because of my failure to respond. Delayed shipments. *Buttercup.*

I'm not sure I truly understood how much Olivia does around the farm, something I'm loath to admit because the *buttercupping* pig is her fault in the first place.

Or how much Olivia *did,* anyway, before she had Asher. I have a newfound respect for her ability to multitask.

It took a week for me to cave and agree to *limited* help from a virtual assistant.

But now, there's nothing limited about Lila's help. She's even scheduling my phone calls, which has somehow stopped me from feeling like all I do is put out fires other people started. *Believe it or not, boss, you can solve people's problems on your timetable instead of theirs,* Lila messaged me when she first set up the schedule.

The woman is a machine. Efficient. Competent. And a good communicator. She also has good intuition, often taking the tasks I've given her one step further. I think it must be her age.

I don't know exactly how old she is, but the avatar she uses in the app we use to communicate is an illustration of a woman with graying hair, pearls, and glasses. Which tracks. Lila seems grounded in a way that can only come from years of experience. Though, her age is probably also the cause of her ridiculously *punny* sense of humor.

Brody would love her apple-themed jokes. Me? I'll tolerate them if it means she's getting her work done.

I reach over and grab an apple out of the overflowing bushel basket in the seat beside me. Windows down. A cool breeze. A bright sky edged with the smoky blues and greens of the rolling mountains in the distance. Fall colors in every direction. I bite into the apple and smile.

I might not be as experienced as Dad, but I know a good apple when I taste one.

For a short minute, I almost forget about all the stress waiting for me back at the farm. I forget the gnawing loneliness that's been consuming me since Olivia had Asher, and Brody got married. I even forget the annoyance of my ex-wife emailing me—repeatedly—about the stupid high school reunion happening next month. I can't figure out why Jocelyn cares so much that I attend. So she can gloat, probably. Parade her happy life in front of me and make me realize what I'm missing.

Or what she thinks I'm missing, anyway.

It took a few years, but I'm finally starting to accept that I'm better off without her. I loved Jocelyn. And I don't doubt that she loved me. Just not enough to be okay when I told her I wanted a different life—one that didn't involve the corporate games she wanted to play. I didn't expect it to end things. I thought she'd understand me wanting to go in a different direction. Instead, she begged me to hang on a little longer, then she plotted her escape.

The betrayal still burns—a thick coil of festering heat that lives deep in my gut, pulsing whenever I think about her. Whenever I realize how foolish I was, how many signs I missed.

My hand tightens on the steering wheel, but I force my grip to loosen, rolling my shoulders to shake out some of the gathering tension. It's over and done with. And I'm better for it. I realize that now.

Seconds later, I tense right back up when my truck lurches and jumps. I slow my speed, immediately recognizing the sound and feel of a blown tire. *Freaking buttercupping buttercup.*

I pull onto the shoulder and get out to assess the damage. The tire isn't salvageable, but luckily, I've got a full-size spare. I move to the back of the truck to get the tire and everything else I'll need and—*oh no.*

I search the truck bed. Every logical place and then every illogical place.

I do have a full-size spare. But thanks to my idiot brother who took mine and forgot to put it back, I don't have a jack.

I'll put it right back, Lennox said. *You'll never know it was gone.*

I climb into the truck and drop my head onto the steering wheel. Of all the stupid days to blow a tire. When I'm way out here in the middle of nowhere. Without the one thing I need to make changing a tire possible.

I call Lennox first, but he's right in the middle of a training run with his kitchen staff and can't leave for another two hours or more. Brody's phone goes straight to voicemail, which means he's probably on the river with his after-school kayaking club. Mom is at physical therapy with Dad. Tyler is in a meeting. I even tried calling Brody's new wife, Kate, but she's in Asheville doing an interview. She can stop by on her way home, but it'll be dinnertime before she's finished.

The whole situation feels like a strange and uncomfortable repetition of the night I battled Buttercup alone. Why does it feel like everyone has someone but me?

The only person I haven't called is Olivia. But all calling her would do is make her feel guilty that she isn't available to help. Or else it would make her put her month-old baby in the car and come to my rescue, something I won't ask her to do until I'm really desperate.

I'm looking up numbers for the nearest roadside assistance when Olivia calls me. It's a video call, which means I might get to see Asher. A glimpse of my nephew might be the only thing that could put a smile on my face right now.

"Hey, Liv," I say, answering the call. "What's up?"

"Mom just called. Have you found someone to rescue you yet?"

I shouldn't be surprised that word traveled so fast. Not when it comes to my family. "I'm looking up roadside assistance right now."

"If you're still stranded in an hour, I'll send Tyler, once his meeting is over. Or I could just come. Asher's sleeping, but he'd probably stay asleep in the car."

"Don't wake your baby up. Isn't that some kind of cardinal rule? You never wake a sleeping baby?"

Olivia yawns. "Sounds about right." She perks up. "Ohh! You know who you should call? Lila. She lives in Hendersonville, right?"

I frown. "I'm not sure that falls under her realm of responsibilities."

"Whatever. She's your assistant. When have you ever needed assisting more than you do right now?"

"It's not the same thing," I say, shaking my head. "She's a virtual assistant. She can't send me a car jack in a direct message."

"But don't you have any desire to meet her in person? See what she's like?"

"I know what she's like."

"You do?"

"Sure. She's older. Gray hair. She likes to crochet."

She yawns again. "She could still bring you a jack. Even little old ladies know how to drive."

"Go take a nap, Liv. You look exhausted."

"K, but promise you'll call if you can't find someone to help you. I'll come, Perry. I don't mind."

"I'll figure it out. Don't worry about me."

I hang up with my sister, my finger hovering between the app I use to communicate with Lila and the search I already started for roadside assistance. Better to start with that. If it's going to be a while, or if I can't find anyone close by, maybe I'll consider calling my assistant. It just feels wrong to ask this of her, after her business hours, when she specifically said her availability is not flexible.

She could be caring for an ailing husband. Or . . . I don't know, crocheting something.

It occurs to me that I probably ought to make an effort to get to know my assistant a little better. Olivia and Brody are right. This isn't like my situation with Ryan. She clearly isn't the same, and she's very good at respecting my boundaries. She only has access to what I give her, and she isn't even a little bit pushy.

I should try to be more friendly.

But do I really want to start that effort on the side of the road in the middle of nowhere?

Except, I really do need help.

Shoving aside the last of my hesitations, I pull up her number and hit *call*.

Chapter Five

Lila

Jack and I are playing a game of Sleeping Queens—his favorite card game and one of the many sacrifices I make because I love him—when my phone rings, the screen lighting up with an unknown number. The city name attached to the number catches my eye because it reads Silver Creek, NC.

I only know one person who lives in Silver Creek.

It could be a coincidence.

A spam call from someone wanting to sell me an extended warranty on my car or asking for a donation to some political action committee. Maybe someone wanting to collect on imaginary debt or refinance the mortgage I don't have.

But my boss *does* have my number. And he's allowed to use it during business hours, should we ever need to communicate.

We never have. Perry is an expert DM'er and a total phone-avoider. At least so far.

It can't be him.

Can it? My palms are sweating, my heart beating so hard, I think Jack could probably see it pounding if he looked closely.

"Oh, this is ridiculous," I say out loud.

Then I answer the call. "Hello?"

"Hello?" a deep voice replies. "Is this Lila?"

My heart drops into my stomach, and a queasy feeling starts swirling.

I've never heard Perry Hawthorne's voice, but somehow, I know it's him anyway. And his voice is every bit as sexy as I imagined it would be.

What I don't know is why my body is acting like "Is this Lila?" actually means, "Hey, beautiful. Want to have dinner with me?"

Can a voice really do that to a person—cause such a visceral response?

"Hello?" Perry repeats. "Are you there?"

I clear my throat. "This is Lila."

There's a long pause before he responds. "It is?"

"Well, who else would I be?"

"No, I know. You just sound . . . younger."

"Younger than who?"

"Your profile picture, er, avatar?"

Oh. Right. I fake a laugh as my hand flutters to my chest. I look at my hand as if some alien life form has taken over my body and turned me into a swooning Southern belle. Is it actually *fluttering?!*

"Oh, that. Right. I get that a lot," I say, dropping my voice into a slightly deeper register. It makes Jack look up, his expression saying he's as confused by my voice as I am by my inexplicable hand fluttering. "How can I help you, Mr. Hawthorne?"

"Actually, I need a favor. I know this is completely inappropriate, and I promise I will compensate you for your time. But I'm stranded in Hendersonville with a blown tire and no car jack to help me change it. I'm hoping you're close enough to give me a hand?"

"Oh, I don't know anything about changing tires." Apparently, I am both a Southern belle and a complete idiot.

I can change a tire. I can change ALL my tires if I need to.

I didn't always love being a military wife, but it did teach me how to get stuff done.

"Right. I don't need you to *change* the tire, but if you have a jack I could borrow, that would be great."

"A jack." I sit down. Stand back up. Sit down again.

"Mommy?" Jack says.

"You know what?" Perry says, backpedaling. "Don't worry about it. I don't think I'll have to wait too much longer for roadside assistance to show up."

"No, no, that's okay," I practically shout into my phone. "I can bring you a jack!"

"What?" Jack says, dropping his cards. "You can bring me where?" He stands up. "Who are you talking to, Mommy?"

"Not *you,* Jack, *a* jack," I whisper to him, shooing him back into his seat.

"What was that?" Perry said.

"Nothing. Everything's fine," I say. "You need a jack. I have a jack."

"Great," he says after a long pause. "Should I, um, text you my location?"

"Yep. Perfect. I'll be right there."

As soon as the call ends, I bluster around the apartment, picking up couch cushions and folding blankets. Jack, clearly sensing that something is up, jumps up beside me, gathering his cards and putting away his backpack.

Wait. *Wait.* I'm not bringing Perry back *here.* Which means I'm just being a dummy. Cleaning because I'm nervous about coming face to face with my boss.

My hand does that stupid fluttering thing again, landing on my hair, which—*ohhhh* my hair! I dash to the bathroom, checking my reflection. It is . . . not awful? It could be worse, anyway.

Then I remember Perry's comment from earlier. *You sound younger than your avatar.* Maybe it doesn't matter what my hair looks like. Perry is expecting a pearl-wearing, gray-haired grandma. Maybe the surprise of seeing me instead will negate any judgment he might make on my less-than-stellar messy bun and almost completely bare face.

"Mommy?" Jack says again. "Do we have to go somewhere?"

Oh man. WE do have to go somewhere. Because Jack goes everywhere I go.

Which means my boss is about to learn that I'm not a grandma *and* that I have a kid all at once.

I don't know how I'm supposed to do this.

Logically, I recognize I'm being silly. Assistants and bosses work together in person all the time. They know about each other's families. Kids. Spouses. Even pets. It's not *weird* to know personal details about the lives of the people you work with. And I've been hoping for opportunities to get to know Perry better.

But the concept felt easier behind a mask of anonymity that allowed me to be bold without feeling vulnerable. That little gray-haired avatar lulled me into a comfort I didn't recognize I was enjoying until now, when I'm faced with the mask's imminent removal.

Truth is, my reality requires that I be more cautious, more vigilant in vetting the people I let into my very small circle. I'm all Jack has to protect him. I can't just let anybody in.

But Marley did say the Hawthornes are good people. And so far, Perry has been nothing but polite. Cold. A little stiff. But perfectly professional and respectful.

"We do have to go somewhere," I say. "I have to go help my boss with a flat tire."

"I thought your boss lived in the computer."

I smile. "He lives one town over in Silver Creek. We stay connected on the computer. Come on. Go grab your shoes."

I walk to the garage and double check that my SUV's jack is where it's supposed to be in the back. When I see it tucked securely into the side compartment, I slam the hatch closed and call Marley. Partly because she's my mentor when it comes to this whole virtual assistant job, and partly because right now, she's the closest thing I have to a friend.

Which . . . is *sad.* I grew up in this town. I know tons of people, many who have been friends for years. But I still feel weird hanging out with people.

Most of my friends from high school are married now, or at least in serious, happy relationships. I've tried to hang out with them a few times, but nobody really knows how to talk to me about being a widow. It's bad enough being the single friend. Being the single, widowed, *parent* friend is a can of worms most people don't want to open at all.

"What's up?" Marley asks when she answers. "Everything okay?"

"Um, yes, I think? Perry just called me. He's stranded with a flat tire and needs me to come help."

"Okay," she says, her tone even. "Is that something you're comfortable doing?"

"I mean, you vouched for him, right? He's a decent guy?"

"I've never met him personally, but after meeting Olivia and talking to her about him specifically, I feel pretty good about saying yes. But Lila, this isn't in your job description. You don't have to do this if you don't feel comfortable."

"No, no, it's not that. I mean, it's weird and all. That I'm meeting him in person. But not because I feel uncomfortable. At least, not for the reasons you might think."

"Why else would you feel uncomfortable?"

I scoff. "Have you ever seen a picture of the Hawthorne brothers?"

She chuckles. "I've heard stories, and of course I know what Flint looks like, but I've never looked up the rest of them."

"I'll save you the trouble. They are all equally gorgeous. Every. Single. One."

"I'm still not seeing the problem here."

I sigh. I've been dancing around the problem myself, trying to figure out why I feel so out of sorts because my boss happens to have an attractive face. All at once, the truth crystallizes in my mind, and I say it out loud before I can chicken out. "Marley, I noticed."

"Noticed what, honey?"

"That he's handsome. And I didn't just notice. When I saw his picture, I felt something."

"What, like attraction?"

I lean against the back of the car, my arms folded over my chest. "Yeah. A glimmer of it, maybe. I don't think it means anything. But it's not so much *him* that's significant but the fact that I felt anything at all. That hasn't happened since . . ." My words trail off, and I shrug. "Since Trevor."

"Oh, Lila. That's a good thing then, right? It's been long enough. It's okay for you to feel something."

"But doesn't this go against your *strictly professional* rules?"

"Technically, you're an independent contractor," Marley says. "My rules are only tips and guidelines to help you achieve success. But beyond that, the happiness and well-being of my assistants will always be more important than anything else. I would never want you to turn away from something—or someone—who truly makes you happy because of work. Do you think what you're feeling is significant? That the glimmer of attraction could turn into something more?"

"With him? Shoot, no. I don't even know if he's single. Even if he is, men like that do not notice women like me. I guess I just feel woken up, you know? And that surprises me."

Jack comes into the garage, his shoes on and tied, and a surge of pride pulses in my chest. "Hey! Great job, kiddo." I open up his car door, and he settles into his seat. "I'll be right back, okay? I'm gonna go grab my bag."

"Perry *is* single. Olivia mentioned something about a divorce a few years back when she was talking about him," Marley says as I hurry back inside.

Divorced. Interesting. *No! Not interesting. Not. Interesting.*

"Also, that whole *women like me* business?" Marley continues. "That's utter nonsense, just for the record."

I won't argue with her, because Marley is paying me a compliment, and my grandmamma taught me it's tacky to toss a compliment back in someone's face. Still, Marley has only seen me on video calls from the waist up. She's never encountered my generous hips in person, and let me tell you, they are a force. Even before Jack, I've never been one of those willowy, wispy people with long, lean limbs. I'm more draft horse than racehorse, and I always have been. Farm stock. Built to last.

Not that I mind. I'm happy in my own skin. (Another gift my grandmamma gave me with the positive affirmations she made me repeat every night before bed.) I recognize the strength and function of my body and do my best (most of the time) to remember its purpose is far greater than just *looking hot.*

But I'm also a realist. Experience has taught me exactly what kind of man will pick a racehorse over a draft horse. When a man looks like Perry Hawthorne, there's no question. He will pick a racehorse every time simply because he can. I've got nothing to worry about when it comes to that man. Not a single, solitary thing.

"Thank you," I say to Marley. "And thanks for talking me through it."

"Anytime. Trust your gut, Lila. You've got good instincts."

I end the call and climb into the car with Jack. "Is your seatbelt buckled?"

"Yep!" he says, his feet swinging.

Despite his turtle-slow pace getting ready in the morning, he's a pretty easy kid, something I'm grateful for every single day.

I catch my reflection in the rearview mirror as I face forward and slide my sunglasses over my face. I can't shake the feeling that something big is about to happen.

But that's stupid. This will probably be nothing. A benign encounter in which I hand my boss a jack and then go on my merry way. Even if he is divorced. And single. And gorgeous.

"And completely out of your league, Lila," I say out loud. "Get a hold of yourself, woman."

"Who's out of your league?" Jack asks from the back seat. "What's a league?"

"Don't worry about it, baby. I'm just talking to myself."

With a deep breath, I shift the car into reverse and back out of the garage.

Ready or not, here I come.

Chapter Six

Perry

It's been twenty minutes since I hung up the phone with Lila, and I'm still doubting the wisdom of calling her. Lila sounded distracted when we spoke. Like there was a lot going on in the background, and she couldn't fully focus on what I was asking of her.

I really *didn't* want to impose. And I don't want to ruin the dynamic of the professional relationship we've built. But desperate times, and all that.

When a blue SUV pulls up behind me and a woman climbs out, I start doubting for an entirely different reason.

If that's Lila, she is . . . *not old*.

She's also beautiful. Dark hair piled on top of her head. Freckled skin. Curves for days.

Something deep in my gut ignites, and I run a hand through my hair. I've dated since my divorce. Mostly to appease my siblings who, at this point, probably think I'm broken beyond repair. But this feeling—a sharp, visceral attraction—is new.

But right behind the attraction is a sense of frustration. It doesn't *really* matter that Lila doesn't look like her avatar. But I've had this picture of her in my head, this idea of exactly who is on the opposite side of my messages. I was comfortable with my imagined version of Lila. But that version just got turned on its head.

If the woman is even Lila. Could she be a daughter, maybe? A neighbor? A friend?

I watch through the rearview mirror as the woman moves to her trunk, likely to pull out the jack she drove out here to give me. I grip the steering wheel a little tighter. This interaction would be so much easier if the avatar-version of Lila had shown up.

This version of her? Or whoever this woman is? I'm not prepared to talk to a woman who is both young and hot. If the past is any indication, odds are pretty good I'm going to say something ridiculous or embarrassing.

My brothers are good at this sort of thing. At small talk with beautiful women. And if I have Lennox or Brody as a wingman, ready to fill in the awkward silences and expand on my monosyllabic answers, I can usually get by. But on my own? I'm too stiff. Too formal. Too direct.

The problem is, I'm also *very* self-aware, so the entire time I'm trying to converse naturally, I fully sense how poorly I'm doing, which puts me in a bad mood. So then I'm not just awkward, I'm also grouchy.

It's honestly a wonder I ever managed to get together with Jocelyn. I think the only thing that saved me was the fact that we knew each other in high school.

But this is Lila. My apple-pun-wielding assistant. (Probably?) Not a woman I'm trying to charm or impress.

Even if I *did* have any idea of her relationship status, which I don't, she's my employee. I just need to treat this like I would any other business meeting. Like she's Preston Whitaker giving me a bushel of apples. Or Calista, Stonebrook's event manager, giving me an update on the weekend's schedule.

I can do this.

I *have* to do this.

And right now.

I might still be awkward, but not as awkward as things will be if I stay in my truck.

I take a stabilizing breath, then climb out.

The woman smiles as she approaches, jack in hand, sparking another flare of attraction in my gut. *That smile.* My eyes flit to her SUV because otherwise I'm going to stare at her, and that would just be weird.

"I guess you're Perry?" she says as she holds out the jack. "I'm Lila. Nice to finally meet you in person."

So she *is* Lila.

Her accent is clearly Southern, but it isn't twangy like you often find along the Appalachians. Instead, her words are soft around the edges, rolling into each other in an easy, unhurried way. She's wearing jeans and a T-shirt cinched up at the waist, accentuating the curves that are, for the record, highly distracting. I am not a man who needs a reminder to keep my eyes up, but this woman is the ultimate test, and it's taking all my willpower not to fail. I fasten my eyes to her sunglasses, but that hardly helps. Now I can't stop wondering what color her eyes are.

Lila's expression shifts to one of confusion, and she pulls the jack back toward her. "You *are* Perry, right? Would you rather I call you Mr. Hawthorne?"

"Right!" I say a little too loudly. "I'm Perry. You can call me Perry."

She eyes me warily. "Okay."

We stand there awkwardly for what feels like a solid minute before I finally blurt out, "You aren't old." I cringe at the harshness of my comment and immediately wish I could take it back. My frustration with Lila has everything to do with me and nothing to do with her.

She presses her lips together. "Sorry about that. The avatar . . ." She scrunches up her nose in a way that's almost adorable enough to make me forget my irritation. She shrugs. "It seemed like a good idea at the time?" She gives her answer like it's a question, like she already *realizes* it isn't a good explanation, but she's hoping I'll buy it anyway.

"It was a good idea to give me the wrong impression?"

She winces. "Yes? I mean, no. But . . ." She looks back toward her SUV. "I wasn't trying to give you the wrong impression. I actually changed the photo before you hired me, so it was more a general thing. To be fair, I didn't really expect to ever meet in person." Her hands move to her waist, where she props them on her hips in a way that shouldn't be so enticing. "Does it matter that I'm not in my sixties?"

"Yes," I say reflexively.

Because you're beautiful. And I noticed. And I'm feeling things I haven't felt in years, and now, every time you message me an apple joke, it's going to land differently.

"No," I quickly amend. "No. Of course not. I just don't understand the point."

She sighs. "It was Marley's suggestion that I make my avatar something a little less personal."

She pushes her sunglasses up onto her head, revealing eyes the same blue as the autumn sky above us. I didn't think it was possible, but her eyes make her even more beautiful.

"My first virtual client was *forward,*" she says, her eyes shifting to the side. "Pointed in his very personal questions. It only took a week or so for him to be so blatant, I immediately quit, and Marley severed his relationship with her company. But the whole thing made me a little more leery. Using an older woman as an avatar seemed safer." Her gaze turns back to her car one more time, where it stays long enough that I half-wonder if she's going to make a break for it. But then she looks back at me, her expression surer than it was only seconds before. She takes a deep breath. "I have a son. And I'm a single mom. I have to protect myself, but more importantly, I have to protect him. The reality is, an old lady avatar makes that a little easier."

The unfounded frustration simmering inside me immediately quiets. She has a kid? He's probably with her. That's why she keeps looking at her car. And she's single?

This point, which matters to me much more than it should, is quickly eclipsed by a sudden and intense desire to find whatever "first client" she had and punch him for crossing a line, for doing anything to make Lila—or any woman—feel unsafe.

"That client was a jerk," I say, almost without thinking.

She nods. "He was."

"I'm not a jerk."

She cocks an eyebrow and grins. "I wouldn't be here if I thought you were. Marley vouched for you. For your whole family, really."

I grunt an acknowledgement and reach for the jack. "Thank you for coming."

Lila hands it over, her fingers brushing mine as she does. I move toward the opposite side of my truck, pretending like I didn't just feel her touch in every cell of my body. "So, are the apple puns part of the old lady facade?"

"Nah. They're all me. I was trying to *branch out* and try something new."

I freeze. "Branch out, huh?"

Lila fights a smile. "I had to do something! It isn't really in my nature to be impersonal, even when using a fake avatar. And you've seemed so determined to keep our interactions as brief as possible,'" she says. "I was just trying to lighten the mood."

I frown, which makes Lila bite her lip, a flash of trepidation crossing her features. Those are my words she's tossing back at me. I *did* want our interactions to be as brief as possible. Because I didn't want to have a stupid assistant in the first place. But how am I supposed to respond? I don't feel the same way *now.* She's helped me too much for me not to acknowledge her value.

I suppose I could just say that. But I'm not sure I trust myself to keep it professional because right now, I'm appreciating a lot more than just her work ethic, which is way more than she needs to know. Especially considering what she just told me about her first client.

Lila clears her throat when I don't respond. "But brief interactions are completely justified," she adds, likely assuming my displeasure based on my silence and my scowl.

Olivia has told me I need to work on my resting face, or I'll never meet another woman. *You look like you want to punch everyone,* she always says. *Just smile every once in a while!*

Lila takes a step backward, away from where I'm crouching beside my tire, loosening the lug nuts. "It's your right to set whatever boundary you're comfortable with, and I'll respect it. And of course, I'll stop the apple puns if they bother you."

This is not going well. I sink back onto my heels and look up, running a hand through my hair. "That's not it. I don't . . . I don't mind them," I grumble.

Lila hovers behind me, her uncertainty clear from her body language. "Okay."

We're silent for a beat before a voice sounds from Lila's SUV. "Mommy? How much longer?"

She glances over her shoulder. "A few more minutes, okay? You're doing great, kiddo. You can grab my phone out of the front if you want to play a couple of games while you wait."

"How old is he?" I say on an impulse. "Would he want to help?"

I have no idea what possesses me to ask. Maybe just that it's the kind of thing my dad did when I was a kid. If there was work to be done, we helped. In hindsight, I realize how much more complicated we probably made things, but I'll never regret the learning I did beside my father.

A thousand thoughts flit across Lila's expression before she finally nods. "Um. He's five. And I'm sure he'd love to help. But I'm just warning you. He'll talk the entire time."

"Okay," I say simply. I don't have a ton of experience with kids. But I do okay when schools come out for education tours of the farm. I'll even volunteer to lead the tours. Sometimes, kids are easier to talk to than adults.

Lila bites her lip, a gesture I've noticed twice now and liked both times, but then her shoulders drop, and she turns back to her SUV. A minute later, a little boy with dark brown hair and wide brown eyes is standing beside me.

"Jack, this is Mr. Hawthorne. Can you say hello?"

"Hi, Mr. Hawthorne," the little boy says.

"Hi, Jack. You want to help? I could really use a little more muscle getting this tire changed."

He nods, a smile creeping onto his face. "I've got pretty good muscles." He curls his arms up to flex his biceps, and I grin.

"Whoa. You aren't lying. All right. Stand back there beside your mom while I jack the truck up, then you can help me get the lug nuts off."

Jack nods as Lila slips a protective arm over his shoulders and pulls him close to her. I quickly position the jack and slowly crank it up, double and triple checking it's secure.

"Okay." I pick up the lug wrench, guessing that since the lug nuts are already loosened, it won't be too tough for Jack to twist them off. "Just like this, all right?" I show him the movement, but he stops me, reaching for the wrench.

"I know how to do it," he says. "Mommy taught me when we changed her tire."

My eyes immediately jump to Lila. I lift an eyebrow. "I thought you didn't know anything about changing tires?"

Her cheeks flush the slightest bit, but otherwise, she seems unfazed by my question. She shrugs. "You put me on the spot."

Her confidence only strengthens her appeal. I can maybe understand the allure of a "damsel in distress." Playing the hero. Riding in to save the day. But I'll take a strong, capable woman over a damsel in distress any day of the week.

Jack finally twists the first lug nut all the way off, and it drops into my waiting palm. "Great job. Want to do the next one?"

He nods, his face determined, and moves to the next lug nut. This one needs a little more muscle, so we work together, holding the lug wrench until the nut is loose enough for him to twist it off by hand.

"Mommy explained what a jack was on the drive over," he says as he works. "I was confused because when she said she needed to bring you a jack, I thought she was talking about me."

"That makes sense."

"How much do you think your truck weighs?"

My eyebrows go up. "I don't know. A few thousand pounds, probably."

"Is that too much for you to lift with your muscles?"

I take the lug wrench and position it over the next nut. "Yep. A little too much."

"What about the tire? Could you lift the tire?"

I look up and make eye contact with Lila whose expression clearly reads *I told you so.* "I could lift the tire," I say.

"Could I?" Jack asks.

"When you're my age, I bet you can."

He purses his lips like he needs to catalog the information. "How old is your age?"

"Jack. Come on," Lila says softly. "You're asking so many questions, Mr. Hawthorne can't get his tire changed."

I wink at Jack and motion toward the lug wrench with a tilt of my head.

He grips it in his hands and twists, letting out a little grunt that nearly makes me laugh. "Just turned thirty-three," I say as I catch the third lug nut.

"Thirty-three?! You're even older than my mom. You're maybe as old as my grandpa."

"Not quite," Lila says, correcting him. "And he's barely older than me, kiddo. Just four years."

"Four years is forever," Jack says matter-of-factly.

The questions don't let up until the tire is fully replaced and the truck is back on solid ground.

Why do I drive a truck instead of a car? Is that the name of my work on the side of the truck? Do we grow apples? Is that why there's an apple tree next to the name? Am I a dad? Do I have a wife? Do I have any brothers or sisters? Or a dog? Or a cat? Or a horse since I live on a farm, and horses can live on farms?

I do my best to answer with a straight face, but by the time I'm handing the jack back to Lila, I've been holding in the laughter so long, I'm ready to burst.

"Okay, little man. Back into the car with you. We've got to let Mr. Hawthorne get back to Stonebrook Farm."

Jack looks up. "Is that far away from here?"

I shake my head. "Just a few miles down the road. About twenty minutes."

"One *Paw Patrol* long?" he asks.

Lila smiles. "About that long."

"Speaking of Stonebrook," I say, before I can stop myself. The idea of inviting Lila out to the farm popped into my head a few minutes ago, growing more and more insistent the closer we got to finishing the tire. I have no idea what I'll do if she agrees. But some part of me wants to see her again. I'm not really sure I'm ready to admit what that might mean, but I'm also not willing to let her drive away and disappear behind her old lady avatar. "If I were to, uh . . . that is, if I had some things I needed you to do at the farm, in person, would you be willing to come out some time?"

I clear my throat, hoping it doesn't sound like I'm asking her on a date. Though, maybe that would have been a better idea. I have no actual clue what kind of work I'll have Lila do in person. If she even agrees to come.

Except, *I can't* ask her on a date. She just told me about a too-forward boss and how uncomfortable he made her. I can't be that guy.

"I suppose I could," Lila says. "If it's during Jack's school hours."

A thrill of victory shoots through me. She said yes. The feeling is followed swiftly by a wave of trepidation. Because *she said yes.*

I nod. "Great. Good. I'll keep you posted."

Jack tugs on Lila's sleeve. "Could I come too?"

"You'll be in school, baby. But we can go to the harvest festival at the farm next month. You loved it the last time we went."

Jack nods, even as he tugs on her arm, pulling her down until she's crouching beside him. He whispers something into her ear, but his whisper is hardly a whisper. "Can I ask him if he wants to be my stairdad?"

"Stepdad." Lila corrects him so quickly, it's clear they've had this conversation before.

She shoots me an apologetic look even as my heart drops into my stomach. The thought is ridiculous. Outlandish. And yet. Something in the back of my heart flickers. It's tiny. So tiny. Tiny enough that I know better than to think it means anything.

Lila pushes her sunglasses onto her head and squares Jack so she's facing him head on, one hand on either of his shoulders. "I know this is really important to you, Jack. But that's a question only grown-ups get to ask each other, okay?"

He shrugs away from her, his tiny hands balling into fists. "But he said he doesn't have any kids. Or a wife. Or even a pet. And I helped him, and he said I had good muscles and . . ."

Tears are hovering in Jack's eyes now, and my heart nearly breaks for the kid, despite the awkwardness of the conversation.

I don't know the whole story, but I can guess. Jack doesn't have a dad around, and he clearly wishes he did.

Jack's lip quivers, and he takes a shuddering breath. "I think he would like me if he got to know me."

Now tears are pooling in *Lila's* eyes. I turn and move a few paces away to give them some privacy, though I'm not so far that I can't hear her response.

I watch out of the corner of my eye as she runs a hand over his hair. "Oh, Jackson. Of course he would like you. I bet he already does. But Mr. Hawthorne couldn't be *just* your stepdad. He'd have to be my husband, too. Do you understand? We would have to get married. And people only get married when they've fallen in love."

He studies me for a long moment. "Is that what Chloe's dad did?"

"I'm sure it is. He met someone, they spent some time together, they fell in love, and then they got married. That all happened before she became Chloe's stepmom."

Jack sniffs. "Do you think if you spend time with Mr. Hawthorne, he'll love you?"

The same attraction that's been spiking every time Lila looks my way roars through me when Jack mentions love. If love were based on physical attraction alone, I'd say odds were pretty good of me falling for Lila. But I know better. Real love is so much more than attraction, and I'm in no position to have any opinions when it comes to this particular conversation.

"Honey, Mr. Hawthorne is my boss. And falling in love—it isn't really something you can plan. It just happens. Now listen, I promise we'll figure something out for the father-son breakfast, but I need you to let this go, okay?"

Ah. At least now I'm starting to understand Jack's motives. Honestly, I'm impressed with how Lila has handled the entire thing. She has every right to feel embarrassed, given that this is our first encounter, and her kid is trying to play matchmaker. But if she *does* feel that way, she isn't letting it preempt what she's saying to Jack. She isn't dismissing him, silencing him. She's down on his level, listening, reassuring, explaining in a way he can understand.

Jack's eyes dart to me before he gives his mom a slow nod. "Okay."

She scoops him up into a hug, lifting him off the ground and swinging his legs back and forth until he starts to giggle. She finally lowers him back to the ground but keeps hold of his hand. "Can you say goodbye to Mr. Hawthorne?"

"Goodbye, Mr. Hawthorne," Jack says without looking up.

"Thanks for your help, kiddo."

Lila ushers him back to the car, then returns to pick up the jack she discarded to answer her son's question. "I'm so sorry about that," she says, avoiding eye contact. "He's got this father-son breakfast thing at school, and it's making him hyper-aware of his fatherless state. But to ask that was so totally inappropriate, and I really need you to know that I didn't put him up to it. Or even talk about the possibility. That was all him."

"I assumed it was. Don't worry about it. I'm flattered, actually. That he would consider me a worthy option."

She nods, eyeing me like my response has surprised her. "Even so, I'm not sure I've ever been so mortified."

"You played it off well," I say. "Jack's dad isn't . . . around anymore?" I don't know what makes me ask the question, but I can't regret it because I really want to know.

Lila's hand falls to her side. "He died a few years back. It's just me and Jack now."

"Oh. I'm so sorry. I'm divorced." I close my eyes and wince. "It's not the same thing. I don't mean to make it seem like it's the same thing."

It occurs to me that blurting out my relationship status has everything to do with me wanting her to know I'm single. It's a weird sensation. I haven't wanted *anyone* to know I'm single in a very long time. "I'm sorry," I say again. "I'm really bad at this."

Her eyebrows goes up. "At what?"

"At talking."

She smiles, and a pulse of desire fills my chest.

"It's okay," she says. "I wouldn't wish what we've been through on anyone, but I imagine a divorce isn't exactly a picnic."

I can't stop the scoff that pushes its way up. "Yeah. That's—" I push my hands into my pockets, unable to finish my sentence. My divorce was awful. Gutting both emotionally and financially. But to lose a spouse? The two don't even belong in the same category. "I should get back to work."

Lila nods. "Of course. We've got a date with *Paw Patrol* anyway."

I narrow my gaze and frown. "With *who*?"

"It's a television show. Jack's favorite, and they just released a movie that he's really excited to see." She cocks her head to the side. "No kids for you?"

"Ah. No. Didn't make it that far."

"Hmm. I wondered. You were so good with Jack."

Warmth spreads across my chest. "He's a good kid."

She smiles, love so evident in her expression, it sends a swell of sharp longing right to my heart. Not for her specifically. Just for *anyone*. For family.

"Enjoy your weekend, Mr. Hawthorne."

"Perry," I tell her again. "Please. Let's stick with Perry."

She nods. "All right. Goodbye, Perry."

I lean against the tailgate of my truck, watching until she pulls onto the road. She lifts her hand in a wave, and I return the gesture, my eyes on her until she disappears around the bend.

Back in the driver's seat, I pull out my phone and stare at the black screen, emotions swirling through me. I should have said thank you one more time. I should have let her know how much I appreciated her taking the time to drive out and help, how much I appreciate everything she's done the past couple of weeks.

But everything that happened with Jack, with the tears and the earnestness of his desire, with the thoughts and feelings it stirred up, I wasn't thinking when she left.

Now she's gone, and all I can think about are the things I didn't but should have said.

I wish I were better at this. At . . . peopling. At not making everyone around me feel uncomfortable. Except I'm not worried about everyone right now. I'm worried about Lila.

The question is, why? Why does it matter so much?

I'm attracted to Lila. I'm not stubborn enough to deny that much. But the reasons for not pursuing a relationship with her are numerous.

She's my assistant, for one, and a good one. I don't want to do anything to screw that up.

She's also got a kid *and* a dead husband, and though it might make me cruel to say it, after my divorce, I'd rather avoid relationships that come with that kind of prepackaged drama. I *like* kids. But liking them and wanting one right out of the gate are different things.

So this feeling—it can't be about that. About anything personal.

But as her boss?

I *do* want her to feel comfortable working for me.

And I don't want her to think her boss is creepy or weird.

I crank my truck, liking where I've landed.

It's natural for me to be concerned about what she thinks and how she feels. That makes me good at my job.

That's all this is.

I'm her boss. She's my assistant.

End of discussion.

Somewhere in the back of my mind, a little voice laughs. *That's all this is . . . for now.*

Chapter Seven

Perry

I RUN MY FINGERS through my hair a few times and roll my shoulders. This shouldn't be that difficult. It's just a picture. I just need to take it, post it, and be done.

I hold up my phone, force out a breath, and take the picture.

Annnnd I look like an ax murderer. Why are my eyebrows furrowed? And why do I look so angry?

"So I need to smile," I say out loud.

I pose again, this time smiling in a way that makes me look like I'm smelling bad cheese.

I drop my phone onto my desk with a sigh and press my face into my hands. No smiling. I just have to make a serious look work. That can be attractive too, right? Broodiness? Not that I necessarily want to look attractive. This is for work. It's better that I look professional. Not smiling should be just fine.

I open up the camera app on my phone and flip it around to face me. Maybe with one hand on my beard, if I turn sideways and look back . . .

"What on earth are you doing?"

I jump when my brother's voice sounds from my office door, and my phone goes flying, clattering to the wood floor beside my desk.

Lennox reaches it before I do and wastes no time pulling up my photo gallery. "Oh, man," he says with a chuckle. "These are so good."

"Shut up."

"Why do you look like you're smelling something?"

"Maybe I was. You were on your way here."

Lennox drops onto the chair opposite my desk. He's wearing casual clothes—jeans and a Red Renegade band T-shirt—and I realize how long it's been since I've seen him in anything but his chef's coat.

"You aren't working today?"

He shakes his head, but his eyes don't lift from my phone. "Gave the staff the day off. They've been working hard. They deserve a break."

"Have you hired everyone you need?" The restaurant opening has been delayed twice now—mostly because Lennox is such a perfectionist—but the plan now is to be ready for a soft opening the weekend before the harvest festival.

"I'm interviewing pastry chefs tomorrow," he says with an ease I've always envied. Lennox *is* a perfectionist, but he isn't a *stressed* perfectionist. He's very good at rolling with hiccups and setbacks, adjusting his schedule accordingly. Though I'm sure it helps that he's got Stonebrook's working capital backing his efforts, so his open deadline isn't exactly do or die. I've told him if he doesn't open by Christmas, he has to work the first three months for free to help offset the cost of paying his ever-growing staff when the restaurant has yet to generate any income.

"Relax. The restaurant will open by festival time," he says, as if sensing the thoughts running through my brain. "It's going to be fine."

I lean into my chair. It will be fine. Olivia and Lennox have worked hard on the restaurant opening, and I trust them. They're good at this. They've thought of everything. But that doesn't mean I don't have a near-constant doomsday narrative humming at the back of my brain. If there is any possible way to fail, my brain will think it up.

As long as I don't think myself into panic attacks, it's actually a pretty useful skill.

You need someone to preemptively troubleshoot your idea? Tell you all the ways it might possibly fail? I'm your guy. It's why my consulting firm did so well, back before Jocelyn cleaned me out, and I came back home to run the farm. I don't have problems shooting holes in things, though Olivia insists I could at least do it with a little more optimism and a little less glee. Pointing out someone's weaknesses is one thing. Projecting their imminent failure is another thing altogether.

"What about you? Is everything with the festival okay?"

I swallow the list of things that could still possibly (but probably won't) go wrong and nod. "For the most part. There's still a lot to do."

"What about taking bad selfies? Is that on your to-do list too?"

I drop my phone onto the desktop in front of me, suddenly too tired to be defensive. "Were they really that bad?"

"I mean, maybe depending on who you're trying to impress." His eyes narrow. "Who *are* you trying to impress?"

"No one."

"Liar. Try again."

I shift in my chair. "It's nothing. It's the software I use to communicate with my virtual assistant. There's a place for a profile picture, and I never put one up."

He nods his head, his expression inscrutable. "Your virtual assistant, huh?"

I turn to my computer and pull up my email. If I look busy, maybe Lennox will leave me alone.

"You met her, right? She's the one who helped you with your flat tire?"

"Thanks to you," I mumble. "Did you put my jack back?"

"Stop changing the subject. What does she look like?"

"Who?"

He rolls his eyes. "Your assistant. Don't play dumb on purpose."

I shrug. "She looks like a woman."

He heaves out an exasperated sigh. "Young? Old?" He pauses. "Beautiful?"

My eyes lift to his, and he grins.

"So she is beautiful."

"That isn't what this is about."

He chuckles. "Right. I'm sure it isn't."

"I just want things to feel a little more personal," I argue, though I don't sound very convincing. "It was nice of her to come out and help. I haven't exactly been kind to her so far, and I'm trying to do better. I don't want to lose her. She's very good at her job."

"All very respectable reasons for wanting to update your profile picture. I still don't believe you."

I breathe out a sigh. "Please don't make this something it isn't."

"Okay. I won't. But if you start to date her, I'm going to say I told you so."

"I'm not going to date her. She has a kid."

"So you *have* thought about it. Also, a kid is not a reason not to date someone."

"She's widowed."

"Also not a disqualifier."

"Maybe not generally, but for me? I don't need complicated, Lennox. You know that."

He studies me. "I hate to break it to you, man. But *life* is complicated. You avoid complicated, you might as well hang up the idea of dating altogether."

"I'm not thinking about dating Lila. Can you please let this go?"

"Only if you admit that seeing her impacted your desire to add a profile picture."

I eye him, hating his smirk. Mostly because I don't want him to be right, and I'm afraid he is.

"I'm not saying I want to date her," I grind out. "But seeing her *might* have influenced my desire to upload my picture."

Lennox's voice shifts, like he's talking to one of those tiny yappy dogs people carry around in their purses instead of his older brother. "Cause you've got such a pretty face, Perry. Yes you do."

"Stop it. She's already seen what I look like. That's not—I just want things to feel a little more personal."

"I'm just saying. If you *did* want to date her, objectively, having your picture in your profile to remind her of your prettiness isn't going to hurt. You're prettier than all of us. Except maybe Flint, but he has a whole team of people to make him pretty."

"Whatever. We all know Brody's boyish charm wins."

Lennox purses his lips as if considering. "True. It was probably better for all of us that he fell in love so young. Taking himself out of the game might be the only thing that made it possible for the rest of us to ever get a date."

I roll my eyes. "Yeah. You really struggle, Len."

He flashes a smile. If Lennox has a superpower, aside from his abilities as a chef, it's his confidence. Though I expect the confidence helps with the cooking, too. He's never afraid to take a risk.

"Come on." He reaches for my phone. "Let's take a picture. I'll help."

"No. I can't do it with you here. I'll feel like an idiot."

"When have you ever cared about looking like an idiot in front of me? Come on. You either let me help you, or I'm calling Liv and telling her what you're doing." He holds the phone up to my face to unlock the screen, jumping back when I try and wrench it out of his hands.

He stands and backs away from my desk, grinning. "Okay," he says, holding my phone up like he's some hotshot photographer. "Maybe try swiveling your chair around so the mountains are visible through the window behind you. And like, lean forward, maybe? Your weight resting on your elbow?"

Somewhere deep in my gut, I feel like I'm going to regret this, but I also really want a good picture to post. "Like this?" I twist my body and lean onto my arm.

"If you want her to think you're a used car salesman, sure. Give us a thumbs up and a cheesy grin, and you're all set."

I let out a frustrated breath. "Then what? I did exactly what you told me to do."

Lennox sits back down in the chair across from me and mimics my stance. "*This* is what you're doing. You're stiff and awkward. Just relax." He loosens his shoulders and gives his arms a shake. "Make it more like *this.*"

That *does* look better. I shift my body so I'm sitting exactly like Lennox.

"Yes! Better," Lennox says, jumping up. "Now, don't move. Except, maybe tilt your head down a little? And put your hand on your jaw like you're thinking."

"Should I smile? Olivia tells me I don't smile enough."

"Can you smile without the weird expression?"

"I don't know. Does my smile always look like that?"

"You never smile, so how would I know?"

"Never? I'm not that bad."

"You are that bad. The line between your brows says so. But yes. Let's try a smile."

I reach up and touch my forehead, frowning even deeper when I feel the deep crease between my eyebrows. I stretch my forehead and try for an easy smile, but it feels so forced, I don't hold it for long. "This is stupid. There's no way I don't look stupid right now."

"You don't look stupid. Think of the moment when Lila first showed up to help you. What did you think when she got out of her car?"

My mind goes back to that moment, to the surprise I felt over her *not* being a little old lady. Then the moment shifts to when she first lifted her sunglasses, revealing the deep blue of her eyes. She has visible freckles, which I like, and a wide, friendly smile.

"Oh man," Lennox says, lowering the phone. "You like her."

I shake myself and relax my pose. "I do not. I hardly know her."

Lennox cocks his head. "You've been working with her for what, two weeks now? Three?"

"Almost three. But it's not the same thing. I've only seen her in person once."

Lennox sets the phone on my desk and slides it toward me. "All I'm saying is I haven't seen *that* expression on your face in a very long time."

I look at the picture Lennox just took. My expression is—I don't know what it is. I'm not quite smiling, but I still look happy. Or content, maybe?

"Post it," Lennox says. "You look hot. She'll eat it up."

"That's not the point."

I look at the picture one more time. It isn't half-bad. Good enough that I probably *will* post it. But not with Lennox watching.

"I didn't even ask what you were doing here," I say.

Lennox breathes out a sigh. "Just came to see what you were doing. You want to get food later?"

"You really don't know how to spend a day off, do you?"

"You're one to talk. What do you say? Lunch? Dinner? I'll take anything. I'm booooored, Perry."

"Fine. Dinner. Now go and let me work."

It takes five more minutes to boot my brother from the room, which is honestly weird. Lennox has never struggled to entertain himself before, though to be fair, he lived in Charlotte for a long time, a city that has a lot more to do than Silver Creek. If you're willing to climb the mountain, Hendersonville isn't that far away, and Asheville is just beyond that, but here in town? There's only a handful of restaurants, and a pretty much nonexistent social scene. Especially if you're single.

A particular struggle for Lennox. He's chronically and intentionally single, but he's a master at playing the field. When he first moved back, he was always driving up to Asheville, dragging Brody and me—at least until Brody married Kate—along. But he hasn't done that in weeks. Maybe longer?

I don't have time to puzzle out what's going on with my brother. Not right now. But that doesn't mean I won't ask him about it later. Especially if Brody comes to dinner too. He'll have a harder time deflecting questions from both of us.

A notification on my phone alerts me to a new message from Lila, and a wave of anticipation washes over me. Which is stupid. It's a message from my virtual assistant. *Calm down, Perry.*

Before I read the message, I take Lennox's advice and post the new photo to my profile. When I pull up my messages with Lila, the tiny circle next to my messages has already updated with the new picture.

A sense of vulnerability tightens my gut. Lila was probably staring at the chat thread when the photo updated. Should I say something?

I should say something.

But what could I possibly say that wouldn't look like I want her to notice the picture? Even though I really want her to notice the picture.

Better to say nothing at all. Maybe she won't notice. Maybe she . . . *oh man.*

In the seconds I've been staring at the screen, completely ignoring her last message because I've been obsessing over my stupid profile picture, *her* profile picture updated.

To a real picture.

Her hair is down and loose around her shoulders. She's looking directly at the camera, a knowing smile on her lips, and she is . . . stunning.

My phone chimes with another notification, and a second message pops up under Lila's first.

Lila: Hey look. We're real people after all. ;)

I shouldn't be so excited about her message.

I rub a hand across my face.

I'm *very* excited about her message.

At least Lennox already left, so he can't see how much this is affecting me.

My fingers hover over the keyboard, and I clear my throat. I'm just going to keep it professional. Businesslike.

Perry: What does your day look like tomorrow? I have a pretty big project I could use your help with, but it would require you to come out to the farm.

It isn't a lie. I need to update last year's festival layout to reflect the vendors, food trucks, and attractions we're hosting this year. I probably *could* do it by myself, but it will be easier with her here in person to help me.

At least that's what I'm telling myself.

It takes over a minute for Lila to respond, which doesn't sound like a lot of time, but trust me, when you're living it, watching those dancing dots appear and disappear and reappear, a minute is eternal.

When her response finally comes through, I breathe out a sigh of relief.

Lila: Okay. I can do that.

Lila: This is going to sound like a dumb question, but what should I wear? Business attire?

I smile at her question. I don't know her all that well, and yet it still feels very Lila.

Perry: Come in whatever you're comfortable in. But it's a farm, and we'll be outside. Don't dress up on my account.

Lila: Noted. Just a reminder, I'll need to leave by two to get home in time to meet Jack's bus.

Perry: No problem.

Lila: In the meantime, did you see my earlier message? Sorry to be pushy. Just want to make sure you don't miss pertinent info.

I scroll back up to her initial message. It reads:

Lila: I've emailed over a list of diesel mechanics who do onsite repairs. Also, I got a second email about your high school reunion. Are you sure you don't want me to respond?

I pull up the email and look over the list of mechanics. We've been using the same garage in Silver Creek to service our work trucks and farm equipment for years, but the owner recently retired, and we haven't found a decent replacement yet. I was planning on researching myself, but the fact that Lila has already narrowed the list to the mechanics willing to come to us? It's like she knows what I need before *I* know what I need.

But the reunion email. I have no idea how to handle that one. Why does Jocelyn keep emailing? I mean, probably because I haven't responded. But I kinda feel like my lack of response should be a big enough clue. I don't want to go. End of discussion.

It doesn't help matters that Lila is the one getting the emails. Though, if I had just responded to Jocelyn's first message, I could have kept all of this from happening. It probably means something that I'd rather Lila *see* the drama than endure the drama of opening up a line of communication with Jocelyn again.

Perry: Thanks for the list of mechanics. And yes. Respond about the reunion. Tell her I appreciate her invitation, but I have no desire to go.

Lila: Got it. But . . . really? You have no desire to go? There isn't anyone you'd like to see?

A weight settles in my gut, a familiar discomfort creeping over me.

There are people who will be at the reunion who I would like to see. But not half as much as I don't want to see my ex-wife. No old friendship is worth the kind of drama Jocelyn is capable of. You'd think, since she's the one who left me, that she'd be willing to leave things alone. Let bygones be bygones and all that. But as burned as our divorce left me, I sometimes wonder if she's the one having a harder time moving on. She's no longer with the guy she left me for—big surprise there—and that's part of why I'm so uncomfortable with the idea of going. Why does she want me there? What is she trying to prove?

On the other hand, I have to wonder if she's actually trying for the opposite. If her goading is her way of scaring me away, of making sure I don't come. It could honestly go either way with her. With the way she's changed over the last ten years, morphing into a woman I hardly recognize, there's no telling what her motives are.

Either way, I don't need to know enough to endure the drama just to find out. I'd rather avoid the complication altogether.

Perry: Just respond, Lila. Thanks. I'll see you tomorrow.

Chapter Eight

Lila

After my encounter with Perry, I could have written a manual on how to scare off a man.

Step one: Tell him you're a widow. Step two: Let him know you have a child who requires constant care and attention. Step three: Have that child announce you're in the market for a husband ASAP. For bonus points, have the child start calling him DADDY immediately.

I won't lie and say watching the two of them together didn't make me think of the possibility. The man is handsome enough to make my toes tingle. And watching him change a tire while keeping my little boy engaged and entertained? A solid ten out of ten, would highly recommend. Add in the soft flannel he was wearing (Fine. I didn't actually touch it, but it *looked* soft.), those deep brown eyes, and the close-cropped beard that lines his jaw, and I could have watched him all afternoon. Pulled up a chair with a mug of coffee and watched like I was attending my own personal drive-in movie. Movie title: *The Hottest Hawthorne Brother.*

I mean, I can't be certain. He's the only one I've ever seen in person. I just can't imagine *anyone*, celebrity or not, being hotter than Perry.

But acknowledging that my boss is objectively attractive and believing anything could possibly happen between us are two very different things. And I am nothing if not a realist. I mean, *yes,* he did ask if I would be interested in coming out to the farm. Adorably, in fact, in a way that almost seemed like he was asking me on a date. But that was before Jack showed his hand. He's in it to win himself a daddy, come what may.

For three whole days, I refused to let myself dwell on any *possibilities* or *fantasies* regarding my boss. The man is a *Hawthorne.* I know better than to set myself up for that kind of disappointment.

But then Perry messaged me at the end of work today and asked me to come out to the farm tomorrow.

Even after Jack practically proposed on my behalf.

Even after learning about my widowed status.

Even after seeing me in person. *All of me*. Hips and all.

It could just be a work thing. (It's probably just a work thing.)

But something in my gut tells me it might be more. (Maybe that's just indigestion?)

Something in my gut and *maybe* the fact that he added an actual photo to his profile?

I may or may not have spent more than a few minutes staring at the updated picture, because good grief, who wouldn't? But that's not the point. The point is, he added one.

But why? Why now? Was it because he met me in person and decided I was normal enough to trust me with his face? Or could it be because he *wants* me to see his face whenever we communicate?

As soon as the change came through, I felt guilty for leaving my old lady avatar up, so I changed mine too. It's an older picture, taken a year or so ago, but my hair is amazing in it, and I still look enough like that version of myself that I felt okay about using it. It looks more like me than a gray-haired lady in pearls anyway.

Whether it was or wasn't on purpose, whether I'm spinning all of this into something it actually isn't, I one hundred percent did *not* expect him to follow through with the invitation, and now that he has, I'm a little bit of a mess.

First, what am I supposed to wear to work that is comfortable, cute, and farm appropriate? And yes, the cute part is absolutely essential. Because Perry didn't say he had a project for *me*. He said he had a project for us to work on *together*.

I'm more excited about this than I should be. But honestly, who am I kidding? It's not like I didn't see this coming. I saw Perry's photo. I felt the reaction. Then I met him in person, and he was everything I expected him to be.

Serious. Unsmiling. Generally grumpy, but not in a way that's off-putting. He just doesn't seem like a lean-his-elbow-on-the-truck-and-talk-all-night kind of guy.

But he was also kind. Especially when Jack was talking his ear off, though that part maybe did surprise me a little. Jack can be trying even for the people who love him most in the world. Perry was basically a stranger, and he took it all in stride, listening, demonstrating *so much* patience. He even smiled a few times—small ones—but they seemed genuine. (They also made me very anxious to see a real, full smile from the man, though it might be the end of me if I ever do.)

The point is, Perry intrigues me. Interests me. And despite the fear of rejection roiling in my gut, I want to show up looking my best.

Jeans? Jeans and boots? Flannel? Hair in pigtails and a straw hat?

Okay, that last one is probably too much. But SHEESH this is a stressful decision.

I settle on jeans and a flannel, cinched up and tied in a knot around my waist, and my plaid duck boots. They're comfortable enough that I'll be fine wearing them all day and they'll work no matter where on the farm we wind up. At least I hope they will. I don't have a ton of experience as an actual farmhand, though surely manual labor isn't what Perry has in mind.

I'm only slightly alarmed that if manual labor *is* what Perry asks me to do, I'll probably say yes. Assuming he'll be laboring beside me.

I drop Jack off the next morning (on time!) before making my way down the mountains to Silver Creek. I'm dressed to impress and possibly muck out goat stalls. Not exactly an easy balance, but I think I'm pulling it off?

The entire drive down to the farm, I work through everything I know about Perry's upcoming high school reunion. Not because I need to, just because I'm really curious. I responded to the email just like Perry asked. Without any puns or even a tiny bit of snark and immediately received a reply which made me wish I *had* been snarky.

The woman sending the emails—whoever she is—was more than a little snippy, going off on how "just like Perry" it was that he would have his assistant reply without dignifying her with a personal response. I hit reply and was halfway through typing a reply about how Perry was too busy hanging out with his super-hot assistant to give her a passing thought, but I finally came to my senses before actually hitting *send.*

She has to be an ex-girlfriend of some kind. But fifteen years later, she's still bitter enough to be this snotty? I think of the woman's initials in the first email. *JH.* Could the H stand for Hawthorne? Maybe the reunion lady is Perry's ex-wife? Regardless, I can't decide if it's in Perry's best interest for me to show him her reply or not. He isn't going to the reunion. It's over and done.

But that doesn't make me any less itchy to know the full story.

I'm ten minutes away from Silver Creek when it occurs to me that I'm alone in my car. Since I work from home, and it's only Jack and me, I'm almost never alone in my car. And everyone knows the car is one of the very best places to sing at the top of your lungs.

Before Jack, or before Trevor, really, I took just about every opportunity I could to sing in the car. Or in the shower. Or the kitchen, or anywhere, really. There wasn't much that filled me up like music did.

I know that part of me still exists somewhere down deep, but it's been hard to find it lately. I haven't played the piano or sung anything real in years. Not since Trevor sold my piano.

A shot of pain slices through me, and I press my lips together.

I'm fine.

I weathered a storm, and now I'm standing on the other side of it.

I'm *singing* on the other side of it.

I crank up the music, *P!nk*, because *of course,* and sing like my life depends on it. And *oh,* it feels good. So good. I don't stop until I reach Silver Creek. I'm out of breath, and my cheeks are flushed when I catch my reflection in the rearview mirror, but

I haven't felt this good, this much like myself, in longer than I can remember. An image of Perry pops into my mind. I'm not sure what it means that when I'm feeling this good, it's him I think about. Maybe it's that he feels like possibility, and for the first time in a long time, possibility doesn't feel so scary.

I wind my way through the tiny town until I reach the long drive that leads into Stonebrook Farm. The peace I felt moments ago immediately melts into nerves, and I grip the steering wheel a little tighter.

I can do this. I'm *ready* to do this.

I've never been on the property when it hasn't been filled with vendors and food trucks for the harvest festival. I always thought it was a pretty place then, but it's even more gorgeous without all the clutter.

Rolling pastures on either side of the tree-lined drive, surrounded by forests ablaze with fall color. White picket fences, and of course the massive farmhouse sitting up on the hill. I round the bend and pass the entrance to the restaurant opening next month. The exterior is stunning. Exposed beams, fancy rock work, and a modern metal sign over the door that reads *Hawthorne.*

So far, the work I've done for Perry hasn't had much to do with the restaurant, but he did ask me to proofread the final menu, and oh my word, I was near starving by the time I got to the end of it. I know Perry's nervous, but there's no way this restaurant isn't going to succeed. People will drive anywhere for a menu like that one.

I park the car and will my heart rate to slow. I pull down my visor and check my reflection one last time. "There's no reason to worry," I say as I smooth my eyebrows. Do they look bushier than normal today? I lean a little closer. *Oh my word.* They need plucking something awful. I cannot face my hot boss with a unibrow.

Fine. It's not *really* a unibrow, but I do look like I lost my tweezers three months ago and never bothered to replace them.

I bite my lip, debating. I keep tweezers in my car because any woman worth her salt knows natural light is the best tweezing light. Also the best light in which to find horrifying inch-long hairs on my chin that *had* to have grown in overnight because HOW ON EARTH did I miss that thing yesterday?! But right now, seconds before coming face to face with Perry, is *not* the time to think about tweezing.

I snap my visor closed. "You can't pluck what you don't see, Lila. Now get on with it. Hotty Hawthorne is waiting for you."

A light knock sounds on my window, and I jump, a hand flying to my chest.

Apparently, Hotty Hawthorne is standing right outside my car door.

He steps back while I scramble out, tossing my bag over my shoulder, hoping against hope that he didn't hear me calling him *Hotty Hawthorne*. "Hi. Good morning," I say, a little too cheerily. "I hope I didn't keep you waiting."

"Not at all. I was walking back from the barn and saw you. Sorry to startle you."

I wave away his concern. "Don't worry about it."

"Were you, uh . . ." He pushes a hand through his hair. "Were you talking to someone?"

My gut tightens. "Why? Could you hear me?"

Perry doesn't smile, but his mouth twitches just enough for me to think he *absolutely* heard me. "Um, no," he says unconvincingly. "Not at all."

Unconvincing or not, the conversation will end faster if I pretend like he's telling me the truth. I mean, the alternative is coming right out and admitting I've been thinking of him as *Hotty Hawthorne,* and that is not going to happen. "You know. Just giving myself a little pep talk," I say.

He nods. "Right. Absolutely. I do that sometimes too."

He does not. I'm sure of it. But I appreciate him trying to make me feel better anyway.

Perry rocks back on his heels and looks toward the farmhouse. "Shall we go inside?"

"Yes! Absolutely." I fall into step behind him, following as he curves around the house to what looks like a side employee entrance. He's dressed casually, a lot like he was last weekend when he blew a tire. You won't hear any complaints from me though. The man makes jeans and flannel look good. And those jeans make *him* look good.

He holds the door open as I walk into the back hallway of the farmhouse. "The main operational offices are all here on the first floor," Perry says as he leads me down the hallway, pointing at different doors as we go. "Human Resources, Accounting, Event Management, Farm Management. That office at the end belongs to my sister, Olivia, who is out on maternity leave, and this one here is my office."

Perry pauses in the doorway, and I peer inside. It's a warm, comfortable space. A big desk sitting below enormous windows that provide a stunning mountain view, a leather sofa in the corner that looks butter soft, framed watercolors on the walls.

"It's lovely."

"You can leave your things in here if you want," Perry says. "I don't have an office, or even a desk for you, but you can use mine while you're here. Or we'll set you up in Olivia's, since she isn't using it right now."

"Whatever is easiest," I say, just barely managing *not* to squeal at the idea of sharing an office with Perry.

Perry shows me the rest of the farmhouse with methodical precision, detailing the way each of the bigger rooms on the main floor are used for weddings and other events, then launching into a summary of the guest rooms and lounge areas upstairs. Actually, summary isn't the right word. Because Perry isn't leaving *any* details out.

I can't tell if he *really* thinks I need to know the square footage of every bathroom, or if he's nervous and it's making him ramble. Either way, I definitely don't mind listening to him talk.

After the inside tour, we head outside and climb onto this golf-cart-looking thing that Perry calls a Gator. It has enormous tires and a sturdier frame, so a golf cart built for getting around a farm, I guess, which makes sense. We aren't quite touching, sitting side by side like this, but I'm close enough to feel the warmth from Perry's arm and catch faint traces of his scent. He smells exactly like I imagined he would. Like the outdoors and sunshine and pine trees and apples.

"How long would it take for you to show me the whole place?" I say, more out of curiosity than because I actually expect Perry to give me the grand tour. I'm not here on vacation, I'm here to work. Though, I'm also not here to ogle my boss, and I'm managing to do plenty of that. What would a little sightseeing actually hurt?

"Almost an hour, probably." Perry looks my direction. "Do you want to see it?"

"Seeing as how you told me how many towel rods are hanging upstairs in the farmhouse, I thought there might be a quiz later. Do I need to see everything if I have any hope of passing?"

Perry's eyes widen, and his frown deepens. "No, no, there won't be—"

I reach out and touch his arm. "Perry, I'm kidding. I would love to see the farm if we have the time to spare."

His eyes shift to where my fingers are still pressed against his skin, just below the sleeves of his flannel, rolled halfway up his forearm.

I pull my hand away and curl my fingers into my fist. Did he feel that too? That spark?

His mouth twitches the slightest bit before he purses his lips, almost like he's fighting a smile. "Best hold on then. We'll be climbing some hills."

Chapter Nine

Lila

It only takes a few minutes to drive around the public parts of Stonebrook. The giant field where the festival takes place. The restaurant. The farmhouse. I do my best to listen to what Perry is telling me about the farm, but the reality is, the best view around this place is sitting right beside me, and it's hard to focus on anything else.

At the end of a long drive lined with maple trees, we finally cross into an area I've never seen before. A giant barn—where the goats live, Perry explains—is to my right. On the left, there's an enclosure full of chickens, and a second barn, painted just like the first but much smaller. We slowly ramble past the chickens, Perry waving at several people working nearby. When we reach the second structure, Perry slows, pointing toward an enclosure that opens into it. The biggest pig I've ever seen ambles toward the fence, where she presses her giant nose up against the railing.

"Buttercup," Perry says gruffly. "She and I don't get along."

"You don't get along with a pig?"

He shoots me a look. "She isn't just any pig. She's smart. Wily. Conniving."

I press my lips together. "Wily? A pig?"

"Trust me. She's meaner than she looks."

We watch as a farm worker steps up to the railing and scratches Buttercup's ears, the pig leaning into the attention like she's really enjoying it.

"Oh yeah. She looks like a real menace," I say.

Perry only grunts, and I stifle my laughter. I really want to hear whatever story is behind Perry's opinions of Buttercup, and I almost ask him, but then we make a sharp turn onto a narrow path past the barn and climb a steep hill into an apple orchard. Suddenly, I'm too distracted by the view to think about anything else. The higher we go, the more my jaw drops open. The rest of Stonebrook is beautiful, but back here, away from the hustle, it's magical. Beyond the apple trees in nearly every direction, the mountains roll into the horizon, fading into the hazy blue sky.

At the top of the ridge, Perry eases to a stop. I lean forward, taking in the view, the fall colors sparkling in the sunlight. When I finally glance back at Perry, he isn't looking at the leaves or the mountains or anything else. He's looking at me.

Really looking. In a way that makes my breath catch and my heart jump.

I swallow. "It's beautiful up here."

Perry nods, his eyes finally shifting to the horizon. "I never get tired of it."

"Did you always know you'd work here? Growing up?"

He shakes his head. "I didn't really think I wanted to. Not at first. I got an MBA. Did some consulting." He runs a hand across his face. "But then when Dad had a stroke, he needed someone to come back, and I've been here ever since."

"And that's a good thing?" I ask, hoping I'm not asking too much.

Peace settles over his expression, and he nods. "I wanted to come back anyway. Dad's stroke just made it easier. It's where I belong," he says simply, and I believe him. Even more, I can tell *he* believes him.

"To be so lucky," I say. "I mean, to belong to a place like this? I can't even imagine." A sense of longing fills me, reaching all the way out to my fingertips. I had a home growing up. But something like this? All this land. There's a sense of permanence here that I've never experienced, and I suddenly wish for it. For myself. For Jack.

We start moving again, and I settle back into my seat, my shoulder pressing against Perry's. I resist the urge to shift away, wondering what Perry will do.

He doesn't shift away either. In fact, it almost feels like he shifts closer.

"What about you?" he says, even while I try and still my frantic heart. I'm out of practice feeling this kind of excitement. This kind of anything, really. "Where do you belong?" Perry asks.

"Me?" I shrug. "With Jack, I guess."

"Any family anywhere else?"

"My grandparents are in Hendersonville, in an assisted living neighborhood, but they don't get around as much as they used to. They raised me. No mom in the picture, and my dad and I aren't really close."

"So Jack really doesn't have anyone to take him to his father-son breakfast?"

I appreciate the way Perry lets the conversation roll forward. A lot of people want to hem and haw and apologize over my semi-parentless state. But it is what it is, and I don't feel sad about it. I had a happy childhood thanks to Grandma June and Grandpa Jamison. I've never lacked love or security, and that's more than a lot of people can say.

"I've asked his other grandpa, Trevor's dad, if he can come up and take him. Hopefully that will work out."

A question hangs in the air between us. The one that's always there whenever Trevor comes up around people who don't know his story. *How did he die?*

I don't fault people for wanting to know. It's human to be curious, likely connected to some subconscious wish people have to protect themselves and their loved ones from whatever unfortunate fate befell someone else. The tricky part is that asking so that *they* can feel better isn't always what's best for the one who's mourning the loss in the first place.

Sometimes I feel like talking about how Trevor died.

Sometimes I really don't.

Perry doesn't ask. Instead, he points at a narrow trail that cuts steeply up the bank to our left, disappearing into the wood line. "There's a trail there," he says. "Up to the best view on the whole property. It only takes about ten minutes if you don't mind the hike."

It doesn't feel like a dismissal of the conversation we've been having. His invitation to hike feels more like he's putting the ball in my court. I can talk or not talk. Hike or not hike.

I want to hike. *And* talk.

I want to tell him everything.

And that's a realization that scares me more than the butterflies in my stomach or my racing heart ever could.

"A little bit of hiking sounds nice, actually."

He nods and cuts the engine. "Let's do it then."

I climb out after him, glancing at my watch. At this rate, we're barely going to start working before it's time for me to leave again. Not that I'm complaining. Who would ever complain about spending time in such a gorgeous place with someone as gorgeous as Perry?

The climb is steep and rocky, making it difficult to talk for all the focus it takes not to fall flat on my face. But the silence is easy and comfortable, which is a nice thing to notice. I get the sense that Perry is the kind of man who enjoys both silence and solitude, which I can appreciate. At least I can now. I've never minded silence, but with my naturally extroverted nature, I had to cultivate an appreciation for solitude.

As we approach a small clearing, Perry turns, offering me his hand to help me step over one final boulder in the middle of the path. Once I'm steady on my feet, he gives my fingers a tiny squeeze before dropping my hand. I'm so focused on dissecting the meaning behind that squeeze that at first, I don't even notice the view, which is somehow even better than the one down below.

"Seriously?" I say, looking at Perry. "Is this place for real?"

And there it is. A smile. A real, wide, genuine smile that is every bit as overwhelming as I expected it to be. There is pride in that smile. Pride and appreciation and gratitude.

Perry's eyes narrow. "Why are you looking at me like that?"

"Because I can tell you love this place," I say. "And because you have a really nice smile." I bite my lip, hoping I haven't said too much. But of course I did. I always say too much. And you know what? That's me. Perry can take it or leave it.

Perry wipes a hand across his face, and the smile disappears, but the warmth in his eyes stays. "We called it the ledge growing up. We still do, really. I have a lot of happy memories up here. A lot of conversations with my brothers." His head tilts the slightest bit. "My first kiss. My first beer."

My eyebrows lift, and he smiles again, holding up a hand. "*Not* on the same night."

"Glad to know you were clear-headed for that first kiss," I say on a chuckle, but honestly, we have got to change the subject, because the thought of Perry kissing someone is messing with *my* clear head.

We're standing side by side, our shoulders not quite touching, and I swear, despite the blue skies in every direction, you could convince me there was a thunderhead directly above us for all the crackling energy in the air. I want to lean into the feeling, but I also have a strange impulse to flee.

I've forgotten how to do this. How to *feel.*

"Trevor was a fighter pilot in the Navy," I blurt out, my eyes cutting over to Perry. "Or at least training to be."

There's nothing but warmth and understanding in Perry's gaze.

"It was a training exercise. Something went wrong with his ejection seat, and . . . he didn't make it."

Perry is silent for a long moment. "I'm so sorry, Lila," he finally says.

It's gotten easier to say it out loud over the years. To think of the event as a tragedy that happened in my past that no longer has to define my present.

At the same time, I'm still working on letting go of the guilt that fills me whenever I think about my *marriage,* which is different than thinking about losing my husband. My grief counselor told me to expect the guilt to flare up when I start dating again, or even just start considering the possibility of happiness with someone new.

With my eyes still fixed on Perry, I hear my therapist's words repeat in my brain. *You deserve happiness, Lila. It's okay to want it.*

I take a steadying breath. I can do this. I can let the joy in.

I nod and give Perry a small smile. "Thank you. He was very good at his job. And the Navy has changed protocol as a result of his accident, so that's something at least."

"That's no consolation."

It isn't. Not even a little bit. But it's a fact I can easily repeat. More easily than admitting that had my husband not died when he was training in California, I likely would have filed for a divorce as soon as he came home.

"Not a consolation," I agree. "But I'm glad his loss will lessen the likelihood of it happening to someone else. I've taught Jack that his father's service to his country persisted even beyond his death."

"Still. It's a lot for a little guy to go through," Perry says.

I press a hand to my stomach and feel the rise and fall of my breathing. Time to wrap this conversation up, because if I start talking about Jack, I *will* start to cry. I give my head a little shake and force a smile. "So. Where to next?"

The moment I back away like this—because that's enough talking about my dead husband, thank you very much—is usually when people's faces shift into that mournful expression I've grown to know so well. Hands pressed to chests. Fingers covering lips. Eyes turned down and sad. Those expressions are so hard because they can mean *I'm so sorry for your loss,* but they can also mean, *I'm so glad I'm not you.* And sometimes the line between one sentiment and the other is very thin.

True compassion is always welcome.

Pity, or someone making my pain about them, is not.

Fortunately, Perry's guileless expression is only full of understanding. "Next, we get to work," he says, and I relax the tiniest bit. Work sounds good. Work sounds like exactly what I need.

"You lead, I'll follow," I say.

And I do.

All over the north field, clipboard in hand, making notes while Perry walks through the logistical layout for the harvest festival, tape measure and flags to mark the distance between each vendor location in hand. Retail booths. Food stalls. Food trucks. Ticket booths for the hayride and petting zoo. There are so many things to consider. Foot traffic flow. Access to bathrooms. The length of food lines and how that might interfere with access to surrounding booths.

Perry is methodical, quick in his decision-making, and needs very little input from me. In fact, I'm pretty sure he doesn't actually need me here at all. He could be jotting things down on this clipboard just as easily as I am.

"Okay," he finally says after what feels like hours and hours of traipsing around the field. "I think that does it."

My stomach growls as I look over the layout. It's pushing one o'clock, and we didn't stop for lunch. If we were still in the orchard, I'd have grabbed an apple from one of the trees ages ago. "Are you open to suggestions?" I say.

Perry's eyes widen, like he's actually taken aback by the question, but he recovers quickly. "Does the layout really need suggestions? I feel like we covered everything."

"We did. And this will probably work fine. But as someone who's attended the festival with a small child, I might reconsider a few things."

He folds his arms across his chest. "Like what?" he asks, his tone sharp.

Well, okay, Mr. Defensive. You don't have to have an attitude about it.

Looks like the nice, easygoing Perry I spent the morning with got swallowed up by a grump.

I walk forward and hold out the clipboard, flipping the top sheet over to the map of the field printed on the back of the vendor list. "Look at these four things," I say, pointing to four different things on the map. "For anyone coming to the festival with children under five years old, these are the attractions they're going to be most excited about. The petting zoo, the hayride, the 'Make Your Own Caramel Apple' booth, and the face painting."

"Okay. I'm still not seeing the problem."

"Perry, none of these things are close together. It almost feels intentional. Like you're trying to make people walk far on purpose."

"But they'll be walking past craft booths and food stalls. People can shop on their way from one thing to another."

"You've clearly never been anywhere with a three-year-old."

His frown deepens, his hand moving to his jaw, but he doesn't respond.

"I know you can't move the location of the petting zoo," I say, "but you could shift the caramel apple booth and the face painting so it's on this end of the field, next to the ticket booth for the zoo and the hayride. Parents with little kids are all about optimizing the brief, magical hours when kids are happy. And by happy, I mean not tired or starving. Don't make them walk all over everywhere. If they finish the kid stuff and everyone is still happy, then they can go browse and shop. But I promise parents with cranky toddlers aren't meandering through stalls looking for hand-carved cutting boards or homemade apple butter. They're just trying to get home without losing their minds."

Perry huffs. "You seem to know a lot about cranky toddlers, but I'm not sure that qualifies you to make decisions about something this big."

I take a step backward. "Are you implying my child is cranky? Because you've spent time with him, and you know how charming he is. But he's a *human child,* which means I do have more experience with cranky toddlers than you do, and as such, my opinion has some merit, whether you want it to or not."

Perry's expression is stern, like he can't quite believe I spoke so freely.

I bite my lip. He was the one who got defensive first. And my suggestion did have merit. Possibly I could have presented it with a little more tact. But that doesn't make me wrong.

Whoa. Speaking of cranky toddlers.

I don't know who's behaving worse right now. Me or Perry. "I'm sorry," I say, quickly backpedaling. "I haven't eaten since breakfast. I think I might be a little hangry." I give him a pointed look because, let's be real, I'm not the only one in this situation who might be hangry. I won't call him out directly, but if a lifted brow helps him make the leap himself, I wouldn't mind.

His face immediately shifts. "You haven't eaten?"

I glance at my watch. "When would I have? I packed a lunch, but it's back in my bag. In your office."

His shoulders drop, and he runs a hand through his hair, mussing it in a way that shouldn't be quite so adorable but absolutely is. "Of course you wouldn't have. I'm sorry. I'm—" He shakes his head. "Come on. We can be done here. I'll drive you back to get your stuff, and you can head out for the day."

Unease swirls through my gut. "I still have an hour before I have to leave," I argue, not liking that I suddenly feel so dismissed.

Perry is already walking toward the Gator we've been driving all over the farm. "You've more than earned the right to leave early, Lila. Don't worry about it."

Perry is polite but distant as we make the short drive back to the farmhouse. He waits in the hallway outside his office while I retrieve my bag, and I think he'll let me leave without saying anything else at all. But then he stops at the back door, a pained look on his face.

"Can we try this again tomorrow?" he says. "I promise I'll let you eat. And take any other breaks you need." He clears his throat. "I appreciate you being here today. It was—" He pauses, like he can't find the right word. "Helpful," he finally manages.

I didn't particularly feel helpful, and the afternoon definitely ended on a more sour note than it started. But I find myself nodding anyway. "I can come back tomorrow."

"Good. Good. I'll see you then."

I make my way to my car, making sure Perry is well and truly out of earshot before I grumble, "I bet you'll confuse me tomorrow, too."

I drop into the driver's seat with a huff. "It was a good suggestion," I say to absolutely no one. "He didn't have to be so defensive." Because he *was* defensive, his tone all judgy. Even his posture screamed his disapproval, like he couldn't believe I would suggest there was a better way to do something than what came out of his own precious brain.

I shift the car into reverse and back out of my parking space. "And then to dismiss me like that," I say as I pull down the winding front drive, not that I really mind the extra hour of solitude before Jack gets home. But I *don't* like feeling dismissed. Forget *Hotty Hawthorne.* Maybe I should start calling him *Grumpy Hawthorne.*

Still, there *were* moments with Perry today that weren't contentious. When we hiked up to see the view, for one. Did I imagine the energy crackling between us? Imagine him leaning the slightest bit closer so our shoulders touched?

Honestly, I'm so out of practice, it's entirely possible I did imagine it. But what if I didn't? What if there is a spark between us? Can I allow myself to hope for something more than professional, even more than friendship?

I suddenly picture Jack's face, asking me for a stairdad, and my stomach clenches.

Instead of going home, I find myself driving over to Grandma June and Grandpa Jamison's house. I try to stop in a few times a week to say hello and make sure they don't need anything. Their assisted living community does a pretty good job of taking care of the basics, but I still like to be aware. Plus, my grandparents have a way of keeping me anchored, and after the day I've had, I could use a little grounding.

Grandma June greets me at the door, pulling me into a gentle hug. "No Jack today?"

"He's still in school," I say. "I got off work early. Just wanted to stop by and say hi."

She looks toward the living room, a ghost of something unreadable slipping across her face. "You'll make your grandpa's day."

"How is Grandpa?"

Her expression shifts again, and a knot of worry tightens in my gut.

"He's okay," she finally says. "The same, mostly. Just ornery because of all the things he can't do anymore. Yesterday, he grumbled for twenty minutes while the yard maintenance people were cutting our grass, criticizing every little thing. They were doing a fine job; he was just grouchy because it wasn't him doing it."

"I'll go say hello," I say. "See if I can cheer him up."

Grandma June smiles and pats my hand. "You always do. But . . ."

I pause, waiting for her to finish her sentence. "But what?" I finally prompt.

"Maybe just don't mention Jack's father-son breakfast. I haven't told Jamison about it. He'll want to go, but he really can't. He's not stable enough on his feet, even if he doesn't want to admit it. But if he thinks you're stressing about it, he'll insist."

I nod my understanding. "I won't tell him."

Grandma June studies me carefully. "Lila, have you thought about calling your dad?"

I barely contain my scoff. "What? No. Absolutely not."

She presses her lips together. "He's only down in Savannah. It wouldn't be that far of a drive."

"It's not the drive I'm worried about. He hasn't seen Jack since Trevor's funeral. Jack wouldn't be comfortable with it, and I wouldn't be either."

I hate the pain that slices across Grandma June's face. My father is her only son, and the youngest of her three children, a surprise baby born fifteen years after her youngest daughter. Her daughters, my aunts, live over in Asheville, and each have two daughters a piece, all older than me, all happily married and living perfectly adorable lives.

My dad is happily married now too. To a woman barely older than I am with three kids barely older than Jack. She and I were in high school at the same time. She was a senior when I was a freshman, but still. It's weird.

Grandma June thinks it's good for him. That he's finally grown up enough to be a good dad. He and my mama, who hasn't been in the picture since my first birthday, were too young when I was born. Too foolish to really settle down. But he's different now. *He's changed.*

Which, fine. I'm happy for him. I had a happy childhood, thanks to Grandma June and Grandpa Jamison. Dad showed up every once in a while, but in my mind, he was more like a visiting uncle than he was my dad. That role fell squarely on Grandpa Jamison's shoulders, and he did a fantastic job.

But being happy for my biological father doesn't mean I feel any obligation to build a relationship with him. I've had the same cell number since I was thirteen. He knows how to find me if he wants to.

Clearly, he also knows how to ignore me, since that seems to be his preferred choice.

"Truly, I can't fault you wanting to keep your distance," Grandma June says. "I just hate to see you managing so much on your own."

I reach out and squeeze her hand. "I'm not on my own. I have you."

"You know that's not good enough. Not long term." She tugs me toward her so we're standing even closer and lifts a wrinkled hand to my cheek. "You're a fighter, Lila. You always have been. And you're more than enough for that little boy. All by yourself, you're enough."

I sense the *but* to her sentence and wait for it, even though I know exactly where she's steering the conversation.

"But you *can* start dating, honey," she says. "It's been three years. Have you thought about it at all?"

Perry's smile flashes in my mind's eye, and my gut tightens. "Maybe? Honestly, it still feels impossible."

She studies me, one eyebrow lifted. "Why do I feel like there's something you aren't saying?"

I wrinkle my nose. This woman knows me too well. "Fine. *Maybe* I'm starting to think it's time for me to try. I don't know. I think the whole breakfast dilemma has me recognizing how much I want Jack to have a father figure in his life."

Grandma June's eyes brighten. "Oh, honey. Of course you do. You know, my neighbor next door, she's got a couple of granddaughters in high school, and she just mentioned the other day how much money they're making babysitting. I could get their number for you."

Babysitting? I guess it would be necessary if I were going on actual dates, which . . . *oh man.* A wave of fear washes over me. The idea of *Perry* might feel a tiny bit enticing, but pick-me-up-on-the-doorstep dating? Dinners and movies and babysitters? Just so I can dive into the drama of awkward conversations and worry about whether my breath still smells like the onions that were on the cheeseburger I ate at lunch and whether I should expect a kiss at the end of the night? Am I really ready for all of that?

Except, wait—is that even what dating is when you're an adult? I might have a bigger problem on my hands than just the possibility of onion breath. Do people even think about kissing at the end of the night, or is it just assumed? And what about *more* than kissing? First date? Third date? Are there rules about this sort of thing?

Everyone referred to "bases" back in high school, but even back then, I never really figured out what they all were. When my best friend sat down at the lunch table and triumphantly declared she'd made it to second base with her boyfriend, I genuinely thought they'd gone to a baseball game and somehow snuck onto the field. It wasn't until weeks later that I finally figured out what she meant.

As for me, there's only one man who has ever gotten *more*, and I married him when I was nineteen. Needless to say, my experience is limited.

I offer Grandma June a smile I hope is convincing. "Yeah, maybe. I'll think about it."

She lifts an eyebrow, her expression saying she isn't buying my lackluster acquiescence. "Any man would be lucky to have you in his life, Lila. Maybe even that new boss of yours."

I roll my eyes. I've only had one conversation with Grandma June about going to rescue my stranded boss. It only took her about fifteen seconds to turn it into the opening scenes of one of the Hallmark movies she loves to watch so much. "Don't you start this again."

"Start what?" she says innocently. "Stranger things have happened."

Stranger things, maybe. But I don't need Grandma June fanning the flames of whatever hope I've got regarding my very grumpy boss. If I let her or Marley or anyone else encourage me, I'm liable to fall, regardless of whether Perry is actually interested. And that feels like a very good way to both embarrass myself *and* lose my job.

"He's my boss, Grandma. I'm not hoping for anything beyond that."

"Fine, fine," she says with a huff. "You're lying, but I won't push it."

I shoot Grandma June a saucy look before moving into the living room, where I lean down and kiss my grandpa's weathered cheek. "Hey, Grandpa. What's the latest? How are your Spelling Bee numbers this week?" We've been playing the New York Times Spelling Bee online game for the past few months, comparing scores and keeping track of who scores the highest the most frequently.

He grunts a hello, his hand reaching for mine and tugging me onto the couch beside him. I nestle into his shoulder, pulling my feet up under me just like I did when I was a kid. This isn't the house I grew up in, but it is the same couch, and the familiarity of the moment is a balm to my soul. Only the presence of the walker set just to the side of where Grandpa Jamison is sitting reminds me that all is not what it used to be. "I made it to genius level every day this week," Grandpa says, his voice scratchy and thin. "How'd you do?"

"Every day? Are you serious?"

He chuckles. "Didn't do that great, huh?"

I huff. "I only got to genius level once. What was the pangram yesterday?"

"Naïvely ," he says, tossing me a knowing grin.

"Naïvely ? Really? How did I not get that one?"

"You're too smart to be naïve," he says, nudging me with his elbow. "The word wouldn't come to your mind."

Huh. I may not be naïve anymore, but I was naïve enough for a lifetime when I met Trevor. Naïve enough to think pausing my dreams and marrying him was a good idea. Naïve enough to miss all the warning signs for what they were. But there's no point in hashing that out with Grandpa Jamison.

"You want to watch some baseball?" he asks as he reaches for the remote.

"Ugh. Not even a little bit," I say, though even baseball would be better than stressing over my past choices. I just have to remember that Trevor brought me Jack, and he's worth whatever else I've been through.

Grandpa Jamison chuckles. "Want to sit here with me and play Spelling Bee while *I* watch baseball?"

"Now you're talking," I say, tugging my phone out of my back pocket. We've had the same conversation hundreds of times. One of these days I'm going to change things up and say *yes* when Grandpa Jamison asks. Except then I'd have to actually watch baseball, so . . . scratch that. Never mind.

Instead of pulling up the Spelling Bee game, I pull up my text messages. There's a message from an unknown number. Except, it isn't unknown. I've seen the number before. It's *Perry's* number.

He's texting my phone directly instead of using the virtual assistant app, which somehow feels significant.

My hands start to tremble as I open the message, which is just. so. stupid. It's a text! Probably about something very boring and business-related.

Actually, it's *multiple* texts.

Perry: I'm sorry I didn't give you a lunch break.

Perry: It was unreasonable. I'll be more respectful of your time in the future.

Perry: Thanks again for your help.

I turn off my phone and drop it into my lap, trying not to feel disappointed.

I shouldn't be disappointed. His texts are fine. Nice, even. Perfectly professional. And he gave me an apology, which I have to appreciate.

Except, the tone of his texts is so . . . not cold, exactly. But lackluster? Unenthusiastic.

Impersonal.

I scold myself for feeling frustrated. The fact that this bothers me is completely on me. I'm the one who filled my head with visions of Perry spending time with Jack, laughing like they did when they changed his tire. I'm the one who watched him on the farm, in all his soft flannel and denim, the one who admired the perfect amount of beard on his face and imagined his time with me as anything other than work.

It's good that Perry's texts feel like a bucket of cold water.

Clearly, I need it.

And now I don't need to worry about all those questions I have about dating, after all.

That should feel like a relief.

It *is* a relief.

I've figured out how to survive on my own. And I'm good at it. I'm making it. A relationship would only disrupt that, especially a relationship with my boss, of all people.

So why, knowing all of this very logical information, do I feel so disappointed?

Chapter Ten

Perry

LILA DOES NOT RESPOND to my (admittedly lame) apology.

I don't know that I truly expected that she would. But I did . . . hope, I guess?

I have a feeling that hope means something. That the irritability I'm feeling now means something.

I like her.

Which is just aggravating. I don't want to like her. Not because it's her, but because I don't want to like *anyone.* I already did this. Tried to make a life with another person and failed so spectacularly, I'm still suffering the consequences of the implosion. I don't like doing things poorly. I never have. If I can't do a relationship well, I'd rather not do one at all.

What's more, Lila has been through a lot. It seems entirely unfair to ask her to gamble on someone like me, someone saddled with all the baggage and heartache I carry around.

And yet.

I can't stop thinking about her. Every time my phone pings, I wonder if it's her, finally responding to my messages.

In all my poor attempts at dating the past few years, I've never met anyone interesting enough to challenge my determination to remain single. Not until now.

Objectively, I recognized my attraction to Lila immediately. The first moment I saw her getting out of the car to bring me a jack, I felt that tug deep in my gut. It was easier to ignore when I thought it was just attraction, when I believed Lila did not return my interest. But then when she arrived at the farm this morning, I'm pretty sure she called me *Hotty Hawthorne* before she got out of the car. And when she left after our disagreement in the field, there was disappointment clear in her expression.

If she's interested back? I don't think I can keep ignoring the pressure that builds in my chest whenever she's around.

I shove away my phone, tired of checking my notifications every fifteen seconds.

I need a workout. Or maybe just a hard run. Something to distract me. Make me think about something other than the way Lila looked in the field this afternoon, clipboard in hand, her expression indignant as she told me all the reasons why I should listen to her.

She was right, of course. And I did listen to her. It only took me an hour after she left to realize she was right about the setup. I've already adjusted the layout to be more family friendly.

But it isn't her ideas that keep flashing through my mind. It's her eyes, bright blue in the afternoon light, sparking with fire as she spoke. It's the curve of her hips as she hiked up to the ledge. The vulnerability in her eyes when she finally told me how she lost her husband.

Seized by a sudden impulse, I grab my phone and google her husband's name. I have to pull up her profile on the virtual assistant app to make sure I get her last name right.

Trevor Templeton.

It doesn't take long to find a few articles about his death. I skim through them, the same words popping out over and over again. *Highly skilled. Highly decorated. Among the nation's best and brightest. An insurmountable loss.*

I drop my phone onto the sofa cushion beside me. See? I knew I wasn't good enough for her, and finding out how amazing her late husband was confirms it. She was married to a national hero, while my marriage was practically a natural disaster.

Okay. It's definitely time for a run.

It's too dark to hit the curvy mountain road I live on, so I settle for the treadmill in my garage. It came with the house when I rented the place, and it sounds like an airplane about to take off and smells like burning rubber if I go faster than seven miles an hour, but it's better than nothing.

I connect my AirPods to my phone and crank up my music, then intentionally leave the phone on the counter in the kitchen where I won't be tempted to look at it every five seconds.

If Lila were going to respond by now, she would have. I have to move on.

I'm ten minutes into my run when the volume on my music decreases and Siri's voice pipes into my ears. "Text message from *Lila Templeton,*" Siri says in a measured, robotic voice. "Thank you for the apology, but it isn't necessary. You're the boss." I can't decide if the text feels cold and impersonal because Siri read it like she was reciting ingredients off the back of a cereal box, or if it really *is* just cold and impersonal.

I scramble to stop the treadmill, but I somehow miss the stop button, my fingers grazing over it without actually *pushing* it.

Problem: my brain already prepared my feet to STOP.

When the treadmill keeps going, it tosses me off the back, right into the concrete wall of my garage.

I pause long enough to make sure I'm not bleeding anywhere, yank the safety key out of the treadmill to stop the stupid thing, then run to the kitchen to grab my phone. I'm going to be bruised tomorrow in so many places. But I don't even care.

Lila responded.

She read my dumb apology and still decided to message me back.

I sit at my kitchen table and read her response for myself, imagining the words in *her* voice instead of Siri's.

Lila: Thank you for the apology, but it isn't necessary. You're the boss.

It isn't terrible, exactly. But it isn't good, either. I key out a quick response before I can overthink.

Perry: Being the boss doesn't make me right all the time, nor does it justify forcing you to work without breaks.

Lila: Well, that's a relief. Guess I don't need to fill my pockets with Lucky Charms before coming to work tomorrow.

I grin at her response, happy to move even this tiny sliver past the weird tension I created between us with my earlier stupidity.

Perry: Lucky Charms?

Lila: Of course. They're magically delicious.

Lila: They're also Jack's favorite. Sometimes I forget everyone doesn't have a pantry full of kid food.

Seized by an idea that could be brilliant but could just as easily be stupid, I type out my next message and send it before I can talk myself out of it.

Perry: I definitely prefer my cereal a little more *hard-core.*

Lila: Hardcore?

Perry: Apple Jacks, Lila. You of all people should apple-solutely understand.

Lila: WAIT. HardCORE cereal? I don't know if I can laugh at that one, Perry.

Perry: Come on. That was a very a-peeling pun.

Lila: STOP. Is this what it feels like when I send you apple puns? I TAKE THEM ALL BACK.

Perry: Nah. They're starting to GROW on me. They always PRODUCE a laugh.

Lila: I've created a monster.

Lila: I've got to go put Jack to bed. Thanks again for reaching out. See you tomorrow?

Perry: I'm looking forward to it.

I send my last message and drop my phone onto the kitchen table before throwing my arms overhead in victory. I could be wrong, but that felt like a very good text exchange. Not flirty, exactly, but almost? And now I'm going to see her tomorrow, and I have no idea how to act.

All of my doubts come roaring back. Her military hero husband. My trash heap marriage. My complete inability to be charming, though I did just incorporate apple puns into a text conversation. Not exactly my MO, so maybe there's hope for me after all?

There are so many reasons why this could go badly, but this is the first time since my divorce that I've felt any real hope when it comes to the idea of a relationship.

Maybe I'll screw everything up.

Maybe she won't reciprocate.

Maybe we'll never date, *and* I'll lose her as an assistant.

But I think I have to try. Shelve my doubts and see what happens.

A new excitement pulses in my chest. I'm going to do this. Actually *pursue* a woman.

I put my phone down and rest my hands on my knees. The thought buzzing around in my brain annoys me. I don't want it to be true, even though I know it is.

If I want to stand a chance, I need help.

I reach for my phone again, swallow every ounce of my pride, and pull up the running text thread I share with my brothers.

"Here goes nothing," I say out loud before sending the first text.

Perry: Brothers. I need help. I met a woman, and I don't know what I'm doing.

Lennox: I KNEW IT. YOU LIKE HER.

Brody: Wait. Hold up. Why does Lennox know something the rest of us don't?

Lennox: It's his virtual assistant. He met her in person when he was stranded with a flat tire and no jack.

Perry: Huh. Stranded without a jack. I wonder how that happened? I feel like someone took it and forgot to put it back. I just can't remember who.

Brody: Lennox?

Flint: Lennox?

Lennox: I APOLOGIZED. And you met a woman because of it, so maybe you should thank me.

Flint: Right. Back to the woman. Name? Age? Family of origin? Aspiring actress? Willing to sign a nondisclosure agreement?

Perry: Flint. What.

Flint: Sorry. Those are the questions my manager makes me answer when I meet someone new. Just answer the relevant ones.

Perry: Her name is Lila. She's twenty-nine? I think? Not an actress. She's my assistant.

Lennox: I feel like there's something you aren't saying here. Something along the lines of LENNOX, YOU WERE RIGHT.

Perry: LENNOX, YOU'RE AN IDIOT. How's that?

Brody: I say go for it. Though it's been so long since you've been interested in anyone, you could tell me you wanted to date Ann down at the feed and seed, and I'd probably say go for it. So.

Lennox: Hey. No knocking Ann. I'm this close to getting her to share her sugar cookie recipe.

Perry: Can we please focus? I need a plan.

Brody: You can't just ask her out?

Perry: I don't think we're there yet. She came out to the farm today, and things didn't go so well.

Flint: Elaborate.

Perry: I forgot to give her a lunch break.

Perry: And we argued about something stupid.

Flint: ELABORATE

Brody: Agreed. This would be easier if you'd give us a little more information.

Perry: She had an idea about how to change the layout for the harvest festival, and I shot her down.

Lennox: This all tracks.

Perry: STOP. I'm trying here. I want to fix things, and I don't know how.

Brody: Maybe start with apologizing?

Perry: I already did that.

Flint: Did you apologize like a human? Or like a robot?

Perry: Hold on. I'll copy and paste. I said:

Perry: *I'm sorry I didn't give you a lunch break.*

Perry: *It was unreasonable. I'll be more respectful of your time in the future.*

Perry: *Thanks again for your help.*

Lennox: So...

Lennox: Like a robot. Got it.

Perry: How was that robotic? I said I was sorry. That I'd try to do better.

Brody: It's a fine apology if all you want is to be her boss. If you want more, you have to up your game.

Perry: I realize that. That's why I'm texting you idiots.

Lennox: Okay. Let's get specific. What do you know about her?

Perry: That she works for me. And she has a five-year-old kid. And she drives a blue SUV.

Brody: That's it, and you know you want to date her?

Lennox: She's also beautiful. He's leaving that part out.

Flint: #hotmoms

Perry: She's also . . . I don't know. She's happy. Even though she's been through stuff. I like that about her. And she smiles a lot and includes stupid apple puns in her messages.

Brody: I like her already.

Flint: When will you see her again?

Perry: At work tomorrow.

Lennox: You should send her to the goat barn with Mom. Women love Mom.

Flint: And baby goats.

Brody: This is a good idea. If she falls in love with the farm, she might be willing to tolerate you.

Perry: I don't know why I thought you guys could help me.

Brody: Wait, wait. I can be serious.

Brody: Make eye contact. Don't be afraid to be vulnerable. Tell her something personal. Compliment her, but not in a creepy way. Ask her questions about herself and listen with your whole body.

Lennox: And for the love, FEED HER. I'll leave a packed lunch in the back of the fridge for you.

Flint: This is good stuff. You should call me over lunch. I'd be happy to say hello.

Perry: Not helpful.

Perry: But lunch would be great, Len.

Flint: What? What woman doesn't want *People Magazine*'s Sexiest Man Alive to tell her hello?

...

...

...

Flint: GUYS. Come on. I was kidding.

...

...

...

Flint: WHATEVER. Your jealousy is showing.

Chapter Eleven

Perry

My brothers were marginally helpful. Scratch that. Brody was helpful. Flint was Flint. And Lennox—at least I got lunch out of the deal. Though it's still a question whether I'll have the nerve to actually invite Lila to eat it with me.

I rub my hands down the front of my pants and pace back and forth across my office. I'm being ridiculous. Lila is just a woman. A woman who works for me and is *only* coming to the farm for that reason. To work.

I need to relax.

If I happen to work up the nerve to invite her to a picnic lunch prepared by one of the region's greatest culinary geniuses? Well, we'll cross that bridge when we come to it. Odds are high I'll chicken out and eat the lunch by myself, hiding on the ledge where no one can report back to Lennox that all his efforts were for nothing.

I grumble and drop into my desk chair. It doesn't have to be this hard. I need to just work. To stop waiting for her and try and get something done.

It takes a few minutes, but I'm finally able to distract myself with an analysis of the farm's quarterly reports, so much so that Lila startles me when she knocks on my open office door.

"Knock, knock," she says lightly.

I look up to see her leaning against the door frame, and my breath catches in my throat. She looks as beautiful today as she did yesterday. "Lila. Good morning."

She offers a reserved smile. "Morning, boss."

Brody's advice cycles through my brain. *Pay her compliments. Be vulnerable.* "You, um—you look nice today."

Her eyebrows go up, then her eyes drop, like she's looking over what she's wearing. "Oh. Thank you."

"I like your, uh—hair thing." *Hair thing? What, am I seven years old now?*

She reaches up and touches her hair. "My braid?"

"Right. Braid."

Her expression shifts again, like she can't quite figure me out. "Thanks," she says again slowly.

This is probably why Brody said not to compliment her in a creepy way. I have to do better than this.

Ask her questions.

I turn in my chair so I'm facing her fully. "How's Jack this morning?"

Her face immediately brightens, and the tightness in my chest eases the slightest bit.

"As cute as ever. He told me at breakfast he's figured out who he's going to marry. She's a fifth grader who rides his bus and, according to Jack, has cool hair that matches her shoes." She smiles, her expression knowing, and lifts her hand to her temple. "I've seen her. She has a strip of blue right here."

Note to self: The ultimate key to Lila is definitely Jack. "Ah. She definitely sounds like marriage material."

Lila smiles. "I'm not sure how London feels about the match, but Jack is sold."

"Her name is London? This girl keeps getting cooler and cooler."

"Right? She definitely has a cool vibe, at least as far as fifth graders are concerned."

I suddenly wonder what would make someone have a cool vibe to Lila. Owning a farm? Working in flannel? Does she think *Perry* is a cool name? It's maybe not as hip as Lennox or Flint, but—*wait.* This is not relevant. *Focus, Perry.* She's standing right in front of you.

Make eye contact.

I hold Lila's gaze long enough for my heart rate to climb and my hope to build. This is going well. I'm smiling. She's smiling. But then Lila shifts and looks down, and my hope fizzles. Am I making her uncomfortable with my questions? Have I waited too long to say something new?

I wish I were better at reading her. At reading *any* woman. Jocelyn always told me how terrible I was at understanding her emotions, at *sensing* what she needed without her having to explicitly tell me. Which sounds more like mind reading than understanding emotions, but what do I know? We wound up divorced so—nothing. Clearly nothing.

I clear my throat. "So, I've got some work you can do inside. Reviewing some reports from accounting, double checking for discrepancies. The event staff is using Olivia's office for some bridal appointments, so if you're okay with it, I thought you could work in here."

She nods and moves into the office, dropping her bag onto the chair on the opposite side of my desk. "Of course. Whatever you need. But won't I be in your way?"

"Not at all. I've got apple shipments going out today. I'll be in the warehouse most of the morning."

Something flashes behind her eyes, and her shoulders drop the tiniest bit, almost like she's disappointed we won't be working in the same space. "All right."

I pull out the reports I need her to review and step away, making way for her to circle around the desk and settle into my chair. She pulls the reports closer as I move to the door.

Nerves prickle along my spine. *Ask her now. Just do it.*

"Lila," I say, pausing with one hand on the door jamb. I can do this. *Eye contact. Be vulnerable.* "Would you like to have lunch with me today? I was thinking we could take a picnic out to the orchard."

Her eyes widen the slightest bit, but she immediately smiles. "Okay. Sure."

"Good. Great. I'll be back at eleven-thirty to pick you up."

I make my way out of my office, a lightness in my step that I haven't felt in ages. For all that I have to get done today, I shouldn't be this excited about taking a lunch break at all, much less a leisurely picnic out in the orchard, but I can't bring myself to truly care. Because Lila said yes to lunch. And even looked excited about it. Maybe excited?

I swing by my parents' house to pick up my dad before heading to the warehouse. Dad is almost entirely retired—a circumstance forced by the stroke he had a few years back. But when he feels up to it, he still likes to do a quality check on the apples before they're shipped out.

Dad's still finishing up his breakfast, so I lean against the counter in the kitchen, scrolling through my email while I wait. My eyes catch on the reunion invite from Jocelyn, but I keep on scrolling. Hopefully Lila has responded by now, and Jocelyn has finally gotten the message.

"What are you frowning about over there?" Mom says, looking up from the dishwasher she's loading.

"Ah, nothing. Just—emails."

"Hmm. Nice lie. Very convincing."

I roll my eyes. Mom always has been annoyingly intuitive. I shove my phone into my pocket and cross my arms. "Jocelyn is throwing the high school reunion happening in a couple of weeks."

Mom's eyebrows go up. "Ah. And you're invited."

I nod.

"And you don't want to go."

"Definitely not. She'll be there. And she's being weird about making sure I'm there too. Why does she care so much?"

Mom shrugs. "Maybe she wants you to have a good time. Maybe she's ready to let things go so you can both move on."

"Sure. And maybe Flint will win an Oscar for the time travel movie he filmed last year."

Mom presses her lips together, trying and failing to hold back her smile. "You be nice. Not every movie can be a hit." She closes the dishwasher and dries her hands, then turns to face me fully. "You really think Jocelyn is up to something?"

"I have no idea. Regardless, I don't really feel like risking it."

"Want to know what I think?" Mom mirrors my stance, leaning against the counter with her arms folded.

"Always."

"I think Jocelyn thought you'd fight for her. She thought you'd come groveling back. Then you didn't. You finally gave her reason to question the power she thinks she has over you."

"She doesn't have power over me." Relief pushes through me as I say the words, because I finally know they're true.

It took me a long time to break whatever spell kept me from seeing Jocelyn for who she was. Our relationship wasn't all bad, not until the end. But even when things were good, she still held all the cards. She had an idea in her head about how our life was supposed to look and didn't want to give me an inch. It was her vision, or no vision. Needless to say, I chose the latter option.

"Not anymore," Mom says knowingly. "Maybe you ought to go to the reunion to show her just that. That you're absolutely fine without her."

"Or I could just *be* absolutely fine without her. Reunion not required."

Mom *tsks.* "That's probably the more mature thing to do, but I sure do love the idea of someone giving that woman what for."

I chuckle. "I'll keep that in mind."

Dad comes into the kitchen, his empty plate in hand, and mom hurries to take it from him. He still isn't as steady on his feet as he used to be. "Let me grab my jacket," Dad says to me before disappearing down the hallway.

"How are things with your new assistant?"

"Good. She's good. Great, even. She's helping me a lot."

"And it's all virtual? I swear, you young people and your technology."

"Mostly virtual, but she's actually here today. Working in person."

"Really? Olivia mentioned she was someone local. An older lady, right?"

Here, I need to tread carefully. If Mom already picked up on the Jocelyn vibes, she'll for sure pick up on whatever I'm feeling—starting to feel?—for Lila. "Um, no, actually. She's younger than me."

"Is that so?" She's trying so hard to play it cool, but I can practically see the questions buzzing around in her brain. "Is she married?" she finally asks.

"Not a relevant question, Mom."

She huffs. "Of course it's relevant. You never leave the farm, Perry. How will you ever meet anyone? The fact that a woman is coming here? Come on. You can't blame me for asking."

It's only a matter of time before one of my brothers—probably Lennox—mentions to Mom that Lila is very single, and I'm very interested. Better to let her find out that way than tell her right now. If she knew, she'd be over at the farmhouse in a minute, doing her own recon work.

"Ready," Dad says, stopping in the kitchen doorway.

I lean down to kiss Mom's cheek. "Bye, Mom."

"Child, we aren't finished with this conversation."

I look back over my shoulder, imagining for a split second how Mom and Dad would respond to becoming instant grandparents to a kid like Jack. I'm getting ahead of myself. *So far ahead.* But it still feels good to know that if it ever came down to it, they'd embrace him as their own without a second thought.

As Dad and I drive over to the warehouse, it occurs to me that it wouldn't just be Mom and Dad becoming instant grandparents. I would also become an instant *dad.*

It's not like I haven't known about Jack from the very beginning. I have. But thinking of Jack as *Lila's* son is very different from thinking about him as *my* son. But he would be, wouldn't he? My stepson, at least. Or my *stairson.* Jack's misspoken word flits through my brain, and I smile.

Smiles or not, it feels ridiculous to even be asking myself these questions when I still have no idea if Lila is even interested. Then again, it's not like the presence of a kid in her life is this changeable factor. Like a job or a living situation. Lila is a mom. She's always going to be a mom.

How do I *not* think about that?

It would be ridiculous—irresponsible—not to.

I sigh and try and swallow down the doubts rising like bile in my throat.

It's just lunch.

Just a woman.

Just a woman with a *kid.*

A woman with a kid whose real dad was a military hero.

Now I'm excited about and dreading lunch in equal measure.

Chapter Twelve

Lila

A FREAKING PICNIC LUNCH in the apple orchard? Am I dreaming right now?

I lean back into Perry's desk chair, my hands sliding down the butter soft leather on the armrests. The chair alone probably costs more than all the furniture in my house, and yet, nothing about Perry's office feels opulent. The whole farmhouse feels nice, comfortable, but not excessive. I wonder if the office is designed to match Perry's preferences or if he inherited the space from his dad and didn't change anything,

Somehow, it *feels* like Perry, though that could be wishful thinking because I'm pretty sure I could live in this office with its tasteful simplicity and easy comfort. Slide a twin bed into the corner and give me a mini fridge, and I'll be set.

It took me hours to finally respond to Perry's text last night. Because my feelings were hurt that he dismissed my ideas and that even though he did apologize, his apology felt so sterile and businesslike.

Which, of course he should be businesslike. It was only that I'd allowed myself to hope, and his texts squashed that hope right into the ground.

But now?

Now I'm swimming in hope. Practically drowning in it. It's not lost on me that *drowning* isn't actually a good thing. That I am in very real danger of getting swept away. My hope might as well be a fast-moving current on a river after all the snow melts and comes flooding down. And I'm swimming—did I mention I'm not a very good swimmer?—with no life raft. No vest. And no one on the shore to throw me a rope and pull me to safety—*or* to stop me from making bad extended metaphors in my head.

But honestly, how can I not hope?

Perry asked about Jack. He complimented my hair. And last night, he texted me actual APPLE PUNS.

It only takes an hour or so to look over the reports, something which I could have easily done from home, not that you'll hear me complaining. I'll choose to work in a cushy leather chair that smells like my sexy boss any day of the week.

I notate the few discrepancies I find, then pull out my laptop so I can pull up my work email. I haven't checked it since yesterday, so there's probably enough to keep me busy for at least another half hour. I could check it on my phone but responding is so much easier on my laptop. Except, Perry didn't mention Wi-Fi before he left, which means my laptop is basically useless.

I look toward the door. Surely there's someone else close by who could help me get connected. I make my way out of Perry's office and head down the long hallway that leads toward the front reception area. There, I find a lovely woman with shoulder-length gray hair, a pair of glasses perched on her nose, her head leaning close to the computer screen on the reception desk.

She looks up when she sees me, her smile warm and wide. "Hello," she says, looking toward the hallway out of which I just emerged. "I don't think I know you."

"Hi. I'm Lila. Perry's assistant? I'm hoping there's someone who can get me connected to the Wi-Fi?"

"Oh. *Oh!* Well, of course. It's been ages since I've used the Wi-Fi, but I'm sure there's someone here who knows the password." She stands and moves toward me, extending her hand. "I'm Hannah Hawthorne."

"Hawthorne?"

She nods. "Perry's mom."

That's why her smile looks so familiar. It's Perry's smile.

She takes my hand, engulfing it in both of hers.

"Mrs. Hawthorne. It's so nice to meet you. I didn't expect—but then, I guess it makes sense that you would be here."

"Please. Call me Hannah. Usually you'd have to come to the barn to find me, but I needed a computer, and the one I have at the house has a broken power cord. This one I can't seem to make work for me though." She looks over her shoulder at the offending computer.

"Is it anything I can help you with?" I ask. "I'm not a computer whiz by any means, but I'm happy to try."

"Oh. Well, sure, if you don't mind. I just need to upload a few pictures into a shared google drive. But whenever I click on the link, it tells me I don't have access."

I follow her to the computer, looking over her shoulder as she explains further. "See, I've got the pictures here, in my email. And the link to the shared folder is here, in this message. It says it's been shared with my email address, but when I click it—" I watch as she clicks the link and receives a message denying her access.

"Oh, I see what's happening," I say. "It's defaulting to the Stonebrook Google account instead of yours." I reach for the mouse, and she shifts to the side, making room. "But if we click here and switch over to *your* profile, it should let us right in." Sure enough, as soon as I switch the profiles, the shared folder opens up. My eyes catch on the name. *Silver Creek High School Class of 2007 15-Year Reunion Slide Show.* "Is this for Perry's reunion?" I ask.

"You know about it?"

"Only that he's been invited," I say, not wanting to insert myself into Hawthorne family drama. Maybe Perry's mom doesn't care that he's not planning on attending the reunion, but maybe she does. "The invitation came to his work email. Do you want me to upload these photos for you?" I ask, gesturing back to the computer.

"Would you? I guess the slide show is supposed to be a surprise for everyone who attends. One picture from high school and one from childhood."

I pull up the first photo. It's Perry in a football uniform, a helmet under his arm, a wide smile on his face—the same smile his mother greeted me with when she first said hello.

"That was his senior year," she says, her voice gentle. "That smile. He doesn't share it very often, but when he does? It's a million-dollar smile."

If by million-dollar-smile she means a smile that makes my knees feel wobbly and my insides feel like Jell-O then the answer is *yes.* One-million times *yes.* I swallow. "I didn't know he played football."

"Quarterback," she says. "He was a good one, too."

I pull up the second photo, afraid that if I stare at this one too much longer, actual cartoon hearts might explode over my head. Call me crazy, but I'm guessing it wouldn't be smart to be quite so transparent in front of Perry's mother, of all people.

In the second photo, Perry looks close to Jack's age. He's standing next to a man who can only be his father. They have the same eyes, the same dark hair. It looks like they've been hiking, a view of the Blue Ridge Mountains stretching out behind them.

"He looks a lot like his dad," I say.

Hannah nods. "He looks the most like his dad, really. He and Flint."

"He has your smile though," I say as I close out the pictures and add them to the shared folder. "I noticed that the moment you said hello."

Hannah smiles slyly, and my cheeks flush.

Abort! Abort! Back away slowly from the mother of the man I'm not supposed to be crushing on.

When both pictures finish uploading, I close out the window and push away from the desk. "Okay. All done."

She breathes out a sigh. "Thank you. That's been on my to-do list for days, and you just made it seem so easy."

"I'm so happy I could help."

She cocks her head. "Listen. If your need for the internet is particularly urgent, then forget I asked, but if there's nothing pressing, would you like to walk out to the barn with me? I had a couple of late deliveries this year, so I've got some baby goats less than a week old that could use some loving."

Week-old baby goats? Oh, I am so in. Except, I'm not sure that exactly falls in my job description.

"Come on," Hannah urges. "It's an official Stonebrook Farm need. The babies need socializing if they're going to get along with people when they're grown. If it matters, I'll tell Perry I insisted you come with me."

Well. If she *insists.* I point back down the hallway. "Let me just go and message Perry so he knows where I am."

I race back to Perry's office and snag my phone so I can send Perry a quick text. I'm momentarily distracted by the notifications filling the screen. I have a new email. A new *work* email. That's not so significant. Except this one is another message from the high school reunion lady. I glance at the door, not wanting to make Hannah wait, but I'm too curious to ignore the email altogether. Especially after the conversation I just had with Perry's mom.

Perry,

Listen. I think I've figured out what's happening. I know how hard things have been for you. I realize that by pushing you to attend the reunion, I was asking for more than you're ready to give. I should respect your need to heal, to recover from our split, no matter how long it takes. But I'll cover for you, all right? I'll make up an excuse so no one else on the planning committee has to know that I'm the reason you won't come. You have to protect your heart. I understand that now. I'm sure seeing me again would only make getting over me that much harder. I wish you well, Perry.

Much love,

Jocelyn

I read the email once all the way through, then read it again, my annoyance growing with each word. The reunion lady really *is* Perry's ex-wife. Email feels like such an impersonal way to communicate with her ex. Why not text? Or even just call?

Then again, if their divorce was as messy as this email makes it sound, maybe Perry blocked her number so she can't call or text.

If I had an ex this condescending, I'd probably block her too. Unless her email is genuine? Perry doesn't really seem like he's still nursing a broken heart, but we haven't exactly had a lot of conversations about his love life, so I could be entirely off-base.

Still, my instincts are telling me Jocelyn's message is meant to be patronizing, not genuine. I don't know the woman, so I can't know for sure, but to me, her *understanding* reads like thinly veiled presumptions and insults.

I'm tempted to just delete the message.

But a bigger part of me wants to convince Perry to GO to the reunion. Who does this woman think she is, assuming that Perry is still wallowing? Still pining after her? Still so wounded, he can't even bear to be in the same room with her? If I were Perry, I'd want to attend the stupid reunion in a million-dollar suit, with a million-dollar date, driving a million-dollar car just to show her.

It's possible I've read too many romance novels.

But COME ON. He can't let her waltz into the reunion telling everyone her poor ex-husband is still too brokenhearted to show his face.

I pocket my phone and hurry out front where Hannah is waiting for me. I wonder what *she* knows about Jocelyn. And if there's any possible way I could bring her up.

Except that would be meddling.

I shouldn't meddle.

I *really* want to meddle.

Mrs. Hawthorne smiles. "Ready?"

It occurs to me a moment too late that I still haven't sent Perry a message, but I'm not going to pull my phone out and do it now. "Yep. Good to go." I glance at my watch as we head down the massive front steps of the farmhouse. It's only ten-thirty.

Maybe I'll be back before Perry comes for me, and it won't matter.

The farmhouse steps are decorated with pumpkins, tiny hay bales, and baskets of yellow, red, and orange mums. I don't remember noticing the decorations when I arrived, but Perry took me in through the back, so it's possible I missed it. "Everything looks so festive," I say once we reach the bottom. I turn and look back at the house. "It's honestly so beautiful out here."

"Decorating the porch is one of the few things I still like to do," Mrs. Hawthorne says with a chuckle. "It used to be my porch, after all."

"When did you move out of the farmhouse?"

She wrinkles her brow. "Perry was in middle school, so . . . maybe twenty years ago or so? It's a much larger house now than it used to be. Everything to the left of the porch, all the offices, that was all added on after we moved out. We still live on the property though. On the backside, where I don't have to worry about customers wandering into my kitchen."

"Does Perry still live on the property too?"

She eyes me curiously, and I brace myself, wondering if she's going to question my reasons for wanting to know. But then she just shakes her head. "He's got his own place a few miles down the road."

I suddenly wonder what Perry's home is like. Does it have the same comfortable feel as his office? Does he have matching furniture? Throw pillows and art on the walls? Is his bedroom decorated, or is he more a mattress-on-a-frame kind of man?

A wave of heat washes through me at the thought of Perry's bedroom. His *bed*.

I pat my cheeks, feeling the warmth there as an image of Perry lounging around his home pops into my brain.

Bad, brain! Now is not the time!

But my brain doesn't care WHAT time it is or even that I'm standing beside Perry's MOM. It's too wrapped up imagining Perry in lounge pants and a plain white t-shirt—or shirtless—can we go with shirtless?—walking barefoot around his bedroom.

"What about you?" Mrs. Hawthorne asks, startling me out of my reverie. It occurs to me a moment too late that there was a first part to her question that I somehow missed.

The faint heat in my cheeks flames even hotter, which is stupid. Perry's mother is not a mind reader.

I clear my throat and glance over at her. Her eyebrows are lifted, the smirk on her face saying she maybe IS a mind reader.

"I, um, I . . . " *Can't even remember what she asked me.* "I'm sorry. What did you ask?"

She chuckles again. "Do you live around here?"

"Oh. Um, not too far from here. Just up the mountain in Hendersonville. I've only been back a couple of years, but I grew up there, so that's home."

We approach the barn, and Hannah slides open a massive door that leads into a dimly lit space. Stalls line either side of the giant barn, a wide corridor running from where we're standing all the way to the other end. There's a hay loft overhead, the smell of hay and leather and old wood heavy in the air. I follow Hannah to the first stall where she scoops up the tiniest baby goat I've ever seen and, without any preamble, plops the goat into my arms.

"Oh my goodness," I say as the goat bleats and nibbles at my ear. "What is even happening right now?"

Hannah smiles. "Her name is Sweetpea."

I rub Sweetpea's soft ears. "Oh, Jack would love you. Will she be a part of the petting zoo at the festival?"

"Probably not," Hannah says. "I like them to be a few months old before they're exposed to all the noise and traffic of the festival. Who's Jack?"

"Oh! He's my little boy. He's only five—just started kindergarten actually." I hold up the goat so I can look into her face. "And he would love you, Sweetpea."

"You're welcome to bring him by anytime," Hannah says. Her gaze shifts, like there's something she isn't asking. Is she wondering if I'm married? If Jack's father is still a part of my life? Or do I *want* her to wonder because that would mean she's wondering if there might be something between Perry and me? But if that *isn't* what she's thinking, and I bring it up, will it make me look desperate and grabby? Like I'm trying to rope her son into liking me? I'm not wearing a wedding ring, at least. Maybe I ought to just let that speak for itself.

Or maybe I should stop thinking so hard and just cuddle this baby goat and forget about everything else.

"This feels like therapy," I say, nuzzling the goat a little closer.

Hannah laughs. "You aren't the first person to say so. They're pretty sweet. And they don't smell nearly as bad as the rest of the farm. This place makes a pretty decent sanctuary."

"Think Perry would let me move my office out here? I'll set up right here next to Sweetpea's stall."

"Will you be working in person from now on then?" Hannah asks.

"Oh. I don't know, actually. I'm happy to do either. Whatever is going to be the most helpful to Perry."

She nods. "He tells me you're helping with the festival."

"I'm trying. There are so many details to keep straight. I don't know how Perry is doing it all."

"He's always been a details guy. Even when he was little, he was very exacting in the way he did things. It made him a little prickly and controlling when he was a kid—his siblings hated him for it—but as an adult, it does make him very good at his job. He's managed to trim the farm's expenses by close to twenty percent. He's good at spotting the extra. At finding the bloat and cutting it."

I think of the way Perry worked his way through the festival layout yesterday. "That definitely sounds like Perry."

Hannah studies me. "I take it you've already discovered his exacting ways?"

I smile. "Maybe a little."

"Well, you're still working for him. Hopefully that means he didn't hurt your feelings too badly."

I shrug, my lips pressing together as I fight a smile.

"Oh, no. He did hurt your feelings?" She shakes her head. "That boy . . ."

"No, no. It wasn't that bad. And his apology was very convincing."

Her eyebrows lift. "An apology is a good sign."

"He's even taking me out for a picnic lunch in the apple orchard this afternoon." Sweetpea bleats. "And honestly, if I get to snuggle baby goats on a regular basis, I'm happy to handle his exacting ways."

Hannah's expression freezes, her hand lifting to cover her mouth.

My stomach drops. "What? What did I say?"

She clears her throat. "*Perry* is taking you out for a picnic?"

"Yes? Is that . . . should I be scared about that?"

"No, no," she rushes to say. "It's wonderful. I'm sure you'll have a lovely time."

Sweetpea squirms, and I shift, leaning over the edge of the stall to place her back in the hay.

"Lila, honey, are you single?" Hannah asks. "You mentioned a son. I don't want to presume, but . . ."

"I'm single," I say quickly. "Widowed, actually. Jack's dad was a pilot in the Navy. He was killed in a training exercise a few years ago."

Her expression softens. "I'm sorry to hear that." She takes a step forward and reaches for my hands, holding them both in hers. "It seems especially unfair that someone as young as you are should have to weather such a storm." She squeezes my hands, and I squeeze hers right back. I've only just met the woman, but it's clear her kindness is genuine.

She reaches up and smoothes my hair, a gesture that, from anyone else, might seem overly familiar, but from her, it just feels motherly.

"Life sometimes deals us sobering blows," she continues. "Take Perry, for example. It's true he's always been exacting, a little grumpy, but it's been so much worse since his divorce. That woman, she stole the light right out of him."

I bite my tongue, wondering if I should mention the email about Perry's reunion.

"But he'll find it again," Hannah continues. "That light. And when he does, he'll make someone really happy. I truly believe that."

My heart starts pounding in my chest. Is she telling me this because she senses I might be that someone? I barely keep myself from throwing my arm in the air and yelling, *I volunteer as tribute! Me! Pick me!*

Instead, I smile warmly, channeling my cool-as-a-cucumber inner zen. *Just kidding.* I have no inner zen. I might as well be lapping at Hannah's heels like a lost puppy who has finally found home.

"I hope he does," I say, my tone oh-so-chill. "He deserves to be happy. We all do." I add this last part to make it clear I'm talking generally. I have no reason to be *specifically* concerned with Perry's happiness. Absolutely no reason at all.

Hannah eyes me. "You deserve it too, Lila."

Oh my. That did not feel general. Is she actually trying to tell me something? But *no.* She can't be. We just met. She wouldn't be thinking—

I almost jump at the sound of a new voice. A deep voice. A voice belonging to a man I can only pray didn't hear any of that conversation.

"I thought I might find you here," Perry says.

I spin around, tripping over Hannah's foot so that she has to reach out and grab me, her hands latching onto either shoulder to stabilize me. "Perry," I say, my eyes darting to Hannah.

She gives her head the tiniest shake as if to say I have nothing to worry about.

"The reports are finished," I say quickly, not wanting to look like I was slacking off. "And then I tried to get connected to the Wi-Fi so I could check my email and—"

"And then I stole her," Hannah says. "I had a computer issue she helped me sort out, then I thought little Sweetpea here could use some socializing."

"I'm sure it was completely coincidental that you made your way to the farmhouse this morning," Perry says, shooting his mother a knowing look.

I look from him to Hannah and back again, not entirely sure what's happening.

Hannah only shrugs. "I have as much right to be at the farmhouse as anyone else," she says with a casual wave of her hand.

"Mmhmm. I'm sure that's all this was." Perry crosses to where we're standing and leans into the goat stall, scooping Sweetpea into his arms.

Because, you know, he needed something else to make him attractive. The hair and the muscles and the eyes aren't enough. Now he's going to carry around baby farm animals, snuggling them close to his chest, and—*oh my word.*

Did he just KISS the baby goat in his arms?! Does he *know* what he's doing to me?

Hannah nudges me with her elbow. "You're staring, honey," she whispers under her breath. "Rein it in."

I press my lips together and throw my eyes to the wood slats overhead, forcing a few slow, intentional breaths. I'm fine. *JUST FINE.*

"Are you getting hungry?" Perry asks over the top of Sweetpea's head.

"Mmhmm," I mumble, still not trusting myself with words.

Perry eyes me before his gaze shifts to his mom. "Do you need her for anything else? Or can I steal her back?"

Oh, please steal me back. Steal me so we can ride off into the sunset like in those old Westerns Grandpa Jamison likes to watch.

"Son, you need her a lot more than I do," Hannah says, giving Perry a look that can *only* mean one thing.

This is not happening.

I am not standing here in the Hawthorne family barn, listening to Hannah Hawthorne joke about her oldest son *needing* me, of all people.

Perry shoots his mom a look I can't read, his jaw tensing, before lowering Sweetpea back into her stall. He turns to me like nothing in the whole wide world is out of the ordinary. "Ready to go?"

Hannah smiles. "It was nice to meet you, Lila. Hopefully we'll be seeing more of you around the farm."

"Mom," Perry says. "That's enough."

Hannah only chuckles and holds up her hands. "Enough of what?"

I follow Perry out of the barn, stopping next to the Gator he must have driven to find me. "Sorry to disappear on you," I say as I climb in beside him.

"Sorry about my mom," he says gruffly as he starts the engine on the Gator. "She means well, but she . . ." His words trail off, and he shakes his head. "Anyway. I hope she didn't say anything to make you uncomfortable."

I lift my shoulders in what I hope looks like a casual shrug. "I think she's wonderful." I don't even try to hide the wistfulness in my tone. I'd take a meddling mama over an absent one any day.

Perry pauses and looks at me, almost like he's looking *through* me, and his expression softens.

Am I really so transparent?

The reality is, I'd do just about anything to have the kind of family that Perry clearly has. Parents who are still married and fully invested in the happiness of their children. Siblings who speak highly of one another, who are *friends* even when they don't have to be.

I was loved. Cherished, even. But belonging to one or two people is different than belonging to a whole tribe. I want Jack to have siblings. To have a whole village of people he can lean and rely on.

"She is pretty wonderful," Perry says. The words are simple, but his tone says so much more. He gets it. He understands the magic of what he has, and he won't take it for granted.

"I'm beginning to sense it runs in the family," I say lightly, shooting Perry a coy look.

His cheeks pink the slightest bit, and he clears his throat and looks away, but not before I see a tiny smile playing at the edges of his mouth.

It's scary how much I want to see that smile again.

Even scarier how much I want to be the reason behind it.

Chapter Thirteen

Lila

Perry turns the Gator toward the orchard we drove through yesterday when we hiked up to the ledge. This time, instead of climbing, he keeps us closer to the level land near the bottom of the orchard.

After my conversation with Hannah, I am hyperaware of Perry beside me. The way he smells, the way the light catches on the copper hairs in his beard. The way the brown of his eyes looks lighter—more golden—out here than it does inside.

I curl my palms over my knees and force my eyes to the surrounding landscape. I have to think of something else. *Notice* something besides the man next to me, or I'm going to keep staring at him, and that will only make things weird.

We pass row after row of apple trees, moving deeper into the orchard until I can't see anything but trees in every direction. The farther we go, the smaller the trees get.

These trees are full of leaves, but they don't seem to hold any fruit. I can appreciate Perry's logic bringing us all the way out here. Apples are all picked by hand—a fact I learned yesterday that surprised me—and so the more mature half of the orchard is full of people working the harvest.

Perry cuts the engine, motioning to the trees around us. "The trees out here will start to bear fruit next fall. Cameo apples," he says as he climbs out of the Gator. "They're my mom's favorite."

"Is there really much of a difference?"

Perry's gaze narrows, but his expression stays light. "Those are fighting words out here."

I grin. "I mean, I can tell a Granny Smith from a Gala, but beyond that . . ."

Perry sighs and lifts a hand, stopping me as I move to get out of the Gator. "Nope. Sit back down. No lunch for you yet."

"What?" I say on a laugh.

He climbs in beside me. "We're making a slight detour first."

I settle back into my seat and fold my arms across my chest. "You know, starving me yesterday didn't work out very well."

He tosses me a smirk. "I'll take my chances. I know how to handle . . . crab apples."

"Oh man, Perry. That was really bad."

His mouth twitches, but he doesn't smile. "Come on. Buckle up. I've got a point to prove, and I can hear your stomach rumbling from here."

"Then just feed me, you monster," I say, swatting his arm, my fingers (conveniently) lingering just long enough to confirm that *yes,* his flannel is unbelievably soft.

"Nope." Perry eases the Gator in between a row of trees, moving opposite the direction we originally came from. "You're earning your lunch today." He shoots me another look. "Boss's orders."

A surge of heat pulses deep in my gut, and a blush creeps up my cheeks. Maybe he didn't mean to get me all hot and bothered combining his *bossiness* with such a heated look, but *good grief* I can't think straight with him carrying on like this.

Perry stops the Gator between a couple of fully matured apple trees and hops out, grabbing an apple from the lower branches of each of the two trees. He jumps back into his seat and pulls a small, folding knife from his pocket. He opens the blade and slices it cleanly into the first apple, cutting out a perfect wedge.

I had no idea cutting fruit with a pocketknife could be so sexy. But then, maybe it's not so much the pocketknife as it is the ownership. Perry knows this orchard. This farm. And that stirs something in me. Respect, but also longing.

Still, the fear in the back of my brain has me remembering Hannah's words from earlier. *Rein it in.* She meant my staring, but I probably ought to apply it generally. I could be reading this situation all wrong, turning what could be a very casual business lunch between coworkers into something it absolutely isn't meant to be.

But then Perry lifts the slice of apple to my lips. He doesn't just *hand* me the fruit. He feeds it to me, his fingers right next to my mouth, brushing my lips as he places the apple slice on my tongue.

"Close your eyes," he says gently. "Focus on the taste right when it hits your tongue."

I am *not* imagining things.

I can't be. Even with my limited experience, I recognize the warmth in Perry's eyes.

I focus on the very basic task of chewing, tasting, swallowing the apple. I keep my eyes closed, willing myself to focus on the taste instead of Perry's proximity.

"Okay, remember that taste. Think about it."

I open my eyes and nod. "Thinking. Noting. Okay. I'm good."

"Ready for the next one?"

I close my eyes again, parting my lips as he offers me a second bite.

Flavor explodes on my tongue, and I let out a little gasp, my eyes popping open. "It's completely different!"

He smiles, the creases deepening around his eyes. "Why?"

I'm still not used to the full force of that smile—it really is worth a million dollars—and it takes me a moment to answer. I swallow, bringing the flavor of the first apple back to my mind, which is a challenge considering all the other sensory things that are going on here. Perry's touch. His proximity. The heat of his gaze. *Apples, Lila. Think. Apples.* "It's sweeter," I say. "Not as tart as the last one."

He nods. "Good."

"Good?" I raise my brows. "I didn't realize this was a test."

He shifts into drive and moves us through the trees. "Tell me something you love. Something you're good at."

I'm not sure what he's getting at, but I'll play along. "Okay. Um, I like to sing. And play the piano."

"Really?"

"You sound surprised." A shadow of trepidation flits through me, but I will it away. Just because Trevor thought my love for music was silly doesn't mean everyone else will too.

"Not surprised. Just impressed."

Impressed. Such an easy thing for him to say. And he seems like he means it, too.

"Okay, so imagine you're hanging out with someone who insists that music is basically all the same. Genre is irrelevant. A song is a song. If you've heard one, you've heard them all."

I cringe, and Perry shoots me a knowing look.

"Fine, fine, you've made your point. But are you saying that if I try these apples and still feel like they all taste the same, you'll stop hanging out with me? Will I lose my job?"

He lifts his shoulders in a playful shrug as if weighing the pros and cons. "I'd *probably* let you keep your job. But virtual only. Definitely no picnics in the orchard."

"Well now you've told me too much. I love a good picnic. You've given me a reason to lie."

He stops the Gator. "Nah. I watched your expression when you tasted the last apple. I know genuine bliss when I see it."

Ha! Joke's on him. He could have been feeding me snail poop and I'd have had the same look on my face. The apples *are* delicious, but the bliss I'm feeling has a lot more to do with him.

Perry jumps out again, grabbing two more apples like he did before. I could watch him do this all day. *Apple. Knife. Slice. Repeat.* You know. As long as he's also *feeding* me the apples.

This time, he hands the apple slice to me, and a tiny pulse of disappointment fills my chest. But then he holds up a scolding finger. "Don't eat that yet."

I grin, not caring the tiniest bit that he's bossing me around. This is Perry's territory, and I'm happy to let him take the lead.

As he slices the second apple, I notice a scar on the back of his hand, running from the knuckle of his pointer finger past his thumb, nearly to his wrist. Without thinking, I reach out and trace my finger along the scar. "When did that happen?"

"The fourth grade," he says easily—so easily I wonder if the touch impacted him the same way it did me. "Dad was teaching me how to use a pocketknife, and I got cocky." He closes his knife and lifts his hand, flexing his fingers. "Thirteen stitches." He takes the first apple slice back from me so he's holding them both and lifts the first one to my lips. "Okay. Same drill. Eyes closed," he says, in the sexy, commanding tone I'm beginning to *really* love. "It's the first impression that matters the most."

I take a bite, my lips brushing against his thumb. *Focus on the fruit. Focus on the fruit. Focus on the fruit.*

"Okay, this one is the mildest of the three I've tasted." I open my eyes to see him studying me. "Almost no tartness. But it isn't overly sweet either. It tastes like honey."

"You're good at this." He pops the last half of the apple slice in his mouth. Like the two of us sharing food is no big deal. Like he has no idea how much he's affecting me. How close I am to unraveling.

I grin. "Give me the last one."

Perry lifts the last slice to my mouth. I keep my eyes open this time—a smart decision because watching him might be the most intoxicating part of this little game we're playing. I immediately groan. "Oh. This one is my favorite." I lift my hand to cover my lips as I chew.

Perry smiles. "I thought it might be."

"What kind is it?" I reach over and grab the other half from his fingers, popping it into my mouth before he can eat it. Perry laughs before cutting another slice and handing it over.

"Mutsu," he says. "It's my favorite too."

"Mutsu. I've never even heard of that one. What were the others?"

He uses the tip of his knife to point to the other three apples sitting on the dash of the Gator. "Cameo, Jonagold, Crimson Crisp."

"Okay, so here's a question for you, Mr. Apple Know-it-all," I say. "If *you* were to close your eyes, and I made you taste these one by one, could you name them? Identify which is which?"

He doesn't even hesitate. "Absolutely."

"You sure you don't mean apple-solutely?" I say through a smirk.

He shakes his head and folds his arms across his chest in a way that draws my eyes to his biceps. "Low-hanging fruit, Lila."

I gasp. "*THAT* was low-hanging fruit!"

He only grins before shifting the Gator into drive and easing us forward. I slice up the rest of the Mutsu apple as we drive, handing a few slices to Perry, wishing it wouldn't be awkward for me to feed him the same way he fed me. But I like this too. Eating in easy, comfortable silence.

Seeing Perry out here in the orchard, in control of his space, knowledgeable and passionate about his livelihood, it's the last nudge I need to start falling.

Whether I think it's a good idea or not.

Chapter Fourteen

Perry

I DID NOT DRIVE into the orchard expecting to take a thirty-minute taste-testing detour. I *really* didn't expect to hand-feed Lila slices of apple. I'm not even sure what came over me. But I think she liked it. *Really* liked it. Not even Lennox could have written a better script for how things went. For a minute, it almost seemed like I have *game.*

Maybe I'm not as rusty at this whole dating thing as I thought.

But then, there's something about Lila that puts me at ease. I spent so much time trying to be exactly what Jocelyn wanted me to be. But with Lila—it's like she has zero expectations. She's just happy to be with me.

Once we're back to the lunch spot I originally picked out, we work together to spread out the picnic blanket, then I haul out the basket Lennox packed for us. "I actually have no idea what's in here," I say as I open it up, shifting it toward Lila.

"Did Lennox pack it?" she asks, her hope obvious.

"You ask that like you've met him."

"I haven't, but you did have me proofread his menu. Don't hate me for being a teeny bit excited about the possibility of eating his food. I mean, the man's reputation definitely precedes him."

Something like jealousy swarms in my chest, but that's nothing new. I'm never jealous of Lennox's ability to cook. I'm *usually* jealous of Lennox's ability to make and keep friends. To have women scrambling for the opportunity to even just talk to him. It's never been that easy for me to talk to people.

Not until now, I realize. Though I'm pretty sure that has nothing to do with me and everything to do with Lila.

"What do we have?" I say, as I watch Lila unpack the food.

"A couple of sandwiches, but they look fancy. Ohh! They're on croissants. And then—" She pulls a container out of the cooler and lifts the edge, holding it up to her nose. "Ohh, this smells delicious. Some kind of potato salad, maybe? And then some cookies?"

"Almond pillow cookies," I say, looking into the container Lila opens and sets on the blanket between us. "He's famous for those."

"Famous for cookies?"

She immediately lifts a cookie and takes a bite, leaving a tiny dab of powdered sugar on her lip that I immediately want to brush off. Or kiss off, which is a startling thought. That would be going way too fast, but feeding Lila apples was like a gateway drug, and now I can't stop thinking about *more.*

The fact that I'm thinking about anything at all feels big. I've been numb for so many years, but Lila is waking me up.

"Oh my word," she says on a groan. "These are ridiculous."

"Not worried about spoiling your lunch, huh?"

She takes another bite of the cookie and hands me the unfinished half. "I've always wondered about the logic behind that expression. It's not as if the nutritional value of the actual lunch diminishes if we eat our dessert first."

I polish off the last of her cookie in one bite. "I like your way of thinking. But here," I say, reaching toward her. "You've got a little . . ." My hand hovers inches away from her lip. I *want* to touch her, but not if she doesn't want me to.

"What? What is it?" She leans toward my hand—that's permission enough for me—and I brush the pad of my thumb across her bottom lip.

"Powdered sugar," I say, my touch lingering a second longer than necessary. This close, I can see the flecks of navy that pepper her sky-blue eyes.

I hear her breath catch as she leans back, then see her visibly swallow, which somehow makes me feel better. Maybe I'm not the only one with fire coursing through my veins.

We dig into the food, which helps alleviate some of the tension brewing, something I think we both need. Chemistry or not, I'm not making a move on Lila—at least not more than I already did when I decided to hand-feed her apple slices. We've both got reasons to take things slow.

Every bite of lunch is delicious. I don't care how much my brother annoys me; this food can only be helping my cause.

We don't talk about anything too important while we eat. The conversation is comfortable and easy, which is becoming the norm with Lila. It helps that she's so inquisitive, asking questions about the orchard (How do we choose what varieties of apple we grow? How long does it take for an apple to fully mature?) and what it was like to grow up in such a big family.

It isn't until we polish off the last of the almond pillow cookies that Lila leans back onto her hands, her legs stretched out in front of her, and looks at me like she has something important to say.

"I need to tell you something," she says.

"Now would be a good time. I'm full and happy. We've got about fifteen minutes before I remember to be grouchy again."

She laughs lightly. "The thing is, I've heard you *say* you're grouchy more than once, but you don't really come across that way. Not to me."

I lift an eyebrow. "Not ever?"

She purses her lips. "Okay. Our first online conversation, you were a little cold. And yesterday in the field, I wanted to punch you in the nose when you dismissed my suggestions. But most of the time? You're a pretty nice guy, Perry. Like it or not."

"What is it they say about nice guys finishing last?" *Or losing the girl.*

My jaw clenches, but I shake the tension away. I don't regret losing Jocelyn. Not anymore.

Lila shakes her head. "It's not true. Not in the ways that truly matter."

My eyes are down, focused on the stitching in the picnic blanket Lennox left with the basket. It's the same one Mom used when we were kids. I don't know where he found it, but I'm glad he did. "Maybe . . ." I say slowly, too nervous to lift my gaze to hers. "You make me want to be a nice guy."

She's shaking her head when I look up, but I don't miss the smile spreading across her face or the color filling her cheeks. "You hardly know me, Perry."

"Okay," I say boldly. Hopefully not too boldly? "What do you want me to know?"

She winces and bites her lip. "Um, hold that thought? Because I actually *do* need to tell you something. And it might make you change your mind." She barrels on before I have the chance to reply. "Remember when you asked me to respond to the woman emailing about the reunion? I did respond and declined the invite. But the woman emailed again this morning. And it's pretty personal. Personal enough that I know it's your ex-wife who has been writing the messages."

I heave out a sigh, but I'm not surprised that Jocelyn messaged again. I don't even need to read the email to guess at its tone, especially if it made Lila feel like she needed to tell me about it. Jocelyn has always had a manipulative edge to her. Which is the *nicest* way I can currently think of to characterize my ex-wife. I can think of a slew of other ways, none fit for any kind of company, especially the company of the woman I'm currently trying to impress. But I promised my therapist I'd stop dwelling on Jocelyn's more frustrating qualities and try to leave the past in the past, appreciating the good times we had together and moving on from everything else.

Some days, it's easier than others.

"What did she say?" I finally ask.

Lila pulls out her phone. "Here. I can just let you read it."

She hands me the phone, and I skim over the email. By the time I get to the end of it, all I can do is laugh. I hand the phone back. "That's very Jocelyn."

Lila frowns. "You aren't upset?"

"At you? Not at all. I'm sorry you got roped into this drama. I shouldn't have asked you to respond in the first place."

Lila bites her lip. "But, it isn't true, is it? You aren't still wallowing and missing her? That's not why you aren't going to the reunion."

I run a hand through my hair. I don't mind that Lila asked, I just have no idea how to answer. Rehashing the reasons for a divorce isn't exactly first date material, and I'm not even sure I can call this a date. I'd really rather *not* talk about something that might keep an *actual* first date from happening.

"I'm not wallowing," I finally say. "I'm not going to say the divorce wasn't awful, but I don't have any regrets about our marriage ending. But you have to understand, this is how Jocelyn works. She tried to make my *attending* the reunion about her. When it became clear I wasn't going to, she decided she'd need to make my *not* attending about her. Either way, she controls the narrative, which has always been her end goal."

"Doesn't that make you mad?"

I shrug. "If I think about it too hard. Generally, I just don't. Which is why I don't want to go to the reunion."

Lila shifts so her knees are under her and she's sitting back on her heels. She looks poised for action, which makes me suddenly nervous. "No," she says. "I don't like this at all."

I lift my eyebrows.

"Perry, you have to go. She's probably going to tell everyone all these lies about why you aren't there. She can't get away with that."

I sigh. "You sound like my mom."

Lila nods. "I knew I liked her."

"Look. I appreciate the thought. I do. But trust me. It isn't worth the effort. Not with Jocelyn. She always finds a way to twist things."

"Are there other people who will be there who you might like to see?"

I think about all the guys from the football team. A few of them still live in town, but most have moved away. Silver Creek isn't exactly a hotbed of business and industry. It's hard for people to stick around. It would be nice to see them. "Maybe," I finally admit. "A few."

"Then you have to go."

"It's not that simple."

She takes a deep breath and squares her shoulders, her lips pressed together in a show of determination that immediately impresses me. "What if I go with you?"

My heart jumps at the thought.

"As your date," she finishes. "Then Jocelyn can't say anything at all. Because you won't be there alone."

The idea is not a terrible one, but it's possible I'm being unreasonably swayed by the fact that technically, Lila just asked me on a date. Her motivations are suspect—this could be altruism and nothing more—but maybe it *is* something more.

"My date, huh?" I ask. I'm totally digging, but I don't even care.

She smiles. "Come on. Don't pretend like you weren't planning on asking me out at the end of today."

Heat flushes my cheeks, though she's not wrong. I don't know why I feel embarrassed that she figured me out. "Am I really that obvious?"

"I mean, I can't really imagine you hand-feeding apples to your mom."

This woman. I chuckle and shake my head before rubbing a hand across my beard. "A high school reunion isn't much of a date, Lila. Especially since I know my ex-wife will be there. She'll try and talk to you, and there's no guarantee she won't be unkind."

"Perry," Lila says gently. "The first time I met you in person, my five-year-old asked me *out loud in front of you* if you could be his stepdad, and you didn't fire me. I think I can handle an encounter with your ex-wife."

Something about the set of Lila's shoulders says she almost *wants* to handle an encounter with my ex-wife. Like she's ready to be my champion, go in and slay all the dragons on my behalf.

Why is this mental image such a turn-on?

"It's an overnight thing," I say slowly. "Up in Asheville. An evening dinner party with drinks and karaoke, and then a breakfast the next morning. And it's next weekend. You have Jack, Lila. Please don't stress about trying to make this work."

She waves away my concern. "No, I want to. It'll be fine. I can take Jack down to see his grandparents in Columbia. Honestly, he's due for a visit anyway."

"And they'll be fine with you scheduling a visit this last minute?"

"Are you kidding? His grandmother literally texts every week begging me to bring him down. It'll work. I promise it'll work."

"You're sure?"

"Call me crazy, but I think it sounds like fun. I love karaoke, and if we happen to give Jocelyn a little taste of her own medicine? I won't complain."

Weirdly, it *does* sound like fun, which says a lot about Lila. Because if she can make me excited about a voluntary encounter with Jocelyn? That can't be anything but magic.

Chapter Fifteen

Lila

I PACE AROUND MY living room with my heart in my throat and my overnight bag on the couch behind me. The house seems too quiet without Jack here, which isn't helping me feel any less anxious.

Jack is fine. With his grandparents in Columbia and probably getting spoiled rotten. He's stayed with them overnight before, so I know he'll be okay until Trevor's parents drive him back to Hendersonville tomorrow afternoon. I'm just not used to having so much silence to fill with my own thoughts.

And right now, my thoughts are *loud.*

A month ago, I was swooning over my new boss's picture and giggling over the idea of working for someone one very close degree of separation away from famous Flint Hawthorne.

Now, I'm pacing around my living room waiting for Perry to pick me up for an *overnight* date to an event at which his ex-wife will also be in attendance. (Yes, date. I'm wearing shapewear so no matter what Perry thinks about the reunion not counting—IT COUNTS.) There are so many things to process. So many reasons to freak out.

Seized by sudden impulse, I move to my kitchen table and pull out a chair, sitting down to evaluate the stretchability of my shapewear. So far, I haven't done a solid sit test. I wiggle back and forth and try to imagine how this will feel after eating an entire meal. So far, so good. I'm really only wearing it to keep the underwear lines hidden in my—*ahem*—very curvaceous dress, if I do say so myself, and it's managing that quite nicely. Plus, it's moving with me pretty well, and sitting doesn't make me feel like I'm suffocating, so I'm calling this late-night Instagram impulse purchase a win.

I stand up and start pacing again, one hand pressed to my stomach. If nothing else, I can kill time reliving all the little moments that have consumed me over the past nine days. The picnic, of course, since that's where everything started, but there's been so much more since then. Long looks. Tiny, intentional touches across Perry's desk. Random texts that have nothing to do with work. It's all been very friendly. A little flirty, maybe, but nothing that would truly raise any eyebrows. At least not to anyone observing from the outside.

But between us? Every touch has felt like fire, every look so filled with anticipation, it's a wonder we managed to get any work done.

A knock sounds on the door behind me, and I spin around, my heart hammering even faster than it already was, which is saying something.

I force a calming breath.

I can do this.

Everything is *fine.*

"You've got this, Lila," I say as I move toward the door.

The sight of Perry on my doorstep does very strange things to my body. I've never seen him wearing anything besides work jeans and flannel. Now, he's dressed for a party. Dark dress pants and a slim-fitting button down, the top few buttons undone. He isn't wearing a tie, but he doesn't need one. His clothes are perfect. Like they were tailored just for him.

I suddenly feel shabby in the midnight-blue dress I pulled out of the back of my closet, no matter my fantastic non-constrictive shapewear. I should have bought something new. Something that would make me look like I belong standing next to a man this impossibly perfect.

"Um, hi," I finally say, my voice sounding stupidly breathy and light. I quickly step back. "Come in. Glad you found the place."

Perry steps inside, making my very tiny house feel even tinier. I've never actually seen a fully grown man inside these walls.

His eyes skate over me, and panic starts clawing up my throat. He hates the dress. Does he hate the dress? "What's wrong? Is it the color?" I ask, looking down at my dress. "Does it look like I'm going to a funeral? I wasn't sure how fancy I needed—"

"Lila," he says gently, taking a step toward me and shutting the door behind him. He pushes his hands into his pockets. "Your dress is perfect. You look beautiful."

"Oh." *Perfect. Beautiful.* I could get used to all these adjectives. "Okay. Let me just grab my—" My words cut off when my phone rings from where it's sitting on the end table next to the couch. I glance at the screen to see Miranda Templeton's name across the top. "Actually, I need to take this. This is Jack's grandma. Just sit a minute."

I motion to my couch, but then I look closer and immediately regret it. On one end, there's a massive pile of Jack's matchbox cars. On the other, there's a *People Magazine* with Flint Hawthorne's face on the cover. AWESOME.

I lunge for the magazine. Perry can work out how to sit on the matchbox cars on his own. The last thing I want him to think is that I sit around reading articles, or worse, staring at pictures of his famous (and famously handsome) brother. I grab the magazine and toss it into the narrow gap between the couch and the wall before answering my phone.

Nothing to see here! Move along! Move along!

"Hello, Miranda. Is everything all right?" I ask, watching Perry out of the corner of my eye.

His lips twitch as he shifts Jack's cars to the side, but otherwise, he doesn't react. Except, he's *going* to react if I don't—I shift my phone to my other hand and reach over to grab a miniature ambulance before Perry can impale himself with it.

I barely make it, his butt grazing my arm on his way down. I hold up the ambulance like it's some kind of trophy, then realize what I'm doing and toss it behind the couch with the *People Magazine.*

"Everything's fine, dear," Miranda says. "I just wondered why you didn't pack the tennis outfit I bought for Jack last month."

I cringe. "Oh, did I forget? You know, I think it's in the wash," I lie. "I'm sorry about that."

She sighs into the phone. "Well, I suppose I can just buy him a new set. Maybe I'll keep it down here for next time so we'll always have it on hand."

"Miranda, he grows so fast. I'm not sure that's a good idea. He can just play tennis in the clothes I packed for him."

"Not if he's ever going to be a professional," she says, and I almost laugh at how serious she sounds. "He has to dress the part, Lila. He'll take it more seriously if he's wearing the proper attire."

I roll my eyes. Jack is a lot of adorable things. A tennis prodigy is not one of them. I mean, he's only five, so I guess stranger things have happened. But the last time I watched him play, he wouldn't stop using his racket to catch the lizards crawling over the azalea bushes beside the court.

I know Jack's grandmother well enough to realize I'm not going to win this argument, and honestly, if it's not *my* money she wants to waste on overpriced tennis clothes for a completely uninterested five-year-old, do I really care? "Whatever you think is best," I finally say.

"Wonderful," Miranda says. "Jack, would you like to go get some ice cream? We'll do a little shopping on our way." *Ha.* Shopping with Jack? On the one hand, Miranda isn't going to have nearly as much fun as she thinks she is. Jack likes shopping about as well as he likes going to the dentist. On the other hand, she's probably going to blame *me* if he misbehaves in the store. He might do all right if there's the promise of ice cream at the end. Either way, there's nothing I can do about it now.

"Thanks again, Miranda. You guys have fun."

I drop the phone into my lap with a sigh.

"That sounded like a fun conversation," Perry says.

"Did you know that five-year-olds who wear very special and expensive outfits while playing tennis are zero percent more likely to become tennis pros?"

Perry nods seriously. "I'm guessing Jack's grandma doesn't agree with your research?"

"Not even a little. But hey. It's her money."

Perry leans back, stretching his arm across my sofa and looking way too comfortable. "So. Should I be offended you threw my brother's face behind your couch?"

I wince. "I really hoped you didn't see that."

"I mean, at least you tossed an ambulance back there to keep him company. The EMTS can dress his wounds if anything happened to his very pretty face."

This last part almost feels like a dig. Like he's teasing me for having pictures of his brother in my house. Which, I can't really blame him. Except the only reason I have the magazine in the first place is because of him.

I press my lips together. "I bought that magazine because of you, you dummy."

He lifts an eyebrow.

"I don't generally read *People*. But I saw it right after I started working for you, when you were still responding to my messages with one- or two-word sentences. I was trying to learn a little more about you."

"Did it work?"

"Not at all. In a four-page spread, Flint didn't mention his family a single time."

Perry leans forward and rests his elbows on his knees. "I'm sure it was intentional. The farm is a public place. We already have people showing up on a regular basis, just hoping to catch a glimpse of where he grew up. And that's with him hardly talking about any of us."

It's funny. When I first started working for Perry, it was thrilling to think that at some point, I might have the chance to meet Flint Hawthorne in person. But that thrill has dimmed over the last few weeks. The more I get to know Perry, the more certain I'm becoming: he's all the Hawthorne I need.

"Lucky for me, I don't need magazine articles to get to know you now. I finally cracked your stony exterior with my sparkling wit and—"

"Ridiculous puns?" he finishes.

"I was going to say brilliant puns, but I'll allow the substitution."

I reach over and give his knee a quick squeeze. "What do you say? Should we get out of here? I hear there's a happening party over in Asheville."

He gives his head a little shake and chuckles. "I'm still not sure this is a good idea."

"Come on. It's going to be great." I stand up and hold out my hand. "I poured myself into this dress, Perry. I can't let all that effort go to waste."

He takes my hand and lets me pull him up, but then he stops, tugging me back toward him. His hand slips around my waist, and suddenly, I'm standing against him, one hand holding his while the other is pressed against his chest.

He leans forward, his lips close to my ear. "Nothing about this dress has gone to waste," he says slowly, *deliciously.*

His words send goosebumps skittering across my skin.

"Perry Hawthorne, I think you're flirting with me."

He lets me go and picks up my overnight bag, heading for the door. "You started it," he calls over his shoulder.

I gasp. "How did I start it?"

He pauses and turns, the full force of his smile slamming into me like a truck. "You put on that dress."

The Grove Park Inn is nestled into a mountainside in the heart of downtown Asheville. And it is stunning. Fireplaces big enough to stand up in. Luxurious lounge areas. Elaborate gardens and gorgeous hotel rooms and valet parking. It's a lot. More than I'm used to.

I'm nervous when I climb out of Perry's truck, but Perry looks cool as a cucumber. Like he's done this a thousand times before. I even watch him slip a tip to the valet with so much smoothness that had I not been specifically watching, I would have missed it.

It suddenly occurs to me that I know very little about Perry's life *before* he moved back home to Stonebrook Farm. When he was consulting, was this the kind of thing he did with Jocelyn often? Go to places where valet parking was the norm? Where they wore fancy clothes and drank fancy drinks and had important conversations with important people?

Dressed like he is now, Perry looks the part. But he also looks perfectly at home at Stonebrook wearing flannel and feeding me apples straight off the tree. I wonder if there's a version of himself Perry prefers the most. If he misses his former life.

I wait while Perry checks us in and passes our bags to a bellboy who will presumably deliver them to our rooms, then we cross through the posh lobby and approach the ballroom where the reunion is taking place. There's a table just outside the room where several women are checking clipboards and handing out name tags.

Perry's steps slow, and I sense his entire body tensing beside me. I follow his gaze to a striking blond woman standing behind the table. She's holding a clipboard and has an air about her that says she's in charge. Combined with Perry's reaction, it's all the evidence I need to know that the insanely beautiful woman in front of us is Jocelyn.

Any confidence I've pretended to feel regarding Perry having fully and completely gotten over his ex-wife vaporizes into the air. Jocelyn is *stunning.* Tall. Slender. Shiny, frizzless hair. Perfectly contoured cheekbones. She's wearing a very small black dress revealing legs that reach all the way up to her armpits.

I . . . cannot do this. My steps falter, and I grab onto Perry's arm, then tug him around a giant wooden pillar so we're hidden from view. "I changed my mind," I say. "I don't think this is a good idea."

Perry frowns. "What happened? What's wrong?"

I shake my head and lean it against the cool wood behind me. "Nothing. It's just . . . the music feels really loud, don't you think?" The music *does* seem loud—the bass thumping through the ballroom walls and filtering out to the lobby where we're standing, though I've never been one to shirk away from a party before.

But this is different.

"You don't want to go because of the music?"

I don't want to go because his ex-wife looks like she could star in his brother's next box office hit. There's real-world attractive, and there's Hollywood attractive. And Jocelyn is one-hundred percent Hollywood attractive.

I peek around the corner, looking at her one more time, and Perry follows my gaze. "That's her, isn't it?" I ask.

He rubs a hand down his face. "That's her."

"Perry, she's not going to believe you're actually here with me. She's *stunning.* You were married to *her,* and now you're here with me? No. No one is going to buy it." I realize as the words come out of my mouth that I sound like I'm fishing for compliments.

"Lila—"

I hold up my hand. "I don't need you to tell me I'm pretty, Perry. I'm just being a realist here. I know I'm not terrible to look at. But she is *exquisite.*"

Perry leans against the pillar beside me and folds his arms over his chest. "A couple things," he says, "and I'm going to say them in order of importance, so you better pay attention." He nudges me with his elbow, and I smile. "Are you listening?" he asks.

I roll my eyes, but secretly I'm loving that he brought out bossy Perry. "I'm listening."

"First, you are so much more than *not terrible to look at.* You're beautiful. And the more I've gotten to know you, the more beautiful you've become. Which is significant because Jocelyn—and this is point number two—is *only* beautiful until she opens her mouth. You get to know her? She gets ugly really quick."

Heat creeps up my cheeks. It's been a long time since someone has complimented me so openly. Not since before I started dating Trevor. Well, that's not entirely true. There was a two-year stretch before I got pregnant with Jack when I mostly lived on saltine crackers and lemon water in an effort to fit into a dress Trevor encouraged me to buy for one of his military balls. I dropped twenty-five pounds and fit into the dress, high on the compliments my husband was suddenly delivering with unprecedented frequency.

I was also starving.

When I found out I was pregnant with Jack, I'd never been so happy to have a reason to eat like a human again.

Trevor tried, after Jack was born, to coax me back down to the size six I'd been for a very brief moment in time. But by then, I had someone else to live for. Jack needed me healthy more than Trevor needed me skinny.

"Now, if you want to leave," Perry continues, "we can walk out of here right now, hit the burger joint down the street, and sneak back into the hotel and spend the evening watching bad television and eating overpriced Peanut M&Ms out of the minibar."

I chuckle. "That doesn't sound half bad."

"But if the only reason you don't want to go in there is because you don't think you measure up to that woman?" He shakes his head. "You're wrong, Lila. So wrong. I'll be the luckiest guy in the room tonight. And I won't be the only one who thinks so."

"Now you're just talking nonsense."

"I'm really not though. I don't know how to—" He shakes his head like he's trying to find the right word. "To schmooze. To be anything but honest with people. It's why I'm so terrible at small talk. I'm not very good at pretending a conversation—or even a person—isn't boring."

"We make small talk all the time."

He shrugs. "You're never boring."

"You do tell it like it is, don't you?"

"Always." He winces like he isn't happy about his answer. "Even when it isn't a good thing. But I'm trying to work on that. On being kind instead of always being right."

"Nah, I like that I can take you at your word." I take a deep breath and stand up a little taller, my insecurities yielding their grip the tiniest bit.

"You okay?" he says, reaching for my hand.

I nod and lace my fingers through his, letting him tug me out from behind the pillar and toward the welcome table outside the ballroom.

Jocelyn's eyes go wide when she sees us approaching hand in hand. I want to run again, but Perry squeezes my fingers once like he knows exactly where my mind just went, so I throw my shoulders back and go with it.

"Perry," Jocelyn says. "When you RSVP'd for two, I just assumed you were bringing one of your brothers."

Well, okay then. Now I see what Perry meant about her beauty fading as soon as she opens her mouth.

"Hi, Jocelyn." He drops my hand and slips his arm around my waist, tugging me into his side. "This is Lila. Lila, my ex-wife, Jocelyn."

Jocelyn makes no move to shake my hand, so I just snuggle in a little closer to Perry. Might as well take advantage while I'm here. "Hello," I say as sweetly as I can. "I've heard so much about you."

Her eyes narrow, and she purses her lips as she looks down at her clipboard. "Lila is your . . . date?" Jocelyn asks, her pen poised as if this is some required question she has to ask. I almost laugh at her posturing. Does she really think we can't tell what she's doing?

Perry tenses beside me, his fingers pressing into my side, and I squeeze him back, hoping he knows what it means. *I'm here. She's ridiculous. I'm still not opposed to cheeseburgers and overpriced M&Ms.*

"Not just my date," Perry says. "She's my . . ."

He pauses, an uncomfortable silence stretching forward while Jocelyn's look grows more and more smug.

Girlfriend. Just say it, Perry. Better yet, tell her we're engaged and wipe that snotty look right off her face.

I slip an arm around Perry's waist, tucking myself even closer.

"Girlfriend!" Perry finally says, a little too loudly.

Yes. Well done.

"My very serious girlfriend," Perry adds.

Jocelyn's eyes narrow.

Very serious girlfriend might be pushing it, but I'm all in to sell this thing if it means Perry doesn't have to deal with Jocelyn's patronizing smugness. I reach over and pat his chest, smiling up at him. "We're practically engaged."

Jocelyn drops her clipboard, and it clatters to the table, causing the woman sitting to the left of where Jocelyn is standing to swear. "Geez, Jocelyn, be careful."

Jocelyn shakes her head, her eyes looking anywhere but at Perry, and for a moment, I almost feel sorry for her. But then she rolls her shoulders, and her shrewd gaze turns calculating. "A girlfriend just in time for the reunion. How *convenient.*"

She clearly doesn't believe us. Or maybe she just doesn't *want* to believe us? Either way, I'm going to do anything I can to sell this story.

For Perry.

If I happen to have the best night of my life pretending I'm *practically engaged* to Perry freaking Hawthorne? Well, *someone's* got to do the job.

She turns her gaze to me. "Maybe we'll have the chance to get to know each other a little better tonight, Lila. We can swap stories, have real girl talk." She leans forward. "I could even give you a few pointers on how to handle *this guy.*" She points at Perry and rolls her eyes. "Trust me. You're going to need them."

Oh, I hate her.

I snuggle in a little closer. "That's so kind of you to offer. But I think I know *exactly* how to handle him."

Jocelyn openly scoffs but backs down when the woman sitting at the table shoots Jocelyn a wilting glare before leaning forward and offering us a wide smile. "We're so glad you *both* could be here," she says, her voice suddenly louder than everyone else's. "Dinner and wine are covered. There's a cash bar inside if you'd prefer something else. Karaoke starts at nine."

"Thanks, Grace," Perry says. "It's good to see you."

The woman's expression softens. "Sure thing. Enjoy your evening."

I don't know who Grace is, but I want her to be my new best friend.

Perry keeps his arm around me as we move into the ballroom. Once inside, he settles for holding my hand as we weave through the tables. At first, I think Perry is just trying to get us to one of the still-empty tables in the back of the ballroom, but then he passes several empty ones, and I half-wonder if we're making a break for it. We do, in fact, go straight out a side door into a dimly lit garden. Only then does Perry stop and drop my hand.

He lifts a palm to his forehead before spinning around, his eyes full of anguish. "I'm so sorry, Lila. I don't know what came over me. She was just so smug and dismissive, and—"

"Hey," I say, stepping closer. "Whoa. Calm down a sec."

"I shouldn't have done that."

I breathe out a laugh. "Perry, I don't care."

"That I just lied and told my ex-wife you're my girlfriend?"

I shrug. "If you hadn't said it, I would have. So we pretend we're a little more serious than we are. Who cares?" I step closer and lift my hands to Perry's chest. His muscles flex under my touch, but then he relaxes into me, some of the fight draining out of his shoulders. “Put your arms around me,” I say softly.

He immediately complies, his arms circling around my waist so his hands are clasped at the small of my back, but I still see the question in his eyes. “It’s dark in there, but light out here,” I say, “which means it’s likely people can see us.”

He nods. “Good thinking.”

“This doesn’t have to be a big deal. We already know we like each other. So we amp things up a little while we’re here. It isn’t a big deal.”

“People might talk,” he says gruffly. “Everyone here is from Silver Creek. Even if they don’t still live there themselves, their parents probably still do.”

I shrug. “If people talk, they talk. They’re just words. Lucky for us, we get to decide what words mean something and what words don’t.”

He smiles the tiniest smile, and a surge of victory pings in my chest. I really like making this man smile. “I still feel stupid for getting you into this mess,” he says.

I reach up on my tiptoes and kiss the side of his jaw just in front of his ear. “I think I get to spend the entire night pretending I’m Perry Hawthorne’s *very serious* girlfriend,” I say, my lips still close to his cheek. “You know what that makes me?”

His hands shift from my back to my waist where they settle on the curve of my hips. “What?” he says, his tone low and gravely.

I smile. “That makes me the luckiest *woman* in the room.”

Chapter Sixteen

Perry

LILA AND I WIND up eating dinner at a table near the back of the ballroom with a bunch of guys from the football team. They are the ones I wanted to come and see, and it feels good to get to talk and catch up. It feels a little weird lying to them about my relationship with Lila, but with Jocelyn making the rounds, "checking" on tables—I swear she's been to our table five times more frequently than all the others—to make sure everyone has everything they need, we don't really have much choice but to keep the story going.

Honestly, there are worse things. I *like* Lila. A lot. And seeing her next to Jocelyn only confirms how much I appreciate all the things that make her different. That make her *her*. It's easy to imagine us like this for real. Talking, touching. *Together.*

The touching is a definite bonus of our spontaneous fake relationship. I have a ready excuse to keep my hands on her. My arm around her shoulder. A hand resting on her knee or on the swell of her hip.

And she isn't holding back either. Earlier, when my friend James was telling a story about the homecoming football game our senior year, Lila curled her hand around my bicep, her fingers tracing mindless circles on my arm while she listened to James's story.

The contact was maddening. Distracting. Tiny pinpricks of pleasure sending heat right to my gut where it's still simmering, ratcheting up my attraction to Lila at an alarming rate.

"Are you having fun?" Lila leans close as the waitstaff clear away our dessert plates.

I nod. "Thanks to you."

She smiles. "I like your football friends."

"I think they like you."

She shrugs. "It's my superpower."

"Getting football players to like you?"

"Just people in general. My Grandpa Jamison used to call me *Likable Lila.* At first, I thought it was great. That I was so good at making people happy. But then I went through this phase in high school where I worried that being *likable* really just meant being a doormat. For about six months, I became *very* opinionated."

"How did that go for you?"

"It was horrible. Turns out, when my friends would ask me where I wanted to grab dinner, I wasn't saying I was happy eating anywhere because I didn't *want* to assert myself by having an opinion. It was because I was genuinely happy eating anywhere. Most of the time, I just didn't care. Trying to make myself care was so much more stressful."

"I can't even wrap my head around what that must feel like."

"What did *you* say whenever your friends wanted to go get food?" she asks.

I look toward James. "Hey. Where did we eat whenever we went out after football games?"

James immediately rolls his eyes. "Like you ever gave us a choice. Tiny's Tacos every single week."

Lila laughs. "Why did you guys put up with him?"

"Nah, it wasn't like that," James says. "You want a friend who's got your back? Perry's got you."

Loud laughter erupts across the room, and I look up, recognizing the sound.

Jocelyn is at the bar getting another drink, fawning over the bartender. Which isn't like her. The fawning or the drinking. When she's in charge of something—which happened a lot during the seven years we were married—she never drank until the event was over, and she no longer had to be her poised and polished self.

A shot of alarm races through me.

This is my fault. Showing up, flaunting a relationship when she had no idea I'd even started dating again was too much. Not that I owe her updates. But Silver Creek is a small town. Even without really wanting to know, I've stayed pretty up to date on Jocelyn's romantic life.

I keep my eyes on her as she tosses back a shot, then motions for the bartender to give her another.

Lila's gaze follows mine and settles on Jocelyn. "Do you think she's okay?"

"I don't know. It doesn't look like it."

Lila reaches over, her hand resting on my forearm. "Perry, it isn't your fault," she whispers.

Even distracted by Jocelyn, I still notice the burst of warmth that fills me over Lila reading my emotions so accurately. "I sprung our relationship on her," I whisper back. "One that isn't even real."

"And she sent you half a dozen manipulative emails."

"Maybe. But that doesn't mean I have to stoop to her level."

Lila squeezes my arm. "See? You really are a nice guy."

We watch as Jocelyn downs another shot and leaves the bar, walking over to the stage. I hold my breath as she climbs the stairs and makes her way to the microphone. "Good evening, Silver Creek High School Class of two thousand seven!" she practically yells.

A cheer erupts around the room before Jocelyn continues. "Now that we've had a nice, civilized, adult dinner, it's time to really have some fun. Is everyone having fun?"

On the surface, there isn't really anything wrong with what Jocelyn is saying. The crowd is responding, cheering whenever she wants them to cheer. But I know her too well not to sense how close she is to teetering over the edge.

"This isn't good," I say under my breath, and Lila slips her hand into mine.

"Okay!" Jocelyn yells. "Warm up those vocal chords, grab some liquid courage from the bar, and get ready for some karaoke!" She draws out the syllables of *karaoke* so it's almost a song itself, and the crowd goes wild, likely motivated by their clearly drunk emcee. "But not yet," Jocelyn says, holding up a finger. "Because I'm going to sing a song first." She laughs. "Bet you guys can't guess who I'm singing about."

"Oh no," Lila says as Jocelyn walks over to the deejay, leaning down as if to whisper in his ear. Seconds later, Jocelyn's back at the microphone, the opening strains of a song I only recognize because of Brody's crush on Taylor Swift blasting through the speakers.

"I guess she didn't want to go for subtle," I say under my breath.

James leans over and claps me on the back, but he doesn't say anything. What could he possibly say? Every person in the entire room has to know Jocelyn would only sing "We are Never Ever Getting Back Together" to me.

Jocelyn doesn't have a terrible voice, but she's obviously drunk and emotional, and the performance quickly shifts from bad to worse. She keeps losing the lyrics, jumping in at the wrong moment, jumbling her words together.

"Come on," Lila says, tugging on my hand.

"What?"

"We have to help her."

Suddenly, Jocelyn gasps and stops singing. She presses her face into the back of her hand, still gripping the microphone, while the track continues to play.

People around the room are looking at each other, concern on their faces, but no one is making any move to help her or get her off the stage.

No one but Lila.

I nod and stand up, letting Lila lead me around the perimeter of the room to the stage. She waits while I climb the stairs and cross to where Jocelyn is standing. She hasn't sung a word in almost a full minute. I tug the microphone out of her hands and hand it back to the deejay. "Come on, Jos," I say gently. "You don't have to do this."

She sniffs and lets me guide her off the stage, my arm around her shoulders.

There's an empty table behind the stage where Lila is waiting with a clean napkin and a glass of water. Jocelyn drops into a chair. "I'm going to regret this tomorrow, aren't I?" she says, her voice small.

I nudge the water glass toward her. She probably will regret it. I'm not going to patronize her by telling her differently.

"I'm so mad at you, Perry," she says. "Do you want to know why?" She looks up, tears pooling in her eyes. She doesn't give me the chance to respond before she says, "Because you're happy. And I'm still miserable. I'm miserable, and I ruined karaoke." She chokes out a sob.

On second thought, I'm not sure she *will* regret this tomorrow. She probably won't even *remember* it. I've never seen her so drunk. "You didn't ruin anything," I say. "Karaoke is fine."

"It isn't fine," she wails. "No one is singing. Someone needs to sing so people stop thinking about me looking so stupid." She tries to stand up. "I'll just go up and do a different—"

"Nope. You aren't going back up there," I say, gently pushing her back into her seat.

"I can do it," Lila says, stepping forward. "I can sing."

Jocelyn turns her gaze on Lila, and I tense. "Of course you can," she says with a defeated laugh. "And you'll probably sound amazing too. Because of course you will."

Lila looks at me, a question in her eyes.

"Are you sure?" I ask. She doesn't owe Jocelyn anything. Someone else can save karaoke, and we can just leave. That's pretty much all I feel like doing anyway.

Lila shrugs. "Why not? I did say I like karaoke." Her eyes sparkle, and another shot of warmth fills my chest. How many times is that going to happen tonight?

She moves toward the stage, reaching out to squeeze my hand on her way. Then she's climbing the stairs while my heart is climbing into my throat.

The deejay meets her with the microphone, and she whispers to him, probably giving him her song choice. “Okay,” Lila says into the microphone with exaggerated flair. “Who spiked the punch?”

The crowd laughs, and the tension in the room immediately eases. “Y’all don’t know me,” Lila continues, “but . . . well, someone needs to sing, so why not, right? I’m only doing one song though, so somebody better be planning what they’re going to sing next.”

A few people whoop from the crowd, and Lila smiles.

I keep one eye on Jocelyn, who has dropped her head onto the table, then move so I’m better positioned to see the stage. I have no idea what song Lila will sing, but even just seeing her stand there in front of everyone, the way she’s joking and making everything feel easier—she’s amazing.

And then she starts to sing.

Lila isn’t just good, she sounds like a professional. Like this isn’t karaoke but an actual concert. She’s singing an easy, stripped-down variation of "Can’t Help Falling in Love," and she’s . . . I’m genuinely speechless.

I try not to focus too much on the lyrics. It’s too soon to think she chose the song on purpose. That she’s trying to tell me something, but I don’t miss how much I *want* the lyrics to mean something. The crowd is silent when she sings, which never seems to happen in a traditional karaoke setting, but Lila’s voice demands the silence, demands the full attention of everyone in the room.

When she finishes the song, every single person jumps to their feet.

Lila said someone else better be planning to sing, but I can’t imagine anyone wanting to follow her performance.

"Thanks, ya'll," she says when the cheering finally stops. "But I meant what I said. Who's getting up here next?"

Eventually, Todd Weston stands up, dragging a couple of his buddies from the basketball team onto the stage with him. Lila hands off the microphone, laughing as all four guys lift their hands and bow down to the ground as if to worship her.

Goosebumps break out along my skin as Lila descends the stairs and walks toward me. There's a look of uncertainty on her face, like she's not quite sure how I'm going to respond. How I might feel. But as soon as our eyes meet, there's something else happening. Something stronger than uncertainty or fear or anything else. Some unseeable force, a living, breathing thing, weaves its way around us, pulling us toward each other.

The noise of the song Todd and his friends are singing falls away.

For all I know, we're the only two people in the room.

The only two people on the planet.

I'm going to kiss her.

Lila slips into my arms like she's always belonged there. Like it's the most natural thing in the world. Her hands move up to my cheeks, and then she's tugging me down, her body curving into mine as our lips touch for the first time.

Heat roars through me, racing out to my fingertips and down to my toes. I pull her closer, one hand splayed against the small of her back as if to anchor her against me. Only when she drops her hands to my shirt, clutching the fabric in her fists, do I remember where we are.

She pulls back, her breathing shallow as she lifts her eyes to mine. "Hi," she says lightly, her lips curving into a tentative smile.

I pull her against me, moving so my mouth is close to her ear, the floral scent of her hair filling my nose. I breathe deeply. "Should I expect this kind of greeting whenever you say hello?"

"Maybe not. I'm buzzed on the adrenaline of performing. You better take advantage while you can."

"Lila, your voice. That was amazing."

"I haven't done that in a very long time."

I haven't done *this* in a very long time.

I kiss her again, my hand lifting to cradle the back of her head. She breaks the kiss and leans into the touch, exposing the slope of her jaw, the long curve of her neck. If we were anywhere but in a room full of people . . .

Jocelyn moans from somewhere to my left, and Lila and I both turn to face her. "We should get her to her room," Lila says. "It doesn't seem like she's here with anyone else."

I nod, knowing and hating that Lila is right. I begrudgingly release the woman in my arms and step toward my ex-wife.

"Up you go," I say to Jocelyn, tugging her to her feet. "We're going to get you to your room."

With her arm draped over my shoulder, we make our way out a side door and head toward the opposite end of the hotel, where the rooms are, while Lila finds Grace, the woman who checked us in, to ask about Jocelyn's phone and other belongings.

Jocelyn has sobered the slightest bit, but she still isn't steady on her feet. I want to know if she has a friend, someone who could stay with her tonight, but it for sure isn't a job I want to volunteer for, so I don't ask.

We're waiting at the elevator when Lila catches up, holding a phone and small purse that must belong to Jocelyn. "She's sharing a room with Grace," Lila says. "Grace says she'll check on her in a bit, even if the reunion hasn't wound down yet."

"Grace is a good friend," Jocelyn slurs. "And you, Lila. You're a good singer." She lifts her finger, pointing Lila's direction. "But that's no surprise. Bigger girls always have better voices."

I freeze, completely horrified. And furious. I think back on the moment right after we arrived when Lila said she didn't belong with someone like me. It's such a ridiculous thought, and I hate that Jocelyn's careless words probably reinforced it. An intense need swells in my chest—a desire to make sure Lila knows with one hundred percent certainty that she is perfect exactly as she is.

For Lila's part, she seems entirely unaffected by Jocelyn's rudeness. She smiles easily and lets out a lilting laugh. "I'll take whatever perks I can get."

It takes all my patience not to drop Jocelyn in a heap outside her hotel room door, but Lila insists on walking her in. "I'll just be a minute," she says. "I'm just going to help her get settled."

I wait for Lila in the hallway, feeling keyed up, almost jittery from everything that's happened. There is so much to process. Jocelyn's comment about being miserable. I don't *want* that for her—I wouldn't wish misery on anyone—but I'd be lying if I said there wasn't some part of me that feels vindicated. The woman was heartless in our divorce.

Then there's Lila's willingness to help Jocelyn. The way she saved karaoke, the way she's repeatedly shown kindness to someone who has done nothing to earn it. Jocelyn has even done the opposite. She's been judging, critical, downright rude. And Lila has smiled through it all.

Then her performance. Her *voice.*

I've never heard anything like it.

Lila slips out of Jocelyn's hotel room and breathes out a sigh. "Okay," she says. "She should be fine until Grace makes it up to check on her."

I lean against the wall and push my hands into my pockets. "I don't even know what to say. Thank you doesn't seem like enough."

She shrugs and starts moving toward the elevator. "Don't worry about it."

"I'm more worried about you. That was a lot back there. A lot of unexpected—and then the way you just got up there and sang. Lila, you've been amazing tonight."

She pushes the down button for the elevator and chuckles. "For a bigger girl."

I sigh. "I'm so sorry she said that to you. It's not true. You aren't—"

She stops me with a hand to my arm. "Perry, it's okay. I don't need you to apologize on her behalf. I know who I am. I'm *happy* with who I am. Am I annoyed she felt like she had the right to say something? Sure." She shoots me a sly grin. "But I *did* get to make out with her ex-husband tonight, so maybe I can allow her one *tiny* dig."

The elevator doors ding and slide open, and Lila strolls on with easy confidence, looking at me over her shoulder, her expression inviting.

I practically scramble onto the elevator after her. "I don't know what kids are calling it these days, but I'm going to have to kiss you a dozen more times if you want to count that kiss as a makeout."

Lila shifts, her gaze turning to the opposite corner of the elevator. The corner I didn't even glance at for how focused I was on Lila. Two teenage girls stand side-by-side in the corner, their expressions open and curious.

"A dozen, huh?" Lila says under her breath. "Is that a promise?"

The elevator goes down a floor, and Lila and I wait while the teens exit. Just before stepping off, the older one turns back to look at Lila. "*Kids these days*"—she says this part with a dramatic eye roll—"only call it making out if there's tongue."

"Got it," Lila says, her tone genuine. "Good to know."

"I don't even know what is happening tonight," I say with a chuckle as the elevator doors slide closed.

"I don't either, but we're alone, and I think you said something about a dozen more kisses?"

I step closer, my hands moving to her hips as I tug her against me. "Can I tell you again how amazing you were back there? How much I admire you for being so chill in the face of Jocelyn's rudeness?"

"You know what? Let's not talk about her anymore tonight. I only have eighteen more hours until I have to go back to being a mom. I'd like to enjoy them while I can."

I lean down to kiss her, startled to realize that until this moment, I'd completely forgotten about Jack. It's a weird sensation. There is an entire human that she has to think about all the time, cataloging his every need, prepared to drop everything and care for him literally every moment of every day. I suddenly feel selfish that it was so easy for me to forget the poor kid even exists.

A few seconds in, the sweetness of Lila's kiss banishes all thoughts of anything but the taste of her, the feel of her hands pressing against my chest, the way her body so perfectly melds to mine.

We're still kissing when the elevator doors open into the lobby.

I growl the tiniest bit when Lila pulls away, and she laughs even as she tugs me off the elevator.

I can already hear the music thumping from the ballroom, and my steps slow. Why did we come back down here again?

I look at Lila. "Do you want to go back to the party?" I try for an even, neutral tone, but I don't think I have her fooled.

Luckily, she immediately sighs with what can only be relief. "Not even a little bit. I haven't worn heels this long since Trevor's funeral. I'm ready to call it a night if you are."

I hesitate, a wave of insecurity washing over me at the mention of her late husband. I don't feel threatened, exactly. Just inadequate.

A loud cheer erupts from the ballroom, followed by raucous laughter.

I'm definitely ready to leave the party. I'm *not* necessarily ready to leave Lila.

But we're in a hotel. I can't exactly invite her up to my room, not without giving her the wrong impression, and it would be the *wrong* impression. First and foremost, Lila will be the one to set the pace in this relationship—if we can even call it that yet. She has more reason to take things slow than I do, and I will not pressure her. But honestly, even if Lila *were* ready for more, I'm not sure I am. The last woman I even *kissed* before Lila was Jocelyn.

So. Now we know how sad and lonely my life has been the past few years.

Lila leans against the same wooden pillar we hid behind when we first arrived, her posture speaking of just how tired she is. I reach for her hand and press a kiss against her fingertips. “Let me go get you your room keys.”

“Didn’t you already check us in?”

“I checked *me* in. There was only one room on the reservation, but I’m sure it was just a mix-up. Did you reserve your room under your own name, maybe?”

"Both rooms should be under your name. Would the confirmation number help? It's in your email.”

Huh. Well, this complicates things. “Let me go talk to them again. I’m sure they have an open room somewhere. I’ll go sort it out, then maybe we can grab a drink before we crash?”

“Or share the overpriced mini bar M&Ms?”

“Now that sounds like a plan.” I give her hand a quick squeeze. “I’ll be right back.”

She nods, her smile warm. “I’ll be right here.”

My heart thumps steadily as I move to the hotel’s front desk, warmed by the promise in Lila’s words and the memory of her lips on mine.

I’ll be right here. It occurs to me that I don’t just want her to be here. I want her to be everywhere else I am, too. Not that I plan on confessing all those feelings and driving us right into a DTR. I meant what I said about respecting Lila’s need to move slowly. But for the first time, the thought of spending my life with another person doesn’t scare me.

And that means something.

Maybe that Lila is magic.

Or maybe that I’m finally—*finally*—ready to move on.

Chapter Seventeen

Lila

THE THING IS, I'M used to people appreciating my voice.

I've done enough singing in public spaces to have grown comfortable in my ability. But no amount of applause from the general public can compare to what I felt when I walked off the stage and into Perry's arms. There was real, raw admiration in his eyes. That alone felt like a shot of adrenaline straight into my veins. But I also saw hunger. *Desire.* And then he was there, and we were kissing, and . . . I've never been kissed like that.

Not ever.

Not until he kissed me on the elevator, which was even a tiny bit better because we were alone.

The whole night feels like a dream. Well. Except the parts that read a little more like a nightmare.

I mean, I just tucked my boss's very drunk ex-wife into bed. Gave her aspirin. Pushed her still-perfect hair out of her eyes. Unstrapped her complicated heels—the kind with straps that go all the way up your calf and make your legs look ridiculously long. Or, they make *Jocelyn's* legs look ridiculously long. On me, they would only make my very sturdy legs look stumpy.

It's all about elongating when you're shaped like I am. Heels are great. The more neutral the tone, the better. But ankle straps? They're always going to be a no for me.

Which, *fine*. I'm happy to work with what I've got, and I've learned a lot about how to do it well. High-waisted anything to accentuate my tiny waist. V-necks to show off my great collar bones and broad shoulders.

Bigger girls always have better voices. I force the words out of my brain, not wanting Jocelyn's small-minded judgment to ruin my good mood.

Perry didn't seem to mind my size when he was kissing me like he wanted to have me for dessert.

My not-so-grumpy-anymore boss makes his way back from the front desk, his frown reminding me of that first day we worked together in person. It's only been a few weeks since then but considering how we've spent the last couple of hours, it feels like it's been so much longer. His smiles came so infrequently at first, but with every day that passes, I feel like I'm seeing more and more of the real Perry.

"No luck?" I ask when he finally stops in front of me.

He shakes his head. "They're completely booked. I showed them the confirmation number, but they're citing some sort of internal error. The good news is they're comping the one room they *do* have for us. But there's still only one." He glances toward the door. "Listen, it's not that far. I could just drive you home. Or you could stay, and I could drive home to sleep, then come back in the morning."

Neither option sounds particularly enticing. I really don't want to stay without Perry, but going home to my empty house? That just feels sad.

We could always go with Option C, the one he didn't mention: us sharing a room like two adults perfectly capable of platonically sharing a room. We'll just pretend like five minutes ago, we weren't making out like fiends.

The heat of the kisses we've shared rushes through me.

So, *fine,* there would have to be some guidelines. He can kiss me a thousand times, but I'm not ready for more. Even if my body feels tempted to think it is.

But then, there's probably a king-size bed inside our one hotel room. We could sleep with our arms and legs fully extended and not touch each other.

I bite my lip. "I hate for the room to go to waste. It's already paid for, right?"

He nods.

"So . . ." I look up to meet his warm gaze. "What if we both stay? Would that be weird? If we share the room?"

He rubs a hand across his face, hesitating long enough that I immediately wish I could take the suggestion back. "*Just* to sleep?" he finally asks.

Oh no. Did he think I wanted more? So soon? Did I give him that impression?

I quickly backpedal. "What? Yes! Of course just to sleep. Only sleeping. Very appropriate boss/employee bed sharing only. No funny business." *Oh good grief. Funny business?* I sound like Grandma June.

Perry lifts an eyebrow, his expression shifting into an easy grin. "I'm not sure I need things to be *that* appropriate."

This, of course, makes me turn the color of Grandpa Jamison's July tomatoes.

Perry hooks his hands around my hips and tugs me toward him. "I would love for us both to stay, mostly because I'm not ready for the night to end."

I slide my hands up his chest. "So we treat it like a slumber party. Stay up all night. Play truth or dare. Share all our secrets."

"If we're playing party games, can we add in spin the bottle?"

I roll my eyes. "I don't think that works if you only have two people."

"It works if those two people really like kissing each other."

I scoff and shake my head. "You're terrible."

And by terrible, I mean wonderful. Perfect. Wonderfully perfect.

"For real though," Perry says, his tone serious. "No expectations." He swallows, and I watch his Adam's apple slide up and down. "Lila, I haven't even kissed anyone else since Jocelyn. Not until you." He flinches the tiniest bit. "Maybe don't mention that to my brothers."

I move my hands to his waist, then slip them around him. "I'm right there with you. Trevor was my first kiss, and then I married him. There's never been anyone else."

He nods. "So we take things slow. No pressure."

The tension drains out of my shoulders. This man is impossibly good. "No pressure," I repeat.

He kisses me, his lips soft and warm, before pulling away and tilting his head toward the elevators. "Come on," he says lightly. "You better not snore."

Our hotel room is stunning. Soft bedding. Overstuffed chairs. Huge windows that will probably provide gorgeous views of the Blue Ridge Mountains once it's light enough to see them. Our bags are situated on the foot of the bed, brought up earlier by the bellman.

I change into my pajamas first, only stressing a little about whether my sleep leggings are thin enough to show the dimples in my thighs. But my sweatshirt is longish. It should totally cover me. Except, when I tug it down to cover my butt, the oversized neck slides down over my shoulder. Which is maybe not a big deal? I'm sleeping in a sports bra—obviously—so . . . *whatever.* It's all I've got, so it has to work. It's not like I'm planning on cranking up the lights and doing yoga poses. I've seen those tests the yoga ladies in the legging infomercials do to prove how *not* see-through the fabric is. There will be NO downward-facing dogs happening tonight.

When Perry emerges from the bathroom wearing lounge pants and a plain white t-shirt, I almost choke on the water I'm drinking, dribbling it down my shirt.

It's like he crawled into my brain and found the *exact mental image* I conjured up that day in the barn when I was hanging out with his mom. Except, it's so much better real and in the flesh.

Perry opens the fully stocked fridge. "Peanut or peanut butter?" he asks. "Or plain." He looks at me over his shoulder. "Does anyone ever choose the plain M&Ms?"

"Not me," I say with a shrug. "Peanut butter for me."

He tosses me a bag, and I open it, trying not to focus on exactly how many pennies each M&M will cost at the overinflated minibar prices. Though, doing math isn't a terrible distraction. It might keep me from staring at Perry. He did look amazing tonight, all dressed up. But I think I like this dressed down version of him best.

I'm sitting on the far side of the bed, leaning against the headboard, so I expect Perry to settle onto the opposite side beside me. Instead, he grabs a few pillows and situates himself so he's propped up, facing me, his head at the foot of the bed and his legs stretched out toward me. Oh, this is a *much better* view.

"Okay, spill it," he says, after popping a few M&Ms into his mouth. "When did you start singing like that?"

I wave a dismissive hand. "Honestly, I felt pretty rusty. I haven't done that in a very long time."

"*That* was rusty? Lila, you were phenomenal. Like, you need to be on stage at *American Idol*."

I roll my eyes. "That was actually my senior superlative. Most Likely to Be on *American Idol*."

"Yes. Definitely. I concur."

"I'm not sure *American Idol* would have me, but thank you. If nothing else, it felt good to be singing again."

"Why haven't you been singing? You should be. Everywhere. All the time."

His praise fills me up like steam filling Grandma June's tea kettle, except instead of whistling, I just want to squeal. And I *never* squeal.

"I sing *some*," I say. "In the shower. In the car. To Jack when I'm tucking him in at night. I'm just not performing like I used to." I take a steadying breath. We are inching toward very dangerous territory. I think I have to tell Perry. I *did* say we would share our secrets tonight, but—

A familiar swell of guilt pushes through me. My truth isn't very pretty, which is why I don't like saying it out loud. I never have. Not even to Grandma June. Only the grief counselor I saw for a year after Trevor's death has heard all the ugly inside of me.

But this thing with Perry feels *good.* Real. After watching him with Jocelyn tonight and sensing the layers upon layers of tricky history between them, somehow, I think he'll understand if I come clean.

He's watching me, as if sensing the telling of this story isn't easy.

I grab a pillow and tuck it against my chest. "I was actually singing in a club down in Columbia when I met Trevor. It wasn't anything big. But I had an agent and was starting to book pretty consistently in smaller venues around the region. Asheville, Greenville, sometimes down in Columbia. The goal was to get to Nashville." I shrug. "But then I met Trevor. He was handsome, charming. A man in uniform and all that. I was only nineteen when we got married, but he was twenty-five, already established in his military career. I moved down to Charleston where he was stationed, and I guess his life sort of swallowed me up. I didn't mean to stop singing, but Trevor didn't—" My words catch in my throat, and Perry reaches over, his hand slipping gently around my ankle.

It's so small. That simple touch, but it somehow grounds me.

"At first, he loved to hear me sing. But then, I think it became something he thought would take me away from him. Something that might impede his control. I didn't see it at first. When you're in love, you *want* to be together all the time. I just thought he really loved me." I let out a laugh. "That I was so lucky to find someone so devoted."

Perry's thumb moves back and forth across my skin, his touch soft.

"After I had Jack, things got a little better. We had this beautiful baby, and of course, when you're a new mom, you just stay at home and breastfeed. Me not going anywhere suited Trevor just fine."

Perry's grip on my ankle tightens the slightest bit, and his expression hardens. "I'm really sorry you went through that."

I shrug. "He was always kind on the surface. It wasn't abuse anyone else could really see, not even the people close to me. It was just little things. Little comments. Digs about my weight. But he always dressed them up. Like, he'd sign me up for a gym membership or book me a day at the spa, but instead of it feeling like, 'Hey, you're a tired new mom. You should take some time for yourself,' it came across as, 'Maybe now you'll stop looking like a tired old hag.'"

"First things first, you do not now, and I'm sure you did not then, look like a tired old hag. But also, I know that feeling," Perry says. "Like just being yourself will never be good enough."

I nod. "A couple of months before he died, Jack and I were out of town visiting my grandparents, and Trevor had some friends over to play poker. He loved poker, and the longer we were married, the riskier he got. It seemed like he was always trying to scrape together the cash he needed to pay what he owed. While I was gone, he lost pretty big and had already tapped what little we had in our savings account. So he sold my piano."

Perry swears, something I've never heard him do. I appreciate the sentiment, but somehow, telling Perry is making the story hurt less than it does when I relive it on my own.

"That's when I decided I was ready to file for divorce. I was tired of feeling so beaten down all the time. But I never did file. Because then he left for training in California, and he never came home."

Perry sits up and runs a hand across his face while I breathe out a shaky breath.

"I've never told anyone that," I say, my voice wobbly. "How do you say out loud that your military hero of a husband was actually kind of a jerk? Nobody wants to know that. Not now that he's gone."

Perry turns himself around so his back is against the headboard, and he shifts closer. He wraps his arm around my shoulders and pulls me against him, my head resting on his chest just over his heart. He doesn't say anything, which I actually sort of love. He just holds me.

"I don't mean to sound heartless. It was still terrible to lose him. I loved him. I grieved his loss. But my grief was so complicated. All people wanted to do was talk to me about how amazing he was. And he was amazing. He really was an exceptional pilot. He just wasn't very nice to me."

"And you couldn't say that out loud," Perry says. "That must have been so hard."

"For the longest time, I felt so guilty. I still get his military benefits. I'll get them forever. And that feels wrong somehow. I'd already decided to leave him."

"Lila, you more than deserve those benefits. You're raising his kid."

"I know. And that's how I've been able to make peace with the whole situation. Those benefits *are* for Jack. And to his credit, Trevor was always a good dad. For Jack's sake, I have to remember him that way."

He slowly runs a hand down my back. "Have you thought about singing again? Like, really going for it?"

"Nah," I say without any hesitation. "I'm all Jack's got. And now that he's in school, stability is important. Plus, it's such a longshot. I don't think it's worth the sacrifice it might take to even try when there's no guarantee it would work." I lift my head and pull back the tiniest bit so I can look at him. "But I will tell you what I've thought about doing. Someday, maybe. If I can save up enough cash to buy a piano and get started."

"What's that?" Perry says, his hand rubbing slow circles across my shoulder blades.

"I'd love to teach. Piano and voice lessons."

"I bet you'd be amazing at that," he says. "You should totally do it."

"I don't have the degree for it. Or any degree. But if I teach for cheap at first, prove to people that I know what I'm doing, maybe I can eventually raise prices and build up a studio."

"People just need to hear you sing, and they'll be lining up for voice lessons."

"Knowing how and teaching how are two different things, but I appreciate the vote of confidence." More than he knows. I got so used to Trevor dismissing the things I wanted, it doesn't seem real that Perry could be so supportive. So accepting.

"Do Trevor's parents know how he treated you?" Perry asks.

I sigh and drop my head back on his shoulder. "No. And I don't think I'll ever tell them. They're good with Jack. At least in small doses. And he has so few people in his life, I don't want to risk alienating them."

Perry is silent for a long moment, which gives me time to take stock of my feelings. It's a weird sensation to be both completely relaxed and completely charged at the same time. My mind is at ease, comfortable in Perry's presence, but my body is lit up, aware of every single place we're touching. My head against his chest, his hands on my back, my side tucked against his. Perry smells like sandalwood, a scent I only recognize because I bought Trevor some aftershave once—citrus and sandalwood—because of how much I liked it, and Trevor returned it.

"Lila, I want to tell you something," Perry says. "And I don't want you to think I'm just saying it to make you feel better. You remember what I said about not being good at schmoozing. Please. I want you to take my words at face value."

I sit up, sensing that I should face him for whatever he wants to say.

"No, don't do that," he says, tugging me back down. "This will be easier if you aren't looking at me."

I chuckle as I snuggle back into his chest. "So demanding."

He gives my shoulders a squeeze before clasping his hands around my back. "When I first saw you, when you drove out to bring me a jack, of course I noticed how beautiful you are. But I also—" His words cut off, and he hesitates. "Now that I'm about to say this, it sounds a lot creepier than it did in my head."

"I promise I won't think you're creepy."

"I noticed your curves. Honestly, it took all my willpower to keep my eyes on your face because I *really* noticed. It made you *more* enticing to me. Not less." He shakes his head. "After what Jocelyn said to you tonight, and then hearing how Trevor treated you, I just . . . I want you to know how beautiful I think you are. Just as you are."

Just as I am? This man cannot be real. If I wasn't touching him, I might wonder if he were a mirage. Some fantastical figment of my imagination embodying everything I could possibly desire.

I shift so I can look at him—he can just deal with the eye contact—and smile at the warmth and sincerity I see in his eyes.

"I'm going to kiss you now, Perry Hawthorne."

As I lean in, I think about that moment earlier this week when Perry fed me apples in the orchard. I sensed then that something was happening to my heart. If that day was the start of my falling, this moment might be the thing that propels me clean over the edge.

I should be nervous about that.

But I can't bring myself to feel anything but the thrill of Perry's lips on mine.

Chapter Eighteen

Lila

THERE IS NOTHING FRANTIC or frenzied about this kiss.

Not at first. It's warm. Tender. A kiss that feels like acceptance and understanding.

My story—my truth—it's safe with Perry.

I reach up and thread my fingers through his hair, pulling him closer, feeling my desire build with each passing second.

Perry's tongue skates across my bottom lip, a featherlight touch, and I willingly respond, giving as much as I get, wanting nothing but to be right here, touching him, tasting him, learning the smooth planes of his body, feeling the way he responds to my hands on his skin.

I've known for weeks that Perry is the kind of man I *could* fall in love with. But when I saw him gently lead his ex-wife off the stage earlier tonight, kind even in the face of her unkindness, I recognized that he's the kind of man I *want* to fall in love with.

But *wanting* to love him isn't enough. My life is complicated. Perry can't just love me back. He has to love me *and* Jack. He has to be comfortable pursuing a relationship with someone who will make him an instant father.

Being together *feels* good, but is that enough? For now, maybe, secluded in a private hotel room in a posh resort, miles away from our real lives and responsibilities.

But will this hold up to real life?

I want to believe it will.

I lean into the kiss. I'm *going* to believe it will.

Perry's lips move from my mouth to the curve of my jaw, leaving a trail of kisses to my ear. I lean back, my eyes closed, and he continues the slow and blissful torture, pushing my hair out of the way and kissing his way down my neck and across the top of my exposed shoulder.

"You said it's been how many years since you've kissed someone?" I murmur.

He chuckles against my skin. "Almost . . . four?" He leans back. "Man. That's hard to admit out loud."

"Nope." I pull him back to me. "That was not an invitation to stop. More like me marveling that you're still so good at this with so little practice."

He pauses, his lips only centimeters from mine, and smiles. "Like riding a bicycle."

Perry pulls me against him as we kiss, rotating us so that he's leaning against the headboard, and I'm leaning into him.

This kiss lasts longer than all the others. *And* tests my willpower more than all the others. Perry's hand slips under the hem of my shirt, his palm flat against the small of my back. I resist the urge to flinch and shy away from his touch. I will not let the fear of Perry noticing the softness of my body ruin this moment. He told me he thought I was beautiful just as I am. I have to believe him.

Too much more of this, and I'm liable to stop thinking. Even if I *want* to stop thinking, I have too many reasons to take things slow.

Perry is either reading my mind or feeling the same way, because he breaks the kiss with a low groan. "Okay. We should . . ." His words trail off into a sigh.

"I know," I say softly. "We should."

For a long moment, we stay close, our arms still entangled, our foreheads almost touching.

Perry runs a hand down the side of my face, brushing my hair back. "I think we've checked all the required boxes to call this an actual makeout."

I grin. "Even according to *kids these days.*"

He kisses me one more time, almost as if he can't help himself, but he ends it quickly, shifting himself backward and putting some distance between us. "Okay. Enough of that." He snuggles into the pillows, his head propped up on his elbow. "We should have a very boring conversation now."

I smirk. "Boring, huh?"

"Yep. Baseball stats. Stock market fluctuations."

"Mood killers. Got it. How about . . . my grandmother's Belgian waffle recipe?"

"That'd be pillow talk for Lennox, but—wait, see? Success. Thinking of my brother is a definite mood killer."

"Mission accomplished." I lift my hands up in a tiny mock cheer.

"All right, Lila Templeton," Perry says. "Tell me something I don't already know about you."

I wrinkle my nose. "Hmm. Does it have to be something important?"

"No. Something unimportant," he says in his boss voice. "I feel like we've covered enough heavy stuff for one night."

I don't tell him I'd do just about anything for bossy Perry. We're trying to *kill* the mood, not heighten it. "Yes. Good thinking. Okay. I think olives are disgusting."

"A worthy opinion. Even if you're wrong. What else?"

"I love country music."

He makes a face. "I'll allow it. But only if you're singing it. Wait." His expression turns serious. "This is an important one. College basketball. Yes or no?"

"Yes. Definitely."

"In that case, Duke or Carolina?"

"You mean Crapolina?"

His eyes go wide, and he presses a hand to his chest. "You wound me."

"Seriously? You're a Carolina fan?"

"I'm a Carolina *graduate.* That's where I got my MBA."

I shift like I'm climbing out of the bed. "This was fun while it lasted, but I think it's time for me to—"

He pushes himself up, lunging across the bed after me. I squeal as he hauls me off my feet and playfully tosses me back on the bed. It's not lost on me that he just picked me up like I'm a tiny sack of potatoes. "A Duke fan?" he says. "Seriously?"

I'm on my back, and he's hovering over me, one hand on either side of my head.

I shrug. "A Duke fan. To my core, Perry. To my very . . . *apple* core."

He groans and drops his head. "Lila, you *didn't.*"

I bite my lip, loving this playful side of him. If I wind up marrying this man, I'm going to write apple puns into my wedding vows. "Is Duke really a deal breaker?"

He pops back up and smiles wide. "I can't believe I'm saying this when the blood in my veins runs Carolina blue. But it's gonna take more than pukey Duke to get rid of me."

I lean up and kiss him on the nose. "Your generosity knows no bounds."

After we share a third bag of M&Ms, we spend another two hours talking about everything and nothing, finally circling back to Perry's divorce.

We're snuggled under the covers now, our faces no more than a foot apart, one of his feet draped loosely over mine.

His summary is brief, almost perfunctory, but I can see the hurt in his eyes. It doesn't take much imagination to fill in the gaps of what the whole ordeal must have been like.

"So your assistant was helping her the whole time?" I ask, still disbelieving an employee could be so disloyal.

Perry nods. "By the end, he wasn't just covering for her infidelity. He was funneling her information about what my business was worth, sharing pertinent information about key clients. It was all a part of building her case. When she filed for the divorce, she knew exactly how much to ask for in the settlement. She presented herself essentially as a partner in the business, and added in, on the grounds of her having finished her MBA six months before I finished mine and the effort she made to *support* me through my graduate program, that she was entitled to more than half of my business's net value."

"That's horrible."

He nods. "The judge sided with her, and I had to liquidate everything I had in my portfolio. Stock options, IRAs, all of it, just to pay the settlement."

I huff. "I should have spit in the water I left next to her bed."

When he smiles, I reach out to trace the lines that crinkle up beside his eyes as a result. "You have good lines," I say.

"Pretty sure those are called wrinkles."

I grin. "They aren't wrinkles! They're smile lines. And yours are very handsome."

"Jocelyn once suggested that I get Botox," he says.

"You're kidding."

"I wish."

"Okay, I don't want you to take this the wrong way, but Perry, why did you marry her in the first place?"

"It's a fair question. But the answer is probably similar to why you married Trevor. I thought she was what I wanted. I probably ignored a lot of warning signs, but she also changed a lot too. And I changed. Realized I wanted something different than she did."

"It just goes to show, after all she put you through, money really can't buy happiness. You've got your family. Your farm—"

"A really fantastic assistant," he adds.

"A really fantastic assistant," I repeat, wishing, even though I know it's too soon, that what he had was a really fantastic *girlfriend.* "And what does Jocelyn have? She said she's miserable."

Perry sighs. "For her sake, I hope that was just the alcohol talking."

"See? There's that nice guy again. I think he's completely chased the grump away."

"Nah," he says softly. "I think you chased the grump away."

I smile, even as my eyes drift closed. No matter how much I wish I could talk to Perry all night, I've been waking up at six-thirty every single day since Jack was born—that child is the most accurate human alarm clock on the planet, no matter what time he goes to bed—and it's after two a.m.

"Okay, sleepy head," Perry says. "Time for bed." He turns off the light, and I expect him to settle down on his side of the enormous mattress, but then the bed shifts as he rolls toward me and suddenly, he's next to me, his hand on my cheek. There's enough light coming in through the window that I can see the outline of him, but it's too dark to make out any features. "Goodnight, Lila," he says. His thumb traces my bottom lip before he leans in and kisses me, slow and tender.

"*This* is how I would like to go to sleep every night," I say sleepily.

Perry stills, and I panic, the reality of my drowsy words waking me to full alertness. I wasn't necessarily thinking about going to sleep next to Perry *specifically*. It was more just the kiss, the tenderness. Who wouldn't want someone to love them off to dreamland every night?

I mean, *yes*. It would be better if that person were Perry. But it's probably a little too soon to make that kind of declaration.

Except I just did. *Sort of did?*

Perry's hand skims my cheek as he pulls it away. "You deserve to fall asleep like this every night. Now get some sleep."

Ha. Easy for him to say. And easy for him to do, apparently. Because he's asleep in what feels like seconds. I listen as his breathing slows and deepens. He's on his stomach, one hand stretched across the bed to rest on my wrist. Which naturally means I will stay in this exact position, even if my arm falls asleep and my fingers go numb, for as long as humanly possible.

If he thinks I deserve to fall asleep like this, well, there's a vacancy in the "Kiss Lila to Sleep" department, and he's more than welcome to fill it.

For a very long time, I thought I'd missed my opportunity for a true happily-ever-after. Guilt, shame, doubt, discouragement, some erroneous belief that we only get *one* shot at happiness in life. They all worked together to make me content with a slightly less happy life. I have Jack, and he's brilliant. I have a job, even if it isn't the one I always dreamed I'd have.

It's enough. It *was* enough.

But now, with a sleeping Perry beside me, I let myself revel in the possibility that maybe, just maybe, my life can have *so. much. more.*

And that is the thought that finally sends me off to sleep.

Chapter Nineteen

Perry

After spending almost an entire night getting to know Lila—*kissing* and getting to know Lila—I don't particularly want to go to the reunion breakfast this morning. I'd much rather drive Lila up to the Blue Ridge Parkway, take in the views, and enjoy the last few hours we're together before I have to take her home.

Logically, I know that if any kind of relationship between Lila and me is going to work, it has to work in our regular lives too, and not just when we're tucked away from everything. But that doesn't mean I want the magic to end sooner than absolutely necessary.

But we're here. And the food doesn't look half bad. And if I can swing it, I'd like to provide my ex-wife with the opportunity to apologize to Lila.

The crowd is a little more subdued this morning than it was last night, which isn't surprising. Lila and I left the party just after nine, and the alcohol was already flowing freely. I'm sure it didn't slow as the night wore on.

Lila and I make our way through the buffet line, then sit near the window where we have a nice view of the mountains. I probably ought to be more enthusiastic about talking and connecting with old classmates, but with Lila beside me, it's hard to be invested in anyone but her.

This thing between us is new, but it already feels bigger than anything I've ever experienced before. Anything I've ever *felt* before. That realization leaves me nervous and jittery. I don't know how to stop worrying that I'm going to screw things up, that I might lose whatever this is before it's even started.

"Did you get enough to eat?" I ask when she slides her plate away.

"Probably more than I needed. I don't usually eat a big breakfast."

"Me neither. That French toast was worth it though."

Over Lila's shoulder, I see Jocelyn finally enter the room next to Grace. She looks about as well as expected after the night she had; she's dressed casually, her hair pulled back in a simple ponytail.

I reach out and take Lila's hand. "Hey, will you be okay by yourself for a few minutes? I'm going to go talk to Jocelyn."

Lila squeezes my fingers, warmth in her eyes, and gives me an encouraging nod. "Of course. Take your time."

It occurs to me that Lila trusts me in a way I'm not sure Jocelyn ever did, even after years of marriage. Jocelyn wouldn't have stopped me from going to talk to an ex, but she for sure would have given me some side-eye and probably launched an inquisition after I returned, wanting a minute-by-minute recap of the encounter.

It's just another example of how different Lila is.

And a reminder of how unhealthy my marriage was.

"You okay?" Lila asks, probably because I'm still sitting here staring at her.

I stand up and move around the table, leaning over to press my lips to hers. "I'm good," I say. "I just really like you."

She reaches up and grabs my shirt, tugging me down for another kiss. "Well, that's good," she says. "Because I really like you, too."

When I stand and turn, Jocelyn is watching us.

I leave Lila and slowly make my way toward Jocelyn. I stop a few feet away from where she's leaning against the wall. "Good morning, Jocelyn."

"Is it?" Jocelyn says breezily. "I hadn't noticed."

I push my hands into my pockets. "You owe Lila an apology," I say. It's not like I came over here for small talk. Might as well get right to it.

Jocelyn's jaw tightens, but I can tell by the way she won't look me in the eye that she knows I'm right. "I don't remember much about last night," she says dismissively.

"Trust me. I remember everything about last night, and you owe her an apology."

Jocelyn sighs. "And I suppose you're her knight in shining armor, swooping in to make sure she gets it?"

I don't try to deny it. "I really care about her, Jos," I say, happy that, at least in this, I'm telling the truth.

Jocelyn studies me for a long moment before her shoulders drop the slightest bit. "Yeah," she finally says. "I can tell you do." She wraps her arms around herself, suddenly looking more vulnerable than I've seen her look in a very long time. "Does Lila like the farm?"

I know what she's really asking. Does Lila like this version of my life? The version Jocelyn didn't want.

"You could ask her," I say. "When you go over to apologize."

Jocelyn rolls her eyes, and I finally see a glimpse of the Jocelyn I *do* remember. "Fine," she huffs. She pushes off the wall and walks toward Lila. I stay where I am, watching as Jocelyn drops into the seat I left empty.

Their conversation only lasts five minutes or so, but from where I'm standing, too far away to hear, it might as well be five hundred minutes. Finally, Jocelyn stands and makes her way back to me, and I breathe out a sigh of relief.

She stops in front of me and shakes her head, her hands propped on her hips. "That woman is ridiculously likable."

I can't help the smile that breaks out across my face.

"I'm happy for you, Perry. I still hate you a little bit. But I'm happy for you."

I have imagined a lot of conversations with my ex-wife over the years. Conversations in which I rant and rave and blame and accuse. It's a relief to realize that I have no desire for that anymore. I appreciate that Jocelyn apologized to Lila, and I'm glad she's happy for me. But I don't need her approval. She really doesn't have power over me anymore.

We say our goodbyes, and I head back to Lila. "Ready to go?" I ask, holding out my hand.

She takes it, allowing me to tug her to her feet. I slip my arms around her, pulling her into a hug, and am immediately blown away by how right this feels. It's such a contrast to the interaction I just had, I suddenly feel desperate to hold on—to do whatever it takes not to lose this.

Lila leans in. "Ready when you are."

I say goodbye to a few friends, then we make our way outside, waiting in the chilly October air as the valet brings my truck around. We drive in comfortable silence until we're out of the city and on the interstate heading to Hendersonville.

"Thank you for asking Jocelyn to apologize," Lila says. "You didn't have to do that."

"Yes, I did. She was rude. Apologizing was the right thing to do." Admittedly, it would have been better had Jocelyn felt motivated to apologize on her own, but something is better than nothing. "You deserve respect, Lila. Just because you're good at letting things roll off your back doesn't mean you should have to." I think of her late-night confession about her husband and the way he treated her. "I need you to know that I would never stand by and let anyone speak to you that way. Let alone speak to you that way myself."

She's quiet for a long moment. "That means a lot," she finally says.

After a few more minutes of silence, she asks, "Is it too soon to ask where we go from here?"

My eyes jump to hers. "What, like, *us*? Relationship-wise?"

She nods.

"I mean, I'd like to see you again, if that's what you're asking. And not just at work." A sudden fear pulses through me. Does she think I might not? That this was just some sort of weekend thing? "Lila, I wasn't messing around last night. I'm serious about whatever this is. I'd like to date you. I'd like to see if this can go somewhere."

"No, I know," she says quickly. "I didn't think you were messing around. And I'd like that too. For us to date. It's just . . . dating is a little more complicated for me."

"Okay," I say slowly.

"Because of Jack."

Buttercupping Buttercup.

Jack. Of course Jack complicates things. I've been so focused on Lila, I haven't even thought to factor him into this new dynamic between us. Which can't be a good sign.

"Right. Of course. We have to think about Jack. But I'm sure we can figure it out," I say to convince myself as much as her.

"Perry, I don't want to tell him yet."

The hope that's been filling my chest since last night deflates the tiniest bit.

"Not because you wouldn't be great with him. You would be. You *will* be," she says. "But you saw yourself how fixated he's been on finding himself a stepdad. If he starts spending time with you, it'll only get his hopes up. I can take risks when it comes to my own heart. It's not as easy to risk his."

Everything she's saying makes total sense. And it's better this way. We can find our footing first, *then* I can work on developing a relationship with Jack.

But that thought brings its own wave of mixed emotions.

On the one hand, a part of me is relieved that I won't be expected to immediately jump right into figuring out dad mode. For all I know, I don't even *have* a dad mode.

On the other hand, I don't love that this feels like a wall between Lila and me. She won't really let me in—not completely—until she's ready to let me into Jack's life as well.

"So we take things slow," I say. "Spend time together at work."

She nods. "And I can get a babysitter every once in a while, too. You just won't be able to come over to the house."

I run a hand across my face. "Sure. No, that makes sense."

"You sound disappointed."

I reach over and wrap my hand around hers. "Not at all. Jack is your first priority. Of course you have to do what's best for him." I give her fingers a quick squeeze. "But just so we're clear, between nine a.m. and two p.m., you're *all mine.*"

She smirks. "Whatever you say, boss."

I pull into her driveway and park the truck, mostly happy with where we've landed. I'm not disappointed. And I do understand why she wants to take things slow.

But that doesn't mean I'm not worried about the giant question mark hanging over our relationship. If things progress—and I really want them to—there's no getting around it. Jack won't just be Lila's, he'll be *ours.*

Chapter Twenty

Perry

THERE ARE A LOT of places on Stonebrook Farm fit for kissing.

The apple orchard.

Up on the ledge with mountain views stretched out in every direction.

In the goat barn.

Hiding in my office.

In the walk-in freezer in Lennox's restaurant kitchen. (Don't ask.)

I know it doesn't sound professional to imply I'm spending so much time at work making out. But Lila and I *are* getting work done. Maybe even MORE work done, since kissing has become a sort of reward for completing tasks. Besides, we have to take advantage of every spare moment. It's been two weeks since my high school reunion, and we still haven't managed to go on a real date.

We tried to schedule one last week, but the babysitter fell through at the last minute. We ended up Facetiming half the night anyway, after Lila put Jack to bed, but Facetime isn't nearly as fun as kissing in the apple orchard.

With the harvest festival coming up, plus the opening of Lennox's restaurant, it might be Christmas before we manage a real date.

I look up from the sales numbers from last year's festival when Lila appears in my office doorway, a giant box in her arms.

I stand up and meet her, taking the box and setting it down on the desktop. "What's all this?"

"Samples from the farm store bakery," she says, pulling the top of the box open. "In need of official boss approval."

I stand behind her, wrapping my arms around her waist and nuzzling my nose against her neck as she unpacks the box.

"Mmm, are you trying to distract me?" she mumbles, even as she leans into me and tilts her head, giving me easier access to her neck. "This is very . . . important . . . business."

There is zero conviction in her voice, and I take full advantage, spinning her around to face me, tucking her securely into my arms. I keep waiting for this to feel old. But holding Lila, kissing her, it still feels like a revelatory experience. There is always something more to learn about her. To *love* about her.

Her brilliance, for example. She's self-deprecating when it comes to her qualifications, tossing around her lack of a college education like it somehow diminishes her overall impact, but she doesn't give herself enough credit. She's also funny. And optimistic and engaging and real. She makes people feel good about themselves. She makes *me* feel good about myself.

I kiss her slowly, drawing it out, then nip at her bottom lip until she whimpers.

"Perry Hawthorne, your office door is wide open."

I chuckle. "What's going to happen? No one is going to fire me, and the only person who can fire you is me."

"That makes you sound like an entitled jerk," she says, but her lips are grazing over my earlobe while she says it, so I'm not sure I can take her seriously.

A throat clears behind us, and Lila jumps out of my arms.

"It also makes you sound like a hypocrite," Olivia says from my office doorway. "Since you *do* have a no-fraternization policy for your employees."

Lila raises a questioning eyebrow, peeking out from behind my shoulder. She immediately gasps. "You must be Olivia! Which means this is baby Asher!"

I finally turn and face my sister. Asher is strapped to her chest in a Baby Björn. "Olivia, Lila. Lila, Olivia," I say with all the enthusiasm of someone who is no longer kissing his girlfriend.

Girlfriend? We haven't talked about making things that official, but Lila wouldn't have to ask me twice.

"The no-fraternization policy is for the summer staff living on site," I say, more for Lila's benefit than anything else. "This is different. And I don't recall the policy stopping *you* from making out in Mom's goat barn."

She rolls her eyes. "Funny, I do remember you scolding me for it though."

"No one should be scolded," Lila says, too seriously for the conversation. "The goat barn is a *very* good place for kissing."

Olivia laughs. "Oh, I like you. Sorry I haven't been around to meet you before now. I've heard so many great things about you." Olivia has been holed up at home while Asher fought off a case of RSV. It's good to finally see them out and around again, even if she is going to make fun of me.

"You too," Lila says. "Perry's told me a lot about you."

I reach out and let Asher grasp my thumb, his tiny fingers curling around it. He has his dad's dark hair and wide brown eyes. But he somehow looks like Liv too. He's also so much bigger than he was the last time I saw him.

Olivia starts to unstrap the baby carrier. "You want to hold him?"

I do kinda want to hold him, but that doesn't stop nerves from jumping deep in my gut. I've had exactly two experiences holding babies. And both times it was *this* baby. Once in the hospital, and once right after Olivia brought him home. I've seen him a lot more than that, but he sleeps a lot, and he eats a lot, and well, there are a lot of people in my family who love babies and are always willing to hold him.

I've never felt compelled to fight for my chance, though, when Olivia lifts Asher into my arms, I wonder if I should start fighting more. This is amazing. Asher wiggles the tiniest bit, his foot randomly shooting out, then he yawns, and my heart squeezes.

My eyes lift to Lila's. She's watching me closely, an expression on her face I can't quite read. She's done this whole parenting thing before. She knows what this is like. And maybe that's what her expression is saying. She gets it. She knows how magical this can be.

Asher grunts a few more times and starts to squirm like he's unhappy, letting out a few shrieks that feel a little too much like they could lead to crying. "Okay. Uncle time is over," I say.

Olivia drops onto the couch at the back of my office and closes her eyes. "Just bounce him a little. I only need a minute."

"Bounce him?" I immediately think of bouncing a basketball, but that for sure isn't right.

Asher squirms again, his cries growing more persistent, so I start bouncing. Except, I'm more . . . squatting?

The baby immediately quiets though, so I keep it up. It's working! I calmed him!

I've got at least three more sets of these before my quads give out. That's . . . five minutes of peace? I can give Olivia five minutes.

Olivia chuckles from behind me. "Perry, he's not a free weight. You don't have to do a full-on squat."

"Don't question what's working," I say.

Except seconds later, it *isn't* working anymore. Asher is crying even louder than before, and my quads are starting to shake. Now I look like a bad uncle and a guy who clearly needs to hit the gym more frequently.

Lila comes to my rescue, scooping Asher into her arms. "It's more like dancing," she says, holding Asher upright so his head is resting on her shoulder. She starts lightly bouncing on her toes, swaying back and forth.

Asher quiets, and Lila smiles, her eyes closing as she presses her face close to his tiny head.

I drop onto the couch next to Olivia, a little disappointed to be *so bad* at baby holding, but also content to watch Lila, who looks as natural with Asher in her arms as she did singing on stage at my reunion. I don't know if there is anything the woman can't do.

She starts to sing some sort of lullaby, and Olivia reaches out and squeezes my arm. "Um, are you in love with her yet?" she says under her breath. "Because I've only known her five minutes, and I think *I'm* in love with her."

When Asher's squirming kicks up again, Lila shifts his position and heads toward the office door. "We're going to walk the hallway for a bit. See if that helps him settle."

Olivia lifts a hand, giving Lila a thumbs up.

"She's pretty great, right?" I say.

Olivia nods. "I'm really happy for you, Perry."

My eyes flick away for the briefest moment, but Olivia is too sharp to miss anything, and she immediately zeroes in on my reaction. "Wait. What was that? You did an eye thing. Are *you* not happy for you?"

I glance toward the door, not wanting Lila to hear our conversation, but there's no sign of her. "It's not that. I'm happy. I really like her. But she's still keeping me at arm's length. Which is fine. She said she wanted to take it slow. But I'm seeing her every day, and I'm just . . . I don't know."

"Your feelings aren't taking it slow?"

"She's so different from Jocelyn, Liv. She fits. Not some fancy version of a life defined by jobs or cars or whatever. She fits *me.* I've never had that before."

Olivia nudges my knee. "You should tell her how you feel, Perry."

I quickly shake my head. "It's too soon for that. What would I even tell her?"

"Ummm, maybe try something that starts with an L and ends in OVE? Is she coming to the restaurant opening? You could tell her there. The whole family will be around."

"Even if I did have something to tell her, I wouldn't want to do it in front of the entire family."

Olivia shoots me a pouty look. "Well that's not any fun for the rest of us."

"The rest of you don't need to have any fun. This is my relationship." I hold up a finger in warning. "Don't do anything, Liv. No pressuring Lila. No making public toasts at the restaurant opening."

"So she *will* be there?"

I sigh. I walked right into Olivia's trap. "Yes? I think? I haven't invited her yet. I think I'm worried being with the entire family will overwhelm her."

The restaurant isn't big enough to invite the entire Stonebrook staff to the opening, or else there would only be employees present, so the entire thing has turned into this sort of "invitation only" affair, at least as far as employees are concerned. Most of the people in attendance will be restaurant critics and former associates of Lennox's from when he worked in Charlotte. But my entire family will be there. Even Flint.

On the one hand, I'd love to have Lila with me. On the other, she's met my family while she's keeping me from her kid like I might give him the swine flu. Would coming to the opening fit into her definition of taking things slow?

"Hasn't she already met the entire family?" Olivia asks. "I mean, not Flint, of course, but the rest of us? I thought I was the only holdout."

"No, you are. Or were, I guess. But inviting her feels so official."

Olivia looks at me with all the judgment only a sister can give. "I thought you wanted official. You were just talking about how much you like her."

"But I don't want to pressure her into something official before she's ready."

"But you're perfectly fine kissing her in every corner of the farm?"

I run a hand across my face. "I guess people are noticing?"

"And talking about nothing else. Listen. Don't pressure her. Just *invite* her. Let her decide if she wants to come or not."

"That's not—" I stop, because there isn't actually anything wrong with Olivia's suggestion. I should just invite Lila. I'm overthinking and making this too complicated. "Okay. That's actually a reasonable suggestion."

"Of course it is," Olivia says through a yawn. "My brain cells haven't *all* died from sleep deprivation. Just most of them." She closes her eyes again, her head falling back onto the cushions. "Dad is completely smitten with Lila, by the way. I was over there before I came here, and he couldn't stop talking about all the help she gave him when he was trying to name Preston Whitaker's new apple variety."

"Has he decided on a name?" I ask, suddenly curious.

Olivia scrunches up her face like she's trying to remember. "Sunshine Crisp? Summer Honeysuckle? I can't remember." She stretches her arms over her head, then winces and drops them back down to fold across her chest.

"You okay?"

She nods. "Milk letdown. Time for Asher to eat."

"Wait, does it—it hurts when that happens?"

Olivia shrugs. "A little? But just for a second."

I watch as she moves to the doorway where Lila has reappeared. They talk for a quick second before Olivia takes the baby and scoops up the diaper bag she dropped by the door when she first came in.

"I'm going to my office to nurse and pretend like I actually know what's going on around this place," Olivia says. She smiles at Lila. "It really was great to meet you. Thanks for your help with Asher."

Olivia jokes about not knowing what's going on, but she's surprisingly involved for still being out on maternity leave. It's an easy enough work environment for her coming and going, dropping in and contributing when she can. I'd love to have her back full-time whenever she's ready, but now that Lila's around, it's been easier to balance the workload. Hopefully, Olivia will adjust her schedule to whatever works best for her and her family.

Her *family.*

A swell of emotion tightens my gut as I watch Lila walk toward me. I want that. I *think* I want that?

The same worries and doubts I had on our way home from the reunion come swirling back, just like they do whenever I think about what will come next for Lila and me.

Lila has already done all of this, but I don't know the first thing about how to take care of a baby. I was just doing full squats with Asher in my arms. It was probably all Lila could do not to laugh at me.

She drops onto the couch beside me. "I don't know how I'm supposed to get any work done around this place," she says. "If it isn't you distracting me with kisses, it's your mom distracting me with baby goats, and now Olivia distracts me with a baby? You Hawthornes. Giving me such terrible working conditions."

"Yeah, it really looks like you're suffering," I deadpan.

Lila rolls her eyes. "Listen. Someone has to be responsible around here. And I do need to get the bakery numbers from you by this afternoon. The supply order has to be in first thing tomorrow if we're going to get everything delivered in time for the festival."

I nod, filing away my Perry-doesn't-know-how-to-be-a-dad worries for another time. "I'm just about finished running the calculations. Almost everything sold out last year. We need to make more, it's just a question of how much more. Twenty percent? Thirty? I don't want to make too much and have the extras to go to waste."

"If it were me, I'd go for the higher percentage," Lila says. "Then if there's extra, you can donate it to the food bank and at least take the tax deduction."

"Huh. That's actually a really good idea."

Lila smiles. "Don't sound so surprised. I have one every once in a while."

That's an understatement. All of her ideas are good ones. But that's such an un-Perry-like sentiment, it's possible I'm heavily biased.

I reach over and grab her hand, recognizing that I have to act before my brain can talk me out of it. "Hey, I want to ask you something."

She laces her fingers through mine. "Okay."

"How would you feel about coming to the restaurant opening with me next weekend? Not to work. Not as my assistant. As my date."

Her eyebrows go up, but she doesn't respond right away.

"I know it's on a Thursday night, and that's a school night, which means you'd probably have to get a babysitter for Jack, but my whole family will be together—even Flint—and I just . . . I want you with me."

Was that too bold? Too forward? Too official?

A million different expressions flit behind Lila's eyes before she finally smiles. "Did you really think I'd turn down the opportunity to eat Lennox's food?"

I breathe out an exaggerated sigh to mask the relief-filled real one. "You had to bring him up, didn't you?"

"*And* I get to meet Flint? I'll have to pull the *People* magazine out from behind the couch and brush up on my celebrity facts."

"Sometimes having so many brothers is very annoying."

Lila chuckles and shifts, one foot tucked under her so she's sitting sideways on the couch, facing me.

"I promise you have nothing to actually worry about."

"I don't, huh?"

She smirks and leans close, close enough for her nose to brush against mine, but she doesn't kiss me. "Yep," she whispers. "I already picked my favorite Hawthorne."

I reach out a hand, hooking it around her waist, and tug her a little closer. "Is that right?"

"Mmmhmm," she breathes. "I mean, with that downy soft hair on Asher's little newborn head, can you blame me?"

I freeze. "You are not funny."

She chuckles, her shoulders shaking with soft laughter as she finally presses her lips to mine. "Kidding, kidding," she whispers in between lazy kisses. "I promise you're the only Hawthorne man for me."

I lean into another kiss, wishing I could fully let go. I'm the only Hawthorne for Lila, but that's not really enough, is it? She also needs me to be enough for Jack. To be a father. And if the last five minutes I spent with Asher is any indication, I am *ill-equipped.*

"Okay," Lila says, breaking the kiss and patting my knee. "Back to work. I also need you to approve the budget for the temporary staff we need to hire to run the festival. And as far as I know, the truck that's supposed to pull the flatbed for the hayride still isn't fixed."

"How did I ever do this job without you?"

Lila smirks. "I genuinely have no idea."

I follow her to my desk and try to focus on the multiple decisions that need to be made. But in the back of my mind, one thought pulses steadily, like a giant yellow caution sign.

I *want* to be enough for Lila and Jack.

But wanting and *being* aren't exactly the same thing.

You don't win a race by *wanting* to be the fastest person on the track. You have to do the work. Earn the prize.

And what if I just . . . *can't*?

Chapter Twenty-One

Lila

I STAND IN THE restaurant's newly paved parking lot and stare up at the shiny new building, all lit up from within, the sign that reads *Hawthorne* sparkling above the wide double doors. I've been inside before. But this is different. Now, the restaurant is full of people.

And Perry's family.

I take a few purposeful breaths and smooth down the front of my dress. I really did buy something new this time. An indulgence Grandma June convinced me was completely justified. It's red, off the shoulder, and fitted through the bodice in a way that makes my boobs look amazing without overdoing the cleavage. The A-line skirt hits just above my knee and would flare out a little if I happened to twirl—something I know from firsthand experience because I twirled a dozen times in my kitchen while Jack watched and laughed until he almost fell out of his chair. I might have kept going had the babysitter not shown up.

Rebecca, a high school sophomore and the highly recommended granddaughter of Grandma June's neighbor, immediately put me at ease with the natural way she engaged with Jack. When she had to cancel on me the first time I asked her to babysit, I wondered. But she apologized for that, and since Jack took to her right away, it suddenly feels easier to try and sneak away a little more frequently.

I'm desperate for a real, bonafide date with Perry. Though this possibly counts as a real date. You know. One with Perry's entire family including his very famous younger brother in attendance. NO BIG DEAL.

I give myself one more once-over in the glow of the streetlights and head to the front door.

It took a lot of effort to convince Perry he didn't need to drive up to Hendersonville to pick me up for tonight. The man had enough going on, and I didn't want him to worry about me, but more than that, I just didn't want Jack to see him. While I was getting ready to leave, it quickly became obvious I made the right call.

I was honest with Jack about where I needed to go without him—to a restaurant opening for work—but of course, he wouldn't leave it at that. He asked a million questions. Would Mr. Hawthorne be there? Was there a bar? Would there be other men looking for wives and stepsons?

Poor kid. His pancake breakfast is only ten days away, but in his five-year-old brain, that's still plenty of time to find himself a new stairdad. *Stepdad.* He's said it wrong so many times now, he even has me saying it.

Jack has at least resigned himself to going with his grandfather if a more favorable option doesn't present itself in time. But I can tell he's still hoping.

And maybe I should start hoping too. Trevor's dad still hasn't confirmed he can even make it. The man is about as married to his work as Trevor was. Leaving his law practice on a regular Thursday is a big ask, even if it is to spend the morning with his grandson.

Worst case scenario, I'll take Jack to the breakfast. He would hate it, but it would be better than going alone.

It has occurred to me, once or twice or five hundred times, that I could just ask Perry to take Jack to his breakfast, but I'm still scared to make that leap.

Inside, every table in the restaurant is filled. Servers are moving around the room with an ease and efficiency that does not scream opening night. In fact, it seems like a well-oiled machine. Though, Lennox started hiring waitstaff weeks ago. Everyone working tonight has been through dozens and dozens of practice runs. As my eyes dart around the room, I half wonder if everything is running so smoothly in the kitchen, but then I see Perry standing across the room, and all other thoughts float away.

He looks up and catches my gaze, his smile stretching wide as he begins to walk toward me.

I think I'm in love with him.

The thought catches me by surprise, but it shouldn't.

I've been falling in love with Perry since that first day all those weeks ago when Jack "helped" Perry change his tire and talked the poor man's ear off. So many tiny moments have led me here. Now, I just need the courage to accept them. To *trust him.*

"Hi," Perry says when he finally reaches me. He's rocking a look similar to the one he wore to the reunion—dark gray dress pants and a white button-down, sleeves rolled up, collar open—except his beard looks like it's been recently trimmed, and he might have even gotten a haircut.

Since this afternoon when I left work to go meet Jack at the bus stop.

Perry had a busy afternoon.

"You're looking particularly dapper this evening," I say.

He leans forward and kisses me softly, right there in front of an entire room full of people. "You're looking pretty beautiful yourself," he says, his hand on my waist, heat smoldering in his eyes like a banked fire. "Red is your color."

I'm still not used to the ease and frequency of Perry's compliments, and I immediately flush at his praise. "Thanks," I say, my voice catching. It feels silly to suddenly be so overwhelmed with emotion, especially emotion I'm not ready to say out loud. If I can't get my act together, Perry's going to figure me out, I'll start babbling, and then I'll wind up blurting my emotions in front of everyone.

I try to swallow the lump in my throat, but Perry is too perceptive.

"You okay?" he asks, pulling me a little closer, his arm wrapping around me protectively. Maybe even a bit possessively? The realization does not help calm the flurry of emotions swirling in my chest or dampen the fire he's igniting with every touch.

I lean closer, breathing in the sandalwood scent I love so much, and press a hand to my stomach.

"I'm okay. Just nervous, I think?"

"Lila, my family already loves you. You don't have anything to be nervous about."

Funny. He thinks I'm nervous about his family. What I'm nervous about is *him*. About the growing certainty that probably, I have to tell him how I feel.

I nod, and we start weaving our way through the tables. "How's Lennox holding up?"

Perry looks over his shoulder. "I haven't seen him in a few hours, but I'm assuming no news is good news, and he must have everything under control."

As we approach the table, I spot Flint, sitting to the right of his mother, and my steps falter. I tug on Perry's hand, and he turns around, a question in his eyes.

I pull him closer. "Okay, I'm just reminding you that if I freak out the tiniest bit when I meet your brother, it has everything to do with the fact that he is *any* movie star and nothing to do with the fact that he is *Flint Hawthorne.*"

Perry grins. "Noted. But I can't promise I won't always make fun of you for freaking out."

I swat at his arm, and he chuckles.

Hannah gets up when we close the short distance between us, immediately pulling me into a warm hug. Brody and his wife, Kate, get up next, offering me hugs as they say hello. Olivia and Tyler are on the opposite side of the table, but they both smile and nod in my direction right before Mr. Hawthorne pulls me in for a hug. After he lets me go, he claps Perry on the back, squeezing his shoulder for a long moment while they exchange some meaningful glance I can't interpret.

Flint is the last one to stand and greet me. "Hey, Lila," he says easily. "I know we're strangers, but do you mind if I give you a hug?"

"I don't mind at all," I say easily. I almost want to run a victory lap around the table. LADIES AND GENTLEMEN, I AM HUGGING FLINT HAWTHORNE, AND I AM NOT FREAKING OUT. It is not lost on me that shouting imaginary all caps exclamations to no one might be considered its own form of freaking out, but at least it's a form Perry can't see.

Flint's arms fall away, and he claps Perry on the back just like his father did. "You're right, man," he says, looking back at me. "She is beautiful." He unleashes the smile he's famous for and winks at me before returning to his seat.

I turn to Perry, eyes wide. "Oh, he is shameless," I whisper, only loud enough for Perry to hear.

Perry chuckles. "You get used to him. Under all that sparkly Hollywood exterior, he really is a great guy."

"Who farts and burps and has smelly armpits just like the rest of us," Brody adds.

"Brody!" Kate says, her eyes cutting to me. "You'll eventually get used to the Hawthorne brother dynamic. For now, just focus on the great guy part."

I believe Perry, because Flint is a Hawthorne. And these people are *all* great. It occurs to me, as my eyes drift across the faces surrounding the table, that I am welcome here tonight because of how much this family loves Perry. They want him to be happy. They *care* about his life. They are all invested.

From down the table, Flint mumbles something about his armpits smelling like flowers, and everyone starts to laugh.

A bolt of longing, sharp and deep, pierces my heart, and I nearly gasp from the strength of it.

I want this.

I want *Perry.*

We settle into our seats, and I reach my hand under the table, sliding it over to grab Perry's knee. I give it a squeeze, holding on as if to brace myself against the emotion swelling through me.

Perry's hand finds mine, prying it off his leg and lacing my fingers through his. His other arm drops across my back. "Hey. You sure you're okay?" he whispers.

I nod, even as I choke back a tiny sob and laugh at the tears gathering in my eyes. "I just . . ." I shake my head and drop Perry's hand long enough to grab my napkin and soak up my tears before they can ruin my makeup. "It's just your family. It doesn't even seem real."

"You get used to that part eventually, too," Kate says knowingly from the other side of me. "I was an only child growing up, so all this—" She motions to the table at large. "I've had a lot of moments just like the one you're having now."

I press my hands to my cheeks. "I feel ridiculous," I say, followed by a tiny sniff. Perry's hand rests calmly on my back, but he seems content to let Kate talk me down this time. "I'm an only child, too. It's pretty overwhelming to think of having all these people to love you."

"Overwhelming is a good word. But you *do* get used to it." She shifts her lips to the side and leans closer, her voice dropping in volume. "You might even get bothered by it every once in a while. But I'll give you the same advice Olivia gave me right before I married Brody."

Something stretches in my heart at the mention of marriage. It might be a little premature to give me *this* kind of advice, no matter how much I've decided that's precisely what I want, but I have no desire to discuss the specifics of those emotions at the dinner table with Perry's entire family, so I just smile and nod. "Okay."

"There are going to be moments when you wish everyone would leave you alone."

Brody leans forward. "Just hang those hopes up now. It's never going to happen."

Kate rolls her eyes. "It truly isn't that bad. Well, okay, it can be that bad. Either way, when it does happen, and you need to go dark for a little while, your best bet is to let someone else in the family know so they can cover for you. Because if you just turn off your notifications? Or worse, turn off your phone? You have about two hours before someone will show up at your doorstep to make sure you're okay."

I laugh. "I don't know. That sounds kind of nice."

"Nice like a really heavy blanket," Olivia says from across the table. "It keeps you warm. And it might even be really soft. But if you're in the wrong position . . ." Her voice drops into an exaggerated whisper. "It will absolutely make you feel like you're suffocating."

"I heard that, Olivia," Hannah says, her tone light and lilting.

"How come no one ever comes to make sure I'm okay if I don't respond to text messages?" Flint says.

Hannah puts a hand on Flint's cheek. "Sweetheart, I'd fly to Malibu in a skinny minute if I thought you needed me. And I text your assistant to check on you all the time."

"You do? Really?" Flint asks.

"What do you take me for?" Hannah says, smiling sweetly.

"She's playing it up now," Perry says, "but Mom is actually pretty chill. Dad, too. They're very good at letting their adult children *adult.*"

I lean into him, suddenly curious about something. I drop my voice, hoping I'm speaking quietly enough for only him to hear. "Hey, what was that look about with your dad earlier?" I ask. "That seemed like it meant something."

Perry's expression softens. "Just a conversation we had a while back. Right after I graduated from high school. Ask me later, and I'll tell you what he told me."

"Or you could tell us all now," Olivia says. "I want to know what Dad said to you in your *time to be an adult* talk."

Perry shoots his sister a glare. "Seriously? Do you have supersonic hearing over there?"

"I'm guessing this is one of those times *Perry* wishes he was alone," Brody says evenly, and Kate and Olivia both start to laugh.

I press my lips together, trying to hold in my own laughter. I'm very interested in what Perry was saying, but I also really love the banter between his siblings. "We can talk later," I say to Perry.

"Can I come?" Flint says from down the table. "I want to know what Dad said. I never got a special talk after I graduated. What's up with that, Dad?"

"Seriously? Is *everyone* listening to our private conversation?"

"You did get a talk," Mr. Hawthorne says to Flint, holding up one slightly wobbly finger. I don't often see signs of the stroke Mr. Hawthorne suffered, but I'll occasionally hear a word slur or see a slight tremble in his movements. "Yours was about different things," he goes on to say. "Yours was for you. Perry's was for Perry."

"What was mine about?" Flint asks.

Mr. Hawthorne looks like he's trying not to roll his eyes. "Integrity. Restraint. Humility."

"Ohhh," Flint says, tapping the side of his forehead. "The don't-let-Hollywood-turn-me-into-a-garbage-human talk. I do remember that."

The banter continues around the table, all good-natured jokes and ribbing. As the night progresses, I make a catalog of all the things I love. The things I want for Jack.

Siblings who know him well enough to joke and tease, but only in ways that aren't hurtful.

Meaningful talks teaching him how to navigate the world without being a jerk or missing the moments in life that matter the most. Cousins who can be his friends.

By the time our server is clearing away my dessert, a lemon-raspberry torte that was just as exquisite as the rest of the food, the list has gotten more specific.

Apple orchards to explore. Strawberry fields to roam. Mountains to climb. Baby goats to play with.

Well. And most significant of all.

Perry as a father.

A part of me fears it is only the magic of the evening that has me wanting to take the next step in our relationship. But really, I was already feeling this way. Tonight only helped confirm it.

I'm not saying I'm ready to propose to the man.

I *am* saying I'd like him to start spending time with Jack.

We sit around the table, laughing and talking long after our meal is finished. Only Olivia and Tyler sneak away so they can get home to put Asher to bed. Eventually, the crowd thins enough that Lennox comes out of the kitchen. His family gives him a standing ovation and a round of hugs similar to the one they gave me when I arrived. When it's my turn to offer him congratulations, he accepts the hug, then snaps his fingers like he's just remembered something.

He turns to the closest server, saying something I can't hear, then turns back to me. "I have something for you," he says simply.

"For me?" I look at Perry, but he doesn't seem to know anything more than I do.

Lennox smiles but doesn't offer any explanation until the server returns holding a pastry box tied with shimmery gold ribbon that matches the interior decor of the restaurant. She passes it off to Lennox who hands it to me. "Almond pillow cookies," he says. "Someone mentioned that you really enjoyed them."

"I did, but a whole box just for me? What did I do to deserve this?"

Lennox shrugs with an easy grin. "You tamed the grump."

Perry and I don't manage to steal a moment alone until he's walking me back to my car. It's a school night for my babysitter as well as for Jack. Even though I'm sure Jack's already sleeping, I ought to get home for her benefit if nothing else.

When we reach the car, I unlock the door, and Perry hands me the cookies so I can put them inside with my purse. Once my hands are free, I melt into his embrace.

"That was a really wonderful evening," I say, my words muffled against his chest.

"I'm really glad you could be here."

"Your family is really great."

He chuckles. "I think they really love you. But I know they can be a lot."

"They can be. But I still love it. Growing up an only child, I don't know. This all feels pretty magical to me."

His hands slide up and down my back, warming me against the chilly fall air. I'm wearing a jacket, but my legs are bare. I probably shouldn't stand out here much longer.

"Hey." I lean back so I can look at Perry. "What was it your dad said? Can you tell me now?"

"It wasn't anything groundbreaking. Mostly just stuff about my future. About the farm. My education. But he also gave me some advice about relationships. I remember that more than anything else."

"What did he say?"

Perry's arms tighten around me, tugging me a tiny bit closer. "He told me that when I met the right woman, I wouldn't just know in my head or in my heart. I would know somewhere deeper. He couldn't explain how I would know, he just said that I would."

I almost hate to ask the question dancing on my tongue, but I don't think I can stop myself. "Did you know with Jocelyn?" I ask, my voice sounding too small. Too needy.

Perry's hand lifts to cup my cheek. "I thought I did. But now, I realize I . . ." His words cut off, and he shakes his head. He blows out a breath, like he's trying to work himself up to something. His hands fall away, and he backs up a half-step, turning away from me, his hands propped on his hips.

He's so clearly warming up for something, I half expect him to start bouncing on his toes and throwing a few fake punches.

"Hey," I say, stepping toward him and slipping a hand over his shoulder. "You okay?"

He huffs out a laugh. "Just trying to figure out how much I can say. How much I *should* say."

"Say it all," I say gently, hoping he senses how much I mean it.

"Lila, saying it all does not sound like taking things slow. You said that's what you wanted."

"I did say that. My heart hasn't done a very good job of listening."

His expression sobers as he picks up my hand. He places it against his chest, spreading my palm so it's flat against his heart. "I didn't know what my dad meant," he says. "Not until now. Not until you."

There are so many unspoken words hanging in the air between us, but for now, this feels like enough.

Do I love him? I think so. I would even say the look in his eyes says he probably loves me too.

But I can't say it out loud. Not until I know he can love Jack, too.

Maybe he's holding back for the same reason. Either way, it's time. We can't keep Jack out of whatever is happening between us. Not anymore.

"So I was thinking," I say slowly, my hands sliding up his chest to his shoulders. A tiny thrill of excitement flits through me. I'm still not used to the fact that this man is mine, that I get to touch him like this. "What if I brought Jack to the festival next week? I was thinking we could go together."

"The three of us?" he asks. His voice is hopeful, but I don't miss the fear lacing the edges of his words.

"The three of us," I repeat, willing confidence into my voice. It's the right move. Jack is a charming kid. Of course Perry will fall in love with him. Everyone does.

Perry pulls me into a kiss, his tenderness quickly melting into something a little more fervent. He presses his forehead against mine. "I feel like I'm going to screw this up," he says softly. "I don't know what I'm doing, how to—"

I silence his words with another kiss. "We just have to take it one day at a time, okay? Nothing has changed. I'm still me. You're still you. Now there's just an extra small person we have to consider in all our plans."

He takes a slow, deep breath, and I wonder if I just scared him off. But then he gives his head one small, decisive shake. "Okay," he finally says.

I smile. "Okay?"

He nods. "One day at a time."

Chapter Twenty-Two

Perry

I BOUNCE ON MY feet as I scan the crowd at the harvest festival, anxious to see Lila, but nervous about seeing Lila and *Jack.* It doesn't make a lot of sense. I've been around Jack once before, and I feel like I handled things pretty well.

But this is different. Now, there are very specific expectations.

I don't want to disappoint Jack.

Even more, I don't want to disappoint Lila.

Mom nudges me from where she's standing beside the barnyard gate, allowing kids to enter the petting zoo a few at a time. "She'll get here when she gets here, Perry," she gently scolds. "Just relax."

I shake out my shoulders. "What if I miss her? There are a lot of people here."

There's a lull in the crowd as the last few kids make their way to the farm manager, who is on hand to supervise the animals. Mom takes advantage of the moment and turns to face me. "Perry. You aren't going to miss her. She's coming to see *you.* Is she meeting you here? At the petting zoo?"

I nod, even as my eyes scan over the crowd again.

"Then just be patient. She's wrangling a five-year-old. Her life is ten times more complicated than yours for that reason alone."

Mom's words are meant to be reassuring, but they only make me worry more. "I'm going to walk toward the parking lot and see if I can find her."

Mom scoffs. "Perry, if you leave, then she'll show up here, and you'll be gone. Why don't you just call her?"

I pull out my phone and hold it up. "I will."

But I still walk away. I'm too full of nervous energy to stand in one place, too overwhelmed with the complexity of my emotions. I keep waffling back and forth between fear and inadequacy, and a driving need to be with Lila, to take care of her. Logically, I know there is a balance somewhere. That no relationship exists without *any* fear. But agreeing to spend time with Jack has had a bigger impact on me than I expected it to. It's like it woke up some narrative in my head telling me all the reasons why I'm *not* going to be a good father.

Not so coincidentally, the narrative sounds an awful lot like Jocelyn.

I stop and take a steadying breath, closing my eyes against the whir and hum of the crowd. I don't need my ex-wife in my head right now.

When I open my eyes, Lila is right in front of me, waiting in line at one of the tables selling Stonebrook Farm hot apple cider. My first impulse is to hide, to dive behind the vendor booth to my left, but I don't think Ann from the Feed N' Seed would appreciate me upending her tables of festively decorated sugar cookies.

Finally, Lila looks up and notices me. When she smiles, the narrative in my head, the fear, the doubt, it all quiets and stills, then fades away completely. Now, there's only her.

I can do this for her.

Her eyes dart to Jack before she looks back at me. She's nervous too. I walk closer, watching as she reaches out to take the cider, tucking one of the cups into Jack's waiting hands. She puts the other cup back on the table and reaches into her purse, but I jump forward, stopping her with a hand to her arm.

"These are on the house," I say.

The teenager working the cash box at the table gives me a nod and turns to the next customer. I've never seen her before, but she clearly knows who I am, because she doesn't question.

"Thanks," Lila says as we step away from the booth. She looks down at Jack. "Can you say thank you to Mr. Hawthorne for the cider?"

Jack takes a slow sip, the resulting slurping noise making me smile before he offers me a lopsided grin. "Thank you, Mr. Hawthorne."

"Oh hey, look at that. Have you lost a tooth since I last saw you?" I crouch down so we're eye to eye.

Jack nods. "Yep. This one right here." He points to his left front tooth, sticking his tongue into the hole the missing tooth left behind. "And this one is loose too," he says, wiggling the other.

"Which is why we're drinking apple cider tonight instead of eating caramel apples, huh?" Lila says.

"Mommy says I can have a caramel apple at home when she can cut it into teeny tiny pieces." He holds his fingers up, his thumb and pointer finger creating a tiny bit of space, his little eyes squinting as he shows me just how small his pieces of apple will be.

"That sounds like a great plan." I stand back up, my eyes skating over Lila.

I'm struck again by how effortlessly beautiful she is. Jocelyn used to talk about how much effort it *actually* took to look effortlessly beautiful, but there was never anything effortless about Jocelyn's look, no matter what she called it. She was always perfectly primped and tweezed and polished to shiny golden perfection. It used to mesmerize me how beautiful she was all the time. Funny how little appeal it holds for me now.

"It's nice to see you," I finally say, self-conscious about how long I've been staring at her. "You look nice." Somehow, we're back to those first few days after the reunion, when we were still nervous around each other, still unsure. *Pull yourself together, man. This is Lila.*

Jack reaches up and tugs on my hand. "Do you want to come to the petting zoo with us?" He looks at his mom. "Mommy, can Mr. Hawthorne come to the petting zoo with us?"

Lila and I make eye contact, and she smiles.

"Please, Mommy?" Jack tugs one more time, the movement jostling the cup of cider in his other hand. It starts to tip, and I reach for it without thinking, steadying it, then taking it out of Jack's hands. As soon as he's free of the cup, Jack grabs *my* free hand instead, so now he's standing between Lila and me, connecting us. "Please, please?" he says.

Lila smiles. "What do you say, Mr. Hawthorne? Would you like to join us?"

A lightness fills my chest as I look down at Jack. "Let's do it."

Jack cheers, jumping up and down without letting go of our hands, then tugs us forward. We walk as a trio toward the petting zoo where we bypass the ticket line, despite Lila's protests, and head straight for Mom, who is still standing by the barnyard gate.

She ushers us in, fawning over Jack, making him feel just as special as I knew she would. She leads him through the petting zoo personally, giving Lila and me a chance to hang back the tiniest bit.

"Your mom's a natural," Lila says easily.

"Oh, definitely. She's been counting down the days to grandmahood for years."

"Why didn't you and Jocelyn have kids? You were married for what, seven years? That's kind of a long time."

"I wanted to," I say slowly. "At first. But then Jocelyn got so focused on her career. And on *my* career. She wanted money. Prestige. Kids didn't fit into the picture for her. It was always something she said we'd take care of later. Once we were really established. By that point, I already felt our marriage unraveling, which made kids just seem . . . reckless, I guess?"

She nods. "I think a lot of people have kids thinking it will save their marriage. Change things for the better." She loops her arm through mine, and a tiny thrill shoots through me that she's touching me this way even with Jack around. I like that we aren't hiding. "Why did you stay married if you felt things unraveling?"

I shrug. "I made a commitment. A vow. I was taught to be a man of my word."

She pulls me to a stop, one hand lifting to my cheek. "Perry, you're a better man than she ever deserved." She leans up on her tiptoes and plants a quick kiss on my lips.

"Mommy!" Jack calls from just up ahead. "Come and see this pig! It's bigger than my bed!"

"*Buttercup,*" I grumble, and Lila laughs as she threads her fingers through mine and tugs me forward.

"You seriously have to tell me what that poor pig did to you," she says.

We slowly walk toward the pigpen where Mom and Jack are reaching over the fence, scratching the top of Buttercup's head.

"It isn't much of a story. Just that she escaped her pen one too many times, and the last time, she nearly barreled through the middle of a wedding reception happening in the pavilion."

"And you're the one who had to stop her?"

"The way I heard the story," Mom says as she gives Buttercup a particularly affectionate pat, "he body slammed her and rolled her into the ditch by the side of the main road."

"You body slammed a pig?" Jack asks, his eyes wide with awe, which sends a surge of pride through my chest. It's the first good thing to come out of my wrestling match with Buttercup. I managed to impress Jack.

"I did *try* and coax her back to her pen with apples first," I say. "It's not my fault she wasn't interested in cooperating."

Lila smiles. "Now that's something I wish I got to see."

I nudge her elbow. "You would have appreciated the jokes Brody made right after it happened."

She lights up. "Were they punny?"

"Something about the Olym-pigs?" I say.

"I always knew I liked Brody the most," she says, laughter in her tone.

I raise an eyebrow, and she grins. "After you, of course."

"I'll let Lennox know he'll have to go bigger than almond pillow cookies."

"Oh! The cookies. I forgot about those. Okay. I take it back. Cookies trump puns."

"Wait, so what's the order again? Should I be writing this down?" I ask, and I'm only half-joking. When it comes to Lila, I want to remember everything.

After we leave Buttercup's pen, Mom takes us inside the big barn away from the actual petting zoo so Jack can meet Sweetpea. She's a lot bigger now, but still more of a baby than all the other goats who are outside.

I scoop Sweetpea into my arms and crouch down so I'm right in front of Jack. "Do you want to hold her?"

He nods, brown eyes wide, and holds out his arms.

I pass him the goat, keeping one hand under Sweetpea to help stabilize her, as Jack pulls her against his chest.

Sweetpea leans up and nuzzles his face, and he starts to giggle. "Mommy, can we get one?"

"Goats have to live in a barn, baby, where they have a big pasture outside that they can run around in. But I'm sure we can come visit Sweetpea and the other goats another time."

"You're always welcome," Mom says.

After we visit a few more animals, go on a hayride, and pick up some apple butter for Lila to take to her Grandma June, I walk Lila and Jack back to her car, feeling a little more optimistic about things.

Jack is riding on my shoulders, too tired to make the long trek back to the parking lot. His arms are resting on my head, and my hands are holding loosely to his ankles. I've never carried a kid on my shoulders before, but this almost feels natural.

Lila walking beside me *definitely* feels natural.

Tonight has been fun. *Easy*.

We finally make it back to the car, and Lila reaches up, tugging Jack off my shoulders and depositing him in the backseat.

I reach out and muss his hair before Lila closes the door. "See you later, kid."

Jack smiles through a yawn. "Are you going to take me to my breakfast now?"

My eyes dart to Lila, whose expression is filled with alarm.

"Now that you love my mommy, you can be my stairdad, right?"

"Honey, it's not—" Lila starts, but then Jack shakes his head. "Chloe said that's how you know when people love each other. They kiss. And I saw you kiss Mr. Hawthorne. If you love him, and he loves you, then he can be my stairdad." He shakes his little head in frustration. "I mean my stepdad. That's what you said."

Lila sighs. "These things just take time, sweetie. It's not that simple."

"Why isn't it simple?" Jack says, his lip quivering. "Why do grownups have to make everything so hard?"

Lila takes a slow breath. "Let me say goodbye, okay? Then we'll talk on the way home." She closes the door and looks at me. "I'm sorry he put you on the spot like that. This breakfast has him so keyed up about not having a dad." She presses a hand to her forehead. "I thought this was a good idea, but maybe we should have—"

"Hey." I reach out and grab her arms, giving them a gentle squeeze. "It's okay."

She nods, but her expression is still pained, her eyes filled with worry.

"Lila, I could take him to the breakfast."

She looks up, hope sparking in her eyes, but then she shakes her head, her lips pressing together into a thin line. "I can't ask you to do that."

"Why not? I want to."

Her shoulders drop. "It's big, Perry. Just the two of you? Are you sure you would even be comfortable? And if tonight gave Jack the impression that we're—that you're—" She huffs, but she doesn't need to say the words for me to know the only way that sentence can be finished.

If tonight gave Jack the impression that we're in love, that we're getting married, then me taking Jack to a father-son breakfast will only drive that impression home. The thought should scare me. No, scratch that. The thought *does* scare me. But not as much as the idea of losing Lila.

"Does it scare you to think that's where we're headed?" I ask.

She bites her lip. "It scares me to think of how I'll recover if we're not."

If not for Jack watching us through the window, I'd pull her into my arms right here, kiss her until her fears are gone, whisper promises into her ear. *I love you. I'm not going anywhere. Trust me. Trust us.*

I settle for taking both her hands in mine and threading our fingers together. "If you aren't ready, I won't push. But I'd love to take him to his breakfast. I'm ready to try, Lila."

She takes a slow breath and closes her eyes. "Are you sure?"

I nod. "Apple-solutely."

She rolls her eyes as she smiles and shakes her head. "You're ridiculous."

"Yes. But you started it."

She glances back at Jack, then lunges up for a quick kiss. "Thursday morning. Next week. You have to wear a tie."

"I have a few of those."

"Can you pick him up at the house? Actually, it's probably better if you just drive my car. Then we won't have to move his booster seat."

"Sounds good."

She opens the driver-side door, offering one final wave before backing up and pulling away.

I make my way back to the festival, emotions swirling. The longer I walk, the less certain I feel.

Tonight was fun with Jack. But Lila was here. Whenever Jack asked for something he couldn't have, she knew exactly how to say no and move him on to the next thing. When he whined about the hay on the hayride feeling itchy, she knew exactly how to distract him and keep him happy.

Am I really ready to spend time with Jack alone?

Ready or not, I just committed.

Time to dust off my ties and turn myself into a dad.

Chapter Twenty-Three

Lila

I AM ONE HUNDRED percent positive I am going to be a stressed out, nervous wreck while Perry and Jack are at the father-son breakfast. Which is why booking a yoga class for the hour or so when they'll be at the school was such a good idea. It'll cut into my workday a little bit but seeing as how my boss will be at the elementary school eating pancakes and sausage links with my little boy, I'm banking on him not minding if I show up to work a little late.

The morning of the breakfast, I pull on my favorite leggings and a sports bra before heading to Jack's room to get him ready to go.

The child is *buzzing* with excitement. He's also supposed to wear a tie, which . . . *okay,* I can value the importance of teaching little boys how to dress up and take care of themselves, but I'm not sure the school thought through the menu choices very well. All I can imagine is a whole bunch of kindergartners with ties dragging through the pancake syrup on their plates.

I get Jack mostly dressed, then send him to brush his teeth while I run a Google search on how to tie a tie. I *thought* I was ordering one of those kid-sized ties that adjusts with a zipper, but Amazon sent me an actual *tie* tie. And I have no idea how to make the thing work.

Halfway through a YouTube video walking me through the simplest knot for children's ties, I've paused and restarted the video almost a dozen times. *This* is simple? How on earth does anyone ever wear one of these things?

When Marley's face lights up my phone screen, I gladly click over to answer her call. She's a single mom with a son. Maybe she'll know how to help.

"Hey!" I answer. "Do you know how to tie a tie?"

"What?"

"A tie. Jack has to wear a tie to school today."

"Oh," Marley says. "I always just bought the zipper ones. Or a standard clip-on."

"Ugh." I groan. "That's what I thought I was buying. But now he has to wear one today, and this is all we have, and I have no idea how to tie the stupid thing."

I drop the tie onto the back of the couch and head back to my bedroom to grab my shoes. I'll have to leave just after Perry does in order to make it to my class.

"I think I read somewhere that it's easier if you're wearing the tie. So you like, put it on yourself, tie it, then widen the head hole so you can move it from your head to your kid's head."

"Oh, that's actually a good idea."

"Why does he have to wear a tie to school?" Marley asks.

I slip on my sneakers one-handed, hopping across my room to keep my balance. "It's a father-son breakfast thing. They're all supposed to dress up. Something about dressing for success or being their best selves. I don't remember."

"I think it sounds fun. Is Jack's grandpa coming up to take him?"

I pause. I've been so wrapped up in my new job, in *Perry*, I haven't given Marley an update. *Any* update. Which isn't all that weird. We're friends. It's easy to talk to her, to relate to her, and it always feels like we pick up our conversation like it never really ended. But we aren't the kind of friends who text each other daily updates.

The last time we talked was the day I drove out to rescue Perry from his flat tire.

Since then, I've progressed from assistant to reunion date to exclusively dating, and now to this. To Perry taking my kid to an event designed for sons and their *fathers.*

I do not have time to summarize how we wound up here.

I also won't lie to her.

"Oh, um. Perry is taking him, actually."

There's a beat of silence before Marley says, "Perry, your boss?"

"Yes?"

"Girl, you better give me more of an explanation than that."

I sigh. "I will. I promise, but I can't do it right now. Perry will be here any minute to pick Jack up."

"You cannot drop a bomb like that and expect me to be fine with you explaining sometime in the vague and distant future. At least tell me whether you're dating."

I drop onto my bed. "We're dating."

Marley squeals. "Oh my word. Lila! You're dating Flint Hawthorne's brother!"

"I met Flint, actually. He was at a family dinner a few weeks back."

"Shut. Up."

A knock sounds on my front door, and my heart jumps. "Listen, I really need to go. Was there a work thing you needed to talk to me about? I feel bad for monopolizing the conversation talking about ties."

"No, no. It's fine. It can wait. I just wanted to make sure everything was okay because you haven't been logging in to the management software."

"Oh. Right. I've mostly been working in person."

"Understandably. If I were dating my boss, and he looked like Perry Hawthorne, I'd want to work in person too. Okay. Go be a mom. But Lila, you better call me and give me an update. And soon!"

"I will. I promise."

I end the call and hurry toward the front door to let Perry inside, but I only make it around the corner before I stop dead in my tracks.

Perry is already inside, looking handsome as ever in a navy-blue suit. He's standing in front of the entryway mirror, Jack perched on a chair in front of him. Perry's arms encircling Jack from behind, his larger hands shadowing Jack's smaller ones as he walks him through the steps of tying his tie.

"Like this?" Jack says, his little voice barely loud enough to reach my ears.

"Just like that," Perry says patiently. "You're doing great. Good. Now just loop it through that hole and slide the knot up."

My heart in my throat, I watch Jack's reflection in the mirror as Perry slides the tie into place. Jack's eyes light up. "I did it!"

"Great job, kiddo," Perry says gently. "Now let me see." He takes Jack's shoulders and turns him so they're facing each other. He adjusts Jack's tie, then smooths down his hair. "All right. Looking good. I think we're ready to go."

It's hard to quantify what's happening inside my heart right now. To see them together like this, to see Perry teaching Jack, guiding him, loving him like a father would. I resigned myself a long time ago to the possibility of muddling through all the parenting milestones on my own. I'm not the best person to teach Jack how to understand what's happening to his body when he's going through puberty. I don't have any personal experience shaving my face or working up the courage to talk to a pretty girl. But I was willing to try. To arm myself with videos on the internet and a whole lot of gumption to do the best I could.

But to see Perry stepping up, voluntarily taking this tiny piece from me?

Tears fill my eyes as an ache fills my chest.

I want this so much.

I want Jack to have a dad.

I want us to be a family.

"Mommy, look!" Jack says, jumping off the chair and running over. "Perry helped me tie my tie."

"That's really great, Jack," I say, my hands smoothing over him. "Go grab your backpack, okay?"

Jack hurries toward his room, and I finally lift my gaze to Perry's.

"Jack let me in," he says, as if I need him to explain his presence. "And I hope it's okay that I asked him to call me Perry. I just thought, at the breakfast, it might be weird if he's still calling me Mr. Hawthorne."

"Of course. No, that makes sense." I sniff and wipe my eyes, turning away from Perry.

Which is stupid. There's no way he didn't notice my tears.

He steps closer and reaches for me. "Hey. Come here."

I shake my head as I fall into his arms. "I'm being ridiculous."

"I don't think you are."

"Sometimes I don't realize how hard it is to do everything by myself until I'm not anymore." I pat his chest. "I'm glad you're here," I say simply. "Thank you for being here."

Something like fear flashes behind Perry's eyes, but then he's tucking me into his chest, his hands sliding up and down my back.

My *exposed* back. Because I'm still only wearing a sports bra.

"Oh no," I say, stepping away and spinning around. I grab a folder off my desk and hold it in front of my stomach.

Perry narrows his eyes. "What are you doing?"

"Nothing," I say a little too quickly.

He lifts an eyebrow, his expression saying just how much he doesn't believe me.

I look down at the folder, then back to him, and bite my lip. "Hiding," I finally say.

"Your stomach? Why?"

Jack barrels into the room, his backpack on. "Mommy's stomach looks like a road map," he says matter-of-factly. "Cause when I was in her tummy, I stretched her skin big, *big, big.*" He stretches his arms out in front of him and starts walking around the room like a marshmallow man.

Or maybe that's just what he thinks women look like when they're pregnant?

Perry turns, his back to Jack so his broad body is shielding me from my son's view. He grabs the folder and tugs it from my hands. "Don't hide from me," he says in the same bossy, commanding voice I hear him use at work.

I close my eyes, but I don't resist.

I love my body. I do.

It is strong and capable and beautiful in its own way. I do not spend a lot of time looking at it and hating it. I don't have time for that kind of self-loathing. But I know what the world's beauty standards are. And they are a lot closer to the woman Perry *used* to be married to than they are to me. She probably doesn't have a single stretch mark on her.

Perry presses his palm flat against my stomach. "Lila, open your eyes."

I shake my head no.

"Lila," he says again. It is NOT fair when he pulls out bossy Perry.

I huff out a breath, then finally comply.

His gaze is soft. Warm. "At some point," he says so quietly, there is no way Jack can hear, "I am going to kiss every single one of these stretch marks."

Oh. *Oh.* I take a stuttering breath.

"They're a part of you. They make you real. *Human.*" He smiles. "I tend to like humans."

Real? We're talking about being real? Because this man feels anything but real. Like a dream come impossibly true. How did I ever think he was just my grumpy boss?

"Perry, come on," Jack says from the doorway. "The clock says we're going to be late if we don't leave right now."

"Hey, that's my line," I say to Jack. Literally word for word. Jack has probably heard me say that exact thing a hundred different times.

Jack grins goofily.

"I'll see you when I get back?" Perry asks.

I nod. "Yes, please."

I follow them outside and pause on the front porch, making a conscious effort *not* to fold my arms across my midsection.

Don't hide from me.

That's a moment that's going to stay with me for a *very* long time. I think about him kissing the road map that zigzags across my skin, and a shot of heat pulses through my veins.

Jack waves through the back window as Perry backs out of the driveway, his smile so wide, I almost start to cry again.

I've got a week's worth of emotions rolling around inside me, and it's barely eight in the morning. Forget yoga. With the way my heart is pounding, I'm burning more calories just standing still, letting all these feelings work their way through my heart and mind.

I drop onto my couch and let the thoughts come, filtering through the fears and doubts I should ignore and holding onto the things that feel more certain. Or one thing, really. One unwavering certainty that beats louder than everything else.

I am definitely in love with Perry Hawthorne.

And I'm going to tell him today.

Chapter Twenty-Four

Perry

I AM OVERWHELMED BEFORE we're even out of the car, which can't be a good sign.

I thought I did well with the tie thing, and things were good with Lila and me. But then Jack and I got in the car, and the radio was on, tuned to NPR. I figured Jack wouldn't like news radio, so I tried to find another station, stopping when I landed on a pop song I didn't recognize. Do kids listen to pop music at age five? The song ended, and the deejays started talking about the song, but by that point, we were already approaching the elementary school, so I completely missed what the deejays were talking about until Jack yelled from the backseat, "Perry, what's twerking?"

So. At least now I know. Kids *definitely* don't listen to pop music at age five. At least not *this* pop music.

The entire time I'm circling the elementary school parking lot, Jack talks constantly. I'm trying to listen—is he going to quiz me later on all the random things he's telling me?—but I'm also trying to focus, and doing both at the same time is not easy.

I wind up slamming on my brakes more than once to keep from rear-ending the cars in front of me.

"There's my friend Maddox," Jack says, pointing out the window.

I can't tell which kid he means. There are dads and grandpas and little boys everywhere, most of them already streaming into the school cafeteria.

Meanwhile, I can't even find a place to park. I leave the parking lot and head back out to the street in front of the school. People are parking along the curb, but with all the traffic, I can't stop imagining getting Jack out of the car and *into* the flow of traffic and spending the rest of the day at the hospital. Or worse.

How do parents do this? All day long, make decisions about how best to keep their kids safe?

I finally settle on flipping a U-turn and parking on the other side of the street, then I make Jack crawl across to the opposite side of the car to get out so we aren't standing in the road.

After all that effort, we're five minutes late for the breakfast, and we miss the instructions on how and where we get our food. I usher Jack into line, assuming we'll just do what the people in front of us are doing, but then we figure out that we're supposed to be going through the line *by class,* and Jack's class hasn't been called up yet.

"Should I put my pancakes back?" Jack asks, his expression worried.

I shake my head. "We're already here. Let's just get through the line. They'll have to forgive us for going out of order."

Jack nods, but I can see how uncomfortable he is. He keeps tossing glances over his shoulder, like other kids are going to be mad at us for cutting.

Finally back at the table, we sit down only to realize I forgot to get us silverware.

"Perry, I don't have anything to drink," Jack says. "Did you get me some milk?"

So I forgot silverware *and* milk.

"I didn't. Can you sit right here while I run and grab us some?"

Jack nods, and I hurry back up to the line, cutting to the end to grab the things we missed.

When I get back to the table, several of the other dads are chuckling. I narrow my eyes and look at Jack, who has poured at least twelve servings of syrup onto his plate. It's full to the brim. One more drop, and we'll have a waterfall of syrup pouring off his plate and onto the table.

"Hey, whoa, that's a lot of syrup," I say, lifting the bottle out of Jack's hands. There is no way he's going to be able to eat without getting syrup all over everywhere. I slide his plate away.

"Hey!" Jack says. "Those are mine!"

"These are yours now," I say, moving my plate in front of him. "Let's see if we can get a normal amount of syrup on them, okay?"

Jack sighs and frowns, but he doesn't protest as I butter and syrup his pancakes. "There. All set."

Jack looks at me like I've just grown a third head. "Why did you put butter on them? I don't like butter."

He doesn't like butter.

"Jack. You probably won't even taste the butter. Try a bite."

"I don't want to try a bite. I have pancakes with Mommy all the time, and she never puts butter on them because she knows I don't like butter."

I look back up to the line which has tripled in size now that more classes are being called up. I can't go get him more pancakes. But I also can't take the butter off of *these* pancakes.

"Hey," a dad says from the other side of Jack. He holds up an empty plate that he pulled out from underneath his own. "Do you mind if I help?"

I hold my hands up. "Please. I clearly need it."

The man forks Jack's original pancakes out of the syrup soup they're swimming in and drops them onto the empty plate. "Here you go, little man," the guy says, swapping the new plate for Jack's. "Pancakes, no butter."

This guy makes it look so easy. I tell myself to calm down. It *is* easy. It's pancakes. Just breakfast. I have to *breathe.*

"Here, I'll take that," I say, reaching for the syrup-filled plate. The dad hands it over, and I carefully carry it to the trashcan in the corner.

And I almost make it. Until somebody's kid runs past me, bumping into me from behind and sending a cascade of syrup down my pant leg and into my shoes. MY FREAKING BUTTERCUPPING SHOES.

I swallow the less polite swear words threatening to erupt and take a slow, even breath. I am a grown man. A CEO of a thriving business. I can handle this.

I lift my foot, hearing the squelch of syrup in my sock.

I cannot handle this.

Back at the table, the hero dad who saved Jack's pancakes gives me a knowing look. "Divorced?"

It takes me a moment to process his question. Do divorced guys have a certain look? But then I realize he's assuming I'm divorced *from Jack's mom.* And probably swooping in to attend a breakfast when I am not the full-time parent. Because clearly, I do not look like a full-time parent.

"No, I'm just . . ."

I'm what, exactly? I don't think there's really a title for hopeful, almost-boyfriends.

"He's my stairdad," Jack says in between bites.

"Stepdad?" the dad says.

"Not quite. I'm dating his mom."

"Ah. You're a good sport then. Events like these can be tough even for the seasoned pros."

I nod. "Thanks for your help with the pancakes."

"No problem," he says with a chuckle. "I'm Dave."

He reaches over and shakes my hand.

"Perry."

"Good to meet you. My oldest refused to eat anything with cheese on it until he was ten. We had to get creative to feed that kid. Pizza? Tacos? Mac and cheese? He wouldn't eat it."

"Mayonnaise over here," a dad says from across the table. "Or any condiments, really. No ketchup, mustard, barbecue sauce."

"Dry foods only," the kid sitting next to him says. He picks up a bite of plain pancake and shoves it into his mouth.

I shift and cringe at the feel of syrup still sliding around my shoe. Dry food is cleaner, at least.

The dads at the table keep talking, laughing as they compare picky-eater horror stories. I know these guys are trying to make me feel better by pointing out their kids' weirdo tendencies, but it's only making me feel worse. How do they even navigate all these different opinions and preferences? How do they remember? What if they have more than one kid, and they forget which one hates mayonnaise and which one hates ketchup?

Once everyone has finished eating and our plates have all been cleared away, the kids gather on the stage to sing a couple of songs they've been working on in their music class. While we wait for them to get situated, I'm distracted (again) by a conversation happening between two of the other dads at our table. Now that the kids are gone, their subject material has taken a significant shift.

"It's been weeks," one guy says. "She's always too tired or too stressed or too overwhelmed with the kids."

"I feel you. Then when you finally think you've got a minute alone, there are kids knocking on the door or waking up because they wet the bed or lost their blanket, or—"

"Hey," Dave says, cutting off their conversation. He motions toward me. "You're scaring the new guy."

"New guy?"

"He's dating the kid's mom," Dave says, waving his hand toward the stage where the teachers are still working to corral fifty five-year-olds onto the risers.

The loudest of the two guys raises his hands and shapes them into a megaphone around his mouth. "Get out while you still can!" he whisper-yells before laughing at himself like he's just told the funniest joke.

The guy sitting next to him hits him on the arm. "Don't listen to him. Single moms, am I right?"

I force a polite smile, but I honestly can't decide which one of these guys I hate the most.

"Sure, single moms," the first guy says. "Then they become *married* moms, and you're strapped with a kid. No privacy. No honeymoon period . . ." He shakes his head. "You're a better man than I am, dude."

Right now, I don't feel like a better man. I feel like I'm in way over my head, doing things I've never had to do, with syrup matting my leg hairs and a stain on my probably ruined leather shoes.

The songs help.

Five-year-old voices are very sweet.

But the longer I'm in the school, the more uncomfortable I feel. I tug at my collar, a cold sweat breaking out across my neck. It's been almost an hour. We have to be done soon, right?

The principal stands up, and I breathe out a sigh of relief. She's going to thank us all for coming, and then I can get out of here. "Let's give another round of applause for our kindergartners," she says. Once the applause dies down, she pulls out a sheet of paper. "If you could all remain seated while our teachers take the students out of the cafeteria, we'll then dismiss you to the following locations, where you can say goodbye to your sons"—she holds up a finger—"and grandsons and pick up a very special craft they've been working on this week before you head out. If your student is in Ms. Callahan's class, you can find them in the media center. If your student has Mr. Joy, they'll be in the gymnasium." She continues down the list, but it hardly matters if I'm listening or not.

I have no idea who Jack's teacher is.

I pull my phone out of my pocket. I can at least text Lila and ask. Except there is no cell signal inside the school. I can't decide if it would be faster to go out into the parking lot to get a signal, or find a teacher or administrator *inside* the school who might be able to help.

My *cold* sweat feels like it's turning into a hot one. An anxious one. An I'm-going-to-melt-out-of-my-suit-and-self-destruct one. I hold my phone up, trying again to see if I can get a signal. Maybe if I lean toward the window?

Dave leans closer. "Dude. You all right, man? You look a little green."

"I don't know who Jack's teacher is," I admit. "I don't know where to go."

"Honestly, you probably aren't the only guy here who doesn't," Dave says. "When I was here two years ago with my middle kid, there was an admin lady by the door helping people out. I'm guessing she'll be there again."

I nod and take a deep breath.

"Now, a room full of moms?" Dave says with a chuckle. "You wouldn't have this problem."

Dave shakes my hand when it's time to go, patting me on the back in a fatherly way, even though the guy doesn't look like he's much older than I am. And yet, he's been my lifeline for the past hour.

I stand in line behind half a dozen sheepish-looking dads to ask the admin lady where I need to go to find Jack. The whole time, I can't stop thinking about Dave's words. About a room full of moms knowing their kids' teachers better than dads do.

I don't want to be that kind of dad. I want to know things. Teachers' names. Birthdays. Whether my kid likes butter on his pancakes.

But I also don't know *how* to be that dad. Surely it feels easier when it's something you ease into. Olivia and Tyler, for example, are learning about Asher together. They're figuring things out. Cataloging every day.

Can I really just step in and be what Jack needs?

If this morning is any indication, the answer is a resounding *no.*

Exhibit A: Syrup in my shoes.

Jack's class is gathering on the playground. But not the *regular* playground. Apparently, there's a special playground just for kindergartners.

I'm the last dad—*stairdad? Boyfriend dad?*—to arrive.

Jack comes racing over and throws his arms around my legs. "I thought you weren't coming," he says.

I crouch down in front of him, swallowing away my hesitations. At least for now. "Of course I came."

"I have something for you," Jack says. He turns and hurries over to a table next to the back wall of the school. There's one lone gift bag still sitting on the far corner.

He carries it over, gripping the handle with both hands, his face serious. The sight tugs at my heart. This kid deserves a dad. He deserves everything.

I sink onto my heels when he reaches me.

"Open it," Jack says.

I dig through the tissue paper and pull out the ugliest mug I have ever seen. It's obviously handmade and hand painted, and I love it with my whole soul. "This is pretty amazing," I say.

"I painted it like an apple tree," he says.

And then I see it. The globs of red dotting a green background, a rim of brown circling the bottom of the cup. "I can see that. I really love it, Jack."

"K. I'm gonna go play."

He takes off for the swings, and I lower the mug back into the bag.

I *do* love the mug.

I just don't know if I deserve it.

I drop onto a bench at the back of the playground. A few dads are still standing around, talking, watching as the kids play. I'm ready to leave, but I'm also afraid to go before everyone else does. Will it make me look selfish? Lazy?

I don't know what I expected this morning to be like. How I expected things to go. But I didn't expect to feel so defeated. I didn't expect to be so *bad* at this.

I'm going to sound very arrogant for saying this, but I'm not generally bad at anything. I do things right, and I do things well.

Except for my marriage. I don't think I did anything right when it came to that particular relationship. So maybe it's just people I'm bad at. *Relationships.*

"Perry!" Jack comes barreling into my leg, tears streaming down his face. "It's my turn on the swings, and Grant says it's his turn, but he's already had a turn to one hundred, and he won't get off. And we have to go inside soon because Ms. Kennedy just gave us a five-minute warning, and I'm not going to get my turn."

He looks at me, eyes expectant. Like this is a problem I should know how to solve. "Um, can you just find something else to do? Go down the slide or something?"

Jack's lip quivers. "I don't want to slide. I want to swing."

"And you're sure Grant's turn is up?"

He nods.

A thought pops into my head, and I reach for my wallet and pull out a five-dollar bill. "Here," I say, handing the money to Jack. "Tell Grant he can have five bucks if he gets off the swing now."

Jack's face lights up. "Awesome!" He grabs the money and runs back to the swings where he offers it to Grant. Grant immediately hops off the swing and takes the money.

Jack jumps into the swing and starts pumping his little legs back and forth. When he looks up and catches my eye, he gives me a big thumbs up, his toothy grin reaching me all the way across the playground.

Somewhere in the back of my mind, I'm guessing bribery probably isn't an acceptable parenting strategy. But I'm out of my depth here.

A few more minutes pass before Jack's teacher claps her hands and calls the kids back to the classroom. Jack waves as he lines up, sending me another big grin, but then my eye catches on Grant, the swing thief, who is showing the money to his teacher.

Uh oh.

She calls Jack over who, of course, turns and points at me. Ms. Kennedy is frowning as she leaves her class with another teacher and walks toward me. There's a gate out to the parking lot right behind me. I half consider making a break for it. It's been a very long time since I've been scolded by a teacher. With the mood I'm in, I'm not sure I'm up for the experience now.

"Hello," she says primly, stopping right in front of me. "I'm Ms. Kennedy, Jack's teacher."

I nod. "Nice to meet you."

"You're a friend of the family?"

She has to know I'm not Jack's actual father, and for the purposes of this conversation, I'm okay with us leaving it at that.

I nod. "Something like that."

"Yes, well, I am glad that you came to be with us today, but we don't generally condone bribes as a way to motivate children to behave." She holds out the five-dollar bill. "I think this belongs to you."

I clear my throat and take the money. "Yeah. Sorry about that. Jack put me on the spot. I wasn't sure how else to respond."

"An honest mistake," she says gently. "I always tell parents success with children is about steady, consistent discipline." She eyes me, her gaze catching on the bottom half of my pant leg where the syrup is still clinging to my skin. "But don't worry too much about it. Everyone has a bad day every once in a while."

She turns to leave, but then stops and looks at me over her shoulder. "It took me a moment to figure it out, but you look just like that actor. Flint Hawthorne. Has anyone ever told you that before?"

I force a smile. "A few times."

I head back to my car, Jack's apple tree mug in hand, feeling more dejected than I have in a long time.

Jack needs steady, constant discipline? Do I even know what that means? I couldn't even make it through a pancake breakfast line without falling apart. I gave him *money* to bribe a kid into giving him what he wanted. That's not even behavior I would condone in adults.

But hey! At least I look just like my super famous, successful, little brother.

I drive back to Lila's overwhelmed and frustrated. And *confused.*

I thought I could do this. That I could step up and be a dad to Jack. But now I'm not so sure.

I sit in Lila's driveway a long moment before slowly heading to her door. I'd hoped I could spend a few hours with her before heading back to Silver Creek, but I'm feeling a need to lick my wounds in private.

She swings the door open, her expression hopeful. "Hey! How did it go?"

I force a smile I hope she can't see through. I can't explain. Not yet. Not now. "Great. Great. I think Jack had a good time."

She narrows her eyes, too perceptive. "And you?"

I nod, focusing on the one part of the day I can call a win. "He made me a really cool apple tree mug."

"I'm sure it's amazing. But tell me how you're *really* feeling right now."

I sigh and run a hand through my hair. "I uh, well. I have syrup in my shoes, so that feels awesome. And you maybe need to have a conversation with Jack about twerking?"

Her eyes widen. "He was twerking?"

"No! Not him. He just heard about it on the radio and asked what it was."

She presses a palm to her chest. "Oh. Phew. That I can handle." Her eyes drop to my shoes. "How did you get syrup in your shoes?" She pushes the door open. "You want to come inside? I can help you clean up."

I grimace. I have to get out of here before she can pull me in and make me forget how I'm feeling. "Actually, I've got to get back to the farm. Something came up."

"Oh. Okay. Something I can help with?"

Of course she would ask. She works for me. It's her job to know about things at the farm. "Nah. Just need to touch base with my dad before the pest control people visit this afternoon." It's not quite a lie. I *do* need to touch base with Dad before this afternoon; I just don't need three hours to do it.

I step forward and give Lila a quick kiss on the cheek. "I don't know if you were planning on working today but take the rest of the day off. I'll call you later?"

She nods, but I don't miss the disappointment flashing in her eyes.

It can only be a direct reflection of the disappointment flashing in mine.

Chapter Twenty-Five

Lila

TAKE THE REST OF the day off.

Is the man crazy?

Does he think that's actually going to make my day easier?

Something went down at that breakfast, and I need to know what it is.

But Perry clearly isn't ready to talk about it. Or talk about anything, apparently. Because he hightailed it out of my driveway like he was running from the police.

Or just running from me.

The thought makes me sick. The entire time he was gone, I was practicing an *I love you* speech. And now this?

I can't stop myself from imagining the worst. Maybe I really was being too optimistic. Maybe he really *is* too good to be true.

I get to Jack's bus stop fifteen minutes early, which does not make the time go by faster. After I use up all my Candy Crush lives, I start pacing, walking up and down the sidewalk.

Could Jack have said something that offended Perry? Not likely. The man is intelligent enough not to take anything a five-year-old says seriously.

Could someone else have upset him? A dad? A teacher? Or maybe he just had a really bad time and decided he doesn't want to be a part of Jack's life after all?

"Oh, this is stupid," I say out loud, pulling my phone out of my back pocket. I pull up Perry's number and call him before I can overthink it.

After five rings, the call goes to Perry's voicemail. But then, it's three o'clock. He's probably still out in the orchard with the pest control people.

Or he's ignoring me.

I'd much rather believe it's the pest control meeting, so I'm going with that.

"A perfectly reasonable explanation for not answering my call," I say out loud.

My heart starts to race as Jack's bus pulls up. Will he look sad? Disappointed?

But Jack tumbles off the bus all smiles. His tie is crooked, and there's definitely a syrup stain down the front of his shirt, but otherwise, he looks unscathed.

"Hey!" I say, pulling him into a hug. "How was your day? How was the breakfast?"

"Good," he says simply.

Good? That's all I get?

"Did you have fun with Perry?"

"He didn't know I don't like butter on my pancakes."

"Well, that's okay. He wouldn't know since he's never had pancakes with you before."

"Yeah, another kid's dad had to help him. But then we sang our songs, and my class went to the playground. And Perry gave me five dollars to give to Grant so Grant would get off the swing. But then Ms. Kennedy made Grant give it back, and she gave it back to Perry."

"Perry gave you money?" Oh, the poor man. Solving playground fights on his first day of solo parenting? He was probably so overwhelmed.

"And it worked, too. It was stupid Ms. Kennedy's fault that Grant didn't get to keep the money. And then he was mad at me because he had to give it back."

"Don't call your teacher stupid, Jack."

"Sorry. But I still think it's dumb she wouldn't let Grant keep the money."

"I can see how you might feel that way. But what would it teach Grant to get money when someone wants him to do something? When we're sharing, taking turns, we do it because it's the right thing to do, not because we're getting paid to do it." I reach down and pat his little chest. "We do what feels right in here. In our hearts."

He nods as he drags his backpack up the front steps. "Do you think Perry is going to move in with us soon? Chloe says I can't start calling him Daddy until he moves in."

I pause at the bottom of the steps, a hand pressed to my heart, and do my best to fend off the worry his question ushers in. "I don't know, sweetie. We're still getting to know Perry. And these things take—"

"Time," he says with a huff, cutting me off. "But how much?" He drops his backpack on the floor inside the entryway and starts to tug at his tie.

I pull him closer, loosening the knot so we can slip it over his head.

"Like a week? Or twenty days?"

"I'm not sure there's a specific number, kiddo. We just have to see how things go. What if we invite Perry over to watch a movie with us tomorrow night? Would you like that?"

He nods. "Can we watch *Coco*?"

"We sure can."

This seems to appease Jack, at least temporarily. But it does nothing to make *me* feel better.

What if Perry won't come? What if he doesn't respond? I definitely need a few of the holes in Jack's story about the breakfast filled in, but it doesn't sound like it went all that terribly.

I fix Jack a snack, then turn on some cartoons for him while I try to reach Perry one more time. I text this time, though his meeting should long be over by now.

Lila: Hey. Jack is home and says he had a great time. Thanks again for taking him. Was thinking you might want to come watch a movie with us tomorrow night. Double feature? One with Jack, then one without?

I'm making dinner when Perry finally responds.

Perry: Glad he had fun. Thanks for the invite, but I don't think I can make it. I'm doing a thing with my brothers.

A thing? That feels vague. Is he blowing me off?

I know I've only known Perry Hawthorne for a few months, but he is not the sort of man to blow someone off.

Except, he *did* blow off his ex-wife when she was trying to get him to RSVP to the reunion.

Fear grips my gut, but I will it away. That was different. Jocelyn was hounding him. Pestering him. Making him feel horrible about himself.

I haven't done any of those things.

I think myself in circles all the way through dinner and Jack's bedtime. I haven't texted Perry back, and he hasn't texted me either. So, do we just leave things like this? Is he expecting me to show up to work tomorrow? Work virtually from home? Take another day off?

A part of me wants to feel angry. Why isn't he responding to me? Talking to me about the morning he spent with my kid? But a bigger part of me is just straight up worried.

I need to see him. Talk to him.

And I need to do it face to face.

Rebecca the babysitter, bless her, is at my house by nine, a stack of homework to keep her busy.

'Thanks so much for coming last minute," I say. "He's totally zonked, so you shouldn't hear a peep from him."

"Sounds good! Take your time. I've got enough homework to keep me busy till midnight."

A quick text to Olivia from my driveway gives me Perry's home address. I've never actually seen his house, but I'm too stressed to be curious.

I just want to see him.

Make sure he's okay.

Make sure *we're* okay.

As I drive down the mountain, all I can think is that the only thing worse than a breakup conversation with a man I think I'm in love with would be having to explain that breakup to Jack.

Chapter Twenty-Six

Lila

Perry's place is more cottage than house, nestled into the woods at the end of a narrow, paved road. There are flowers on his porch and ivy climbing up a trellis toward the second floor, and a birdhouse sign bearing the house number and the words "Home, Sweet Home" next to the front door.

I can't be in the right place. Nothing about this house says Perry. Not even a little bit.

I pull out my phone and double check the address Olivia sent over. The house numbers match, but could I be on the wrong road? I send Olivia a quick follow-up.

Lila: Are you sure you gave me the correct address?

Olivia: It's right. He's renting. Saving up to buy a place.

I think of what Perry told me about Jocelyn gutting him in their divorce, and my heart squeezes.

Sliding my phone back into my pocket, I step up to the door and knock.

I hear movement inside, but no one answers, so I try again. If he doesn't come this time, I'll text him and tell him I'm standing on his porch, and I'm not leaving until he comes out to talk to me.

I channel the frustration I felt this morning when he brought the car back and then hightailed it out of town. I think of the moment before he left for the breakfast, the way he touched me, *promised* me.

I think of how much I wanted to tell him I love him.

And *now* he thinks he can ignore me?

I pound on the door a third time, this time like I really mean it.

Finally, the door swings open. "Brody, seriously, I'm not in the mood to—"

I jump back at his tone—grumpy Perry is definitely back—and press a hand to my chest.

"Lila."

"Geez, Perry. You scared me."

"I thought you were Brody."

"I gathered."

"Sorry. I'm sorry I scared you. I didn't—I wasn't expecting you."

I shrug. "You know what Kate said about what happens when you go dark for a couple hours. Someone's liable to show up on your porch."

He lets out a little huff of laughter. "I guess I should have seen that coming."

Perry is wearing jeans and a gray t-shirt, and his feet are bare, and he is so achingly handsome, I almost want to forget why I drove all the way over here and throw myself into his arms. "Can I come in?"

He nods and pushes the door open, and I cross through the entryway into the living room.

The inside of Perry's house is more the house I expected to find. Simple, modern furniture. Clean lines. It has the same elegance of his office, and I recognize how easily I could feel at home here, even if it isn't exactly his house.

"I texted Olivia to get your address. I hope that's okay."

Perry runs a hand through his hair. "Of course. I guess it's weird you haven't been here yet, but . . ." He holds his hands out the slightest bit. "This is it."

"When I pulled up, I thought I'd found the wrong place. The outside looks like a gingerbread house."

This makes him smile the tiniest bit, and the tension around my heart eases. Still, it would ease more if I could go to him. Feel his arms around me. Take whatever is making him distant and throw it out the window.

"Can I get you anything? Something to drink?" he asks.

I shake my head no. "I'm okay."

"Do you want to sit?"

This is stupid. We both know I didn't come over here to sit and chat. He just needs to talk to me. "Perry, can you please tell me what happened this morning? I know something happened. You got so quiet, and then you gave me a lame excuse about going back to the farm, and I can just tell something's wrong. I've been worried about you all day."

Perry's gaze drops to the floor, his hands propped on his hips. "I don't know what you want me to say," he finally says.

"Start with the breakfast."

He looks up but doesn't move closer. "What did Jack tell you?"

"Bits and pieces? Something about butter on his pancakes and bribing a kid on the playground? I'd love to hear your version though."

He scoffs. "No, that about sums it up."

"Perry, come on. What's going on?"

He's quiet for so long, I almost wonder if he's forgotten I'm here. He's turned away from me now, his arms over his head and gripping the top of the door frame leading into what looks like his bedroom. It's not a bad view, what with the way his muscles are bunching under his shirt, but I'm too distracted to enjoy it for long.

Finally, Perry turns around. "Lila, I'm not sure I can do this."

I close my eyes and press my palms flat against my legs, forcing air into my lungs and out again. I'm suddenly afraid I might actually *stop* breathing if I don't think about doing it. "I think I need you to explain a little more than that," I say simply.

And then Perry is across from me, sitting on the ottoman, his expression serious. "It was awful. *I* was awful. We got there late because all the empty parking spaces were on the street and that felt too dangerous for Jack. And then I forgot to get him silverware and milk, and I buttered his pancakes, and I got syrup in my shoe, and I didn't know who his teacher was and had to wait in line with all the deadbeat dads who didn't know so I could ask the admin lady where to find him. And then a kid was bullying him on the playground, and I didn't know how to help. I didn't know how to stop it from happening."

He stands up and starts pacing around the room. "Jack needs steady, consistent discipline, Lila, and I don't know anything about how to provide that. How can I discipline a kid if I can't even stay married?"

Okay. So there's a lot to unpack here. But first of all, Jack needs steady, consistent discipline? I'm guessing that isn't something Perry came up with on his own.

"Were you talking to someone about Jack's discipline?" I ask, already feeling defensive.

"Only Ms. Kennedy. When she scolded me for suggesting Jack bribe a kid to give up his swing."

That explains *that,* at least. That's one of Ms. Kennedy's favorite lines.

"Perry, I'm sure it wasn't that bad. Today was the first time you've ever been alone with Jack. You can't expect to know how to do everything on day one."

He drops back onto the couch. "The dads at our table were talking about how they never get to have sex. Or even just be alone with their wives. And the busy schedules. And weird food things. Like kids who won't eat cheese, even on pizza."

"Yeah, some kids are like that. Usually they grow out of it."

"See?" Perry says, holding up a hand as if to emphasize his point. "You know that because you're a mom. But I'm not a dad, Lila. I don't know anything."

I have had enough freak-outs as a parent, positive I have done and will probably *keep* doing everything wrong, to recognize one when I see one. On the one hand, it means Perry cares. He doesn't want to disappoint Jack, or me, and that matters.

On the other, I *can't* decide that I don't want to try. That being a parent is too hard. Jack is mine, for better or worse, which means I have to keep muddling through, doing the best I can.

But Perry *can* choose. And that's the thought that has nerves swirling in my gut and a thin sheen of sweat breaking out across my lower back.

"Do you know what Jack asked me when he got off the bus this afternoon?"

Perry is leaning forward, his elbows propped up on his knees. I hate how achingly handsome he is right now, tension tightening all the angles of his body. He lifts his eyes to meet mine.

"He asked when you were moving in. If he could start calling you Daddy."

Perry scoffs. "I don't know why you think that's supposed to make me feel better."

I scoot closer and slip a hand onto his leg. "Because, Perry, ninety percent of the stuff you think you screwed up today, Jack didn't even notice. He had a great time. And the other ten percent? I mean, welcome to the club. I've made a million bad calls. And I'll probably make a million more. No parent knows what they're doing all the time."

"Then how do you make it look so easy?"

"You've only spent one evening with Jack and me. I promise. I have my moments." Even as I say the words meant to reassure Perry, I wonder if they'll have the opposite effect and scare him away even more. I also realize with utter certainty that I never should have allowed Perry to take Jack to the breakfast in the first place. Talk about throwing someone into the deep end. Navigating the school—why didn't I tell Perry who Jack's teacher is?—handling a buffet line in an elementary cafeteria. Those school events can be a challenge for anyone.

It was too much, too soon, and that's on me.

I open my mouth to say so, but before I can, Perry says, "When people fall in love, Lila, they get to date. Get to know one another. Build a life together. *Then* they have kids. They ease into it."

Anger flares in my chest. "Yeah, I know. I already did that once," I say sharply. "So you're saying single parents—they only get the one chance at happiness, and then they're done? Alone for the rest of their lives?"

"That's not what I mean. But maybe you date *other* single parents, who already know—"

"Oh my word," I say, standing up. "Do you even hear yourself right now? Perry, you *knew* about Jack from minute one of our relationship. I never hid him from you."

"I know that. *I know.*" He runs his hands through his hair and stands up. "Gah, I'm doing this badly." His broad shoulders drop, his head shaking like all the fight has drained out of him. "I just wish we could go back to when it was just the two of us."

Tears pool in my eyes, and I look up, willing them to stay where they are until I get in the car and cry without this idiot man watching me.

"But it isn't just the two of us," I say. "It never has been." I walk toward the door. "But I hear you loud and clear, Perry. That's too much for you. And I guess it's better we figure that out now than later."

I make it all the way to the front door before Perry calls me back. "Lila, wait."

I turn around, and he rushes toward me, grabbing me by the elbows, his expression pained. "I'm not saying I don't want this. That I don't want *you.*" He pulls me against his chest, and for a selfish moment, I let him. Feel his arms slide around me, lean into the solid warmth of his body.

But I can't. *I won't.* My heart can't take this for too much longer.

I press my palms against his chest and push away. "Perry, I love you. I was ready to tell you that after the breakfast. I practiced how I was going to say it all morning." Something flashes in his eyes when I say the words, but he doesn't say them back. And maybe it's better that way. "*I love you.* But you don't get me without Jack. We're a package deal."

"I know that. *Of course* I know that," he says softly. "But what if I can't do it?"

"What if you can't do it?" I ask. "Or what if you can't do it *perfectly*?"

"You deserve perfect," he says, frustration in his tone. "Jack deserves perfect."

"Wasn't it you this morning who told me our flaws make us real? I don't want perfect, Perry. I just want you."

I lean up and press my lips to his, and he cradles my face in his hands, kissing me with a fervency that only makes the tears fall faster.

It could be a kiss that says I love you.

It could also be a kiss that says goodbye.

I break away and back up until I'm pressed against his front door. He's said too many hard things tonight for me not to be crystal clear.

"I know it's a lot," I say. "Asking you to be a part of Jack's life is a big deal. I won't try to convince you, no matter how much I want to, because it has to be your choice. But I do want you to make that choice with all of the facts." I wipe my tears away with the heel of my hand. "Perry, I love you. And I promise you, if given the chance, I will spend the rest of my life loving you like you deserve." Even just saying the words out loud—owning them—makes me feel steadier on my feet.

"Jack has a soccer game on Saturday morning," I continue. "Ten a.m., at Fletcher Park. His team wears light blue. I can't compromise when it comes to Jack, so if you're in, you have to be all in. Take a couple of days to think about it. If you come to the game, I'll know you want to try." I take a steadying breath.

"If you don't? Then I'll understand where you are and what you want. And I won't be at work on Monday morning."

His eyes lift to mine like this last part surprises him.

I shrug. "I can't be in love with you and still work for you. Not if you can't love me back. Love *us* back." I lean up and kiss him on the cheek. "Goodbye, Perry."

As I walk out to my car, fresh tears streaming down my face, I can only hope it isn't goodbye forever.

Chapter Twenty-Seven

Perry

"LET ME GET THIS straight," Brody says, leaning forward. "She told you she wanted to spend the rest of her life loving you like you deserve, and you let her walk away?"

I drop my empty glass onto the bar in Lennox's restaurant. "It's not that easy." It's late enough that Hawthorne is mostly empty. Brody and I are the only two people at the bar. Another half hour or so, and Lennox should be able to join us. Which means I'll get to hear it from TWO brothers instead of one.

Tyler drops onto the barstool on the other side of Brody. "Sorry I'm late. Did I miss it? Did you convince him?"

Oh great. Make that two brothers *and* a brother-in-law.

"Seriously? You're ganging up on me now?" I say, eyeing Brody.

He shrugs. "Tyler's the only one of us with a kid. His opinion holds more weight."

"His kid is only five minutes old," I argue. "It's not the same thing."

"He's almost three months old, actually, but—" I shoot Tyler a look that immediately silences him. "You know what, I can just sit here and listen. Without talking."

"I still say you're overcomplicating things," Brody says. "She told you she loves you. Just say you love her too, kiss her like you mean it, then ride off into the sunset."

I roll my eyes. "And I say you're oversimplifying things. Don't forget. Before we can ride off into the sunset, we have to stop and pick her kid up from the babysitter."

Brody doesn't respond, which is almost worse. I'd rather he scold me. Insult me. *Something.* Anything would feel better than my own incriminating thoughts and a silence heavy with his judgment.

"That kind of attitude doesn't look good on you, man," he finally says. "I don't understand. You've always wanted kids. Are you really willing to let a woman like Lila get away because she already has one? Are you weirded out that he isn't yours? Is that what this is?"

"That's not it," I say quickly. "I don't care about that."

"Then what is it?"

I twist my empty glass in a slow circle as I think about how best to explain. I've been thinking since Lila left my house last night. Thinking so hard that I stayed home from work—something I haven't done in years—and didn't leave my house until Brody showed up and strong-armed me into coming down to Hawthorne. All that thinking, and I still don't feel any closer to an answer.

"Lila makes me feel like living," I finally say. "I don't even know if that makes sense. But when I look at her, everything is brighter somehow. It just feels right. I've never felt that rightness. Like my body, all the way down to the cellular level, knows we're supposed to be together." I look up. "Is that how you always felt with Kate?"

Brody smiles and drops a hand on my shoulder. "From the very beginning."

I shake my head. "I don't know how you did this for so many years." Brody was in love with his now-wife for a very long time before she moved him out of the friend zone. I'm not sure most men would have been so persistent.

"Love can make you do crazy things, man."

The bartender comes over and offers me another drink, but I slide her my empty glass and decline.

"So, if we've established you want to be with her, we're back to Jack," Brody says.

"Not just Jack. I think I'm afraid that if I have to love them both, I won't be able to love Lila like I should. With Jocelyn, I did everything I could think of to try and make her happy. And it was never enough. Now I have to make two people happy? What if I can't do it? What if Lila winds up miserable just like Jocelyn was?"

"Hold up," Brody says. "Your relationship with Lila is nothing like your relationship with Jocelyn. Is that seriously what you're scared about? That you might fail *Lila*?" He runs a hand across his face. "Man, your ex-wife really did a number on you." He takes me by the shoulders and turns me to fully face him. "Listen to me, all right? What you have with Lila is so much more than what you had with Jocelyn. We all saw that after five minutes of watching the two of you in the same room."

"Everyone who saw you making out all over the orchard would agree," Tyler unhelpfully adds.

"Jocelyn made you miserable, Perry," Brody says. "You know she did. This is different. You have to trust that this is different."

Lennox drops onto the barstool on the opposite side of me. "What's different? Who's different?"

"Lila is different from Jocelyn," Brody says.

Lennox scoffs. "You can say that again. Why are we talking about *her*?"

"I only brought her up as a comparison. Perry has until tomorrow at ten a.m. to decide if he loves Lila enough to become her baby's daddy."

"An ultimatum? Way to boss the boss, Lila," Lennox says. "I should bake her another box of cookies."

"That's not—" My words cut off. Lila didn't mean to give me an ultimatum, but it feels like one anyway. And it should feel like one. I can't play around with her feelings. Or with Jack's.

"I don't understand the hold up," Lennox says. "Are you in love with her?"

"Yes," I say, admitting it out loud for the first time. "Yeah. I am."

Lennox takes a swig of the drink the bartender slides in front of him. "Then what's the problem?"

"He wants to be *enough* for her," Brody says knowingly.

"And Jack," I say. "I want to be enough for both of them."

"And he isn't sure he can be because he wasn't enough for Jocelyn," Brody finishes.

It's painful to hear my brother distill the doubts and hang-ups I've been struggling with for years into one very concise sentence.

But then Lennox shakes his head. "Nah. This isn't about Jocelyn. I mean, she's a piece of work, but right now, this is all about you." He looks me head on, and something deep in my gut shifts, like I know before he even says it that what Lennox is saying is true. "Jocelyn had high expectations, sure. But the only person who has ever expected you to be perfect is *you*. And I'm willing to bet that isn't at all what Lila expects."

The words Lila promised me last night float into my mind. *I don't want you to be perfect, Perry. I just want you.*

"Can I say something?" Tyler says.

We all turn to face him, but he keeps his gaze focused on me. "I know I've only been a father for five minutes, but I do know a little about feeling inadequate. Honestly, I don't know how *anyone* could look at Asher, knowing you have to raise him and teach him everything he's supposed to know about life, without feeling inadequate. But honestly, what's the alternative? If I don't want to fail him, the very best thing I can do is be here."

"But it's not the same thing. Asher is your son."

The words feel flimsy on my tongue. Jack could be my son if I wanted him to be.

Tyler shrugs. "Okay. Then walk away."

I'm already shaking my head. "I don't want to walk away."

I understand what he's doing. The reverse psychology he's pulling on me.

"Why not?" Brody asks, leaning into Tyler's point.

Lennox nods. "Face it. You're already invested, man. You're too far in."

So far, I haven't framed it this way. I've thought about how overwhelming it might be if I stay and commit. I haven't really considered the bleakness of what it would feel like if I didn't. And not just because I'd be walking away from Lila. I'd be walking away from *Jack,* too.

Shock roils through me.

I haven't spent enough time with Jack to love him in the same way I do his mom. But he belongs to Lila. He's a part of her.

Which means, he's a part of me now, too.

I think of the apple tree mug sitting on the kitchen counter back at the house, and the way Jack so easily announced over his pancakes that I was his stairdad. My heart pulls and stretches, and I lift a hand to my chest, rubbing the spot.

"Let go of your doubts, man," Brody says. "Just go for it. Trust that love is enough. That you are enough."

Lennox coughs loudly, the noise shifting into what sounds a little too much like a chicken. Then he makes the sound again. "Bwak, bwak, bwak."

Is he actually making chicken noises at me? Are we in the third grade?

"Bwak, bwak," he whispers.

Brody and Tyler join Lennox's chorus, their arms flapping like tiny wings. "Bwak, bwak, bwak."

I stand up from the bar. "Okay. That's my cue to leave."

Their chicken noises follow me all the way to the door.

"You're all idiots," I call back to them just before pushing my way outside.

"You're welcome," they call back in weirdly synchronized unison.

As I drive home, a new sort of peace settles over me. Idiots or not, my brothers are right. I *am* too invested. I don't want to fail. But walking away would be the biggest failure of all.

Which means I have to figure out how to swallow my doubts and dive in.

And then get myself to a soccer game first thing tomorrow.

Cabbages.

I can't believe CABBAGES are going to make me miss my chance with Lila and Jack.

An entire semi of them, turned over on I-26 and blocking both lanes of northbound traffic.

I'm only a mile outside of Silver Creek, at a standstill because of *cabbage.*

I glance at my watch. It's been twenty minutes already, and I haven't moved an inch.

A pang of sympathy runs through me. That's somebody's harvest on that truck, representing months of work down the drain. But my *life* is going to be down the drain if I can't figure out how to get around this mess.

When an errant cabbage bounces past my window, I give up and call my brother.

"Hey, are you busy?" I ask as soon as Brody answers.

"No, but shouldn't *you* be busy?"

"I'm on my way to the game, but I need you to come pick me up. I'm on the interstate, and there are cabbages everywhere. Traffic is blocked."

"Did you just say cabbages?"

"Details aren't important, man," I say. "The clock is ticking. Can you come?"

"You're just going to leave your truck?" Brody asks.

"Yes! I'll come back for it. This is more important."

"All right. I'm on my way. Where can I meet you?"

"Just go to the Silver Creek exit on I-26," I say, already pulling over onto the uncomfortably narrow shoulder. I park and unbuckle my seatbelt. "But don't get on the highway. We'll have to take 176 into Hendersonville."

"Got it," Brody says. "I'll be there in ten."

I climb out of my truck, lock it, say a little prayer for its safety, and then I start to run.

Brody is already waiting at the shoulder when I make it to the top of the on-ramp. His double cab truck is easy to spot because it almost always has his bright red kayak loaded into the back. As I approach, Kate jumps out of the front seat and climbs into the back, where it looks like several other family members are already crammed inside.

So this is going to be a family affair. *Fantastic.*

"This is so exciting!" she says, squeezing my arm as she passes me.

"For real, cabbages?" Lennox says from the back as I climb in.

Olivia leans forward. "And you said the entire highway is blocked?"

"Seriously?" I say to Brody. "You all had to come?"

"We're happy for you," Olivia says. "Plus, the most exciting thing I've done in the past two months is pump seven ounces out of each boob in one sitting. I need more adventure in my life."

"Too much information, Liv," Lennox says.

"You just don't like it when I say boob."

"Because you're my little sister. You aren't supposed to have boobs, let alone talk about them."

"So the boobs are a problem, but the baby isn't? Got it. Very mature of you, Len. I suppose you think I found Asher in a cabbage patch."

"Speaking of cabbages," Kate says, her voice rising enough to calm the bickering between Lennox and Olivia. "Were there really cabbages blocking the entire highway?"

"Piles of them," I say. "Here, give me your phone." I hold my hand out to Brody. "I'll plug in the address of the park."

He hands it over. "We were at Olivia's visiting Asher when you called. Then Lennox showed up, and they all wanted to come. Sorry if it's overwhelming."

I wave a hand dismissively. What's overwhelming is realizing that even if we hit every green light between here and the soccer field, I'm not going to make it on time.

"At least I left Asher with Tyler and Mom," Olivia says. "Can you imagine if we had a baby with us too?"

I run a hand across my face. This isn't at all how my morning was supposed to go.

"Hey," Brody says. "She's going to understand. You're trying. You'll get there."

I shake my head. "I wanted to be there when the game *starts.* If I'm not there, she's going to think—"

"Hey," Lennox says. "Let go of the *perfect* idea you have in your head and just roll with it. This is going to work out. Lila loves you. She's going to understand an overturned semi full of cabbages."

I nod. He's right. Of course he's right.

"Just call her," Kate says. "Or text, at least. If you don't want her to worry, let her know you're on your way."

I nod and quickly pull out my phone. I wanted to be there. To show up next to her, hold her hand while we cheer for Jack together. But there's no way I'm making it in time.

Lila doesn't pick up, so instead of leaving her a voicemail, I end the call and send her a text.

Perry: I'm coming, Lila. Don't give up on me. I'm coming.

Chapter Twenty-Eight

Lila

I WILL KEEP MY eyes on the field. I will keep my eyes on the field. I will keep my eyes on the field.

In the ten minutes that Jack is warming up, it takes all my effort not to constantly turn and scan the parking lot behind me.

Will he come?

Does he love me enough to come?

It's been a long thirty-six hours since I gave Perry an ultimatum, but I don't have any regrets. We can slow down, ease into him spending time with Jack when the three of us are together, but we can't go backwards. If he wants me, he has to want us both.

Jack waves at me from the field as the referees blow the starting whistle.

Perry isn't here.

The game is starting, and Perry isn't here.

I itch to check my phone, see if I've missed something, but I accidentally left it in the car, and now that the game has started, I don't want to go back for it for fear I'll miss something.

I *could* go back for it. If I run, maybe?

But then Jack has the ball, and he's taking off down the field, and I have to keep my eyes on my boy. What could my phone possibly tell me anyway? Perry is either here, or he isn't.

And he isn't.

When we break for halftime, I decide to leave my phone in the car. At this point, I don't even want to see any explanation Perry might have sent for why he isn't here. Better I focus on Jack. Enjoy the game. Still, in the back of my mind, I keep hoping. Keep imagining that at any moment, he'll show up.

My hope doesn't fully flicker out until the last few minutes of the second half. Jack has done great. He scored a goal, which, considering we started the season just hoping he wouldn't trip over his own feet, is pretty impressive.

And I was the only one here to see it.

I didn't tell Jack Perry might come today.

So this burden—this painful disappointment—I will bear on my own. I wipe tears out of my eyes, hoping the other parents think I'm only emotional because my kid is a soccer rockstar and scored a second goal.

At some point, I'm going to have to tell Jack he won't be seeing Perry anymore. Maybe now that he's already had his father-son breakfast, he won't be so consumed with the idea of getting a new dad.

The final whistle blows, and Jack comes running over, all smiles. "Mommy, did you see me score?"

"I did, buddy. You were amazing."

"Hey, good game, Jack," his coach calls.

Jack runs over to the mom handing out snacks and water bottles to all the kids while I gather up my camp chair and the rest of my things. We head back toward the parking lot, my eyes scanning for Perry's truck the whole time. I dig deep for the determination to force them forward, straightening my spine, making my steps intentional as I lead Jack back to the car. I can't keep doing this to myself. I can't keep looking for him.

Perry made his choice.

And it wasn't me.

I unlock the car, helping Jack into his booster seat before hauling my camp chair to the back of my SUV. I drop everything inside and turn and sit on the back bumper. I close my eyes and press my hand to my chest. Here, just for a minute while Jack can't see me, I let myself feel the full weight of my disappointment. The ache is bone deep, the sadness sharpened by the contrast of the bliss I experienced just a few days ago when I still believed Perry was mine.

"Lila!"

I look up.

Perry is running across the parking lot. Not driving. *Running.*

What on earth? My heart lifts at the sight of him, but then I remember our conversation the other night, and uncertainty fills me all over again.

If he wanted to be here, why didn't he come on time? Did he show up late to give me a *thanks, but no thanks?* Then again, he *is* running. Maybe something happened to his truck, and that explains why he's so late?

He stops a few feet away from me and drops his hands onto his knees, his breathing labored. "I'm here," he manages between breaths. "I'm so sorry I'm late, but I'm here."

He's here. Peace settles over my heart. *He's here.*

"Um, did you run the whole way?"

He stands fully upright and holds up a finger, like he's really struggling to catch his breath. I turn back to my car and pull out one of the extra water bottles left over from the last time I had to bring snacks to one of Jack's games. I take a few steps forward and offer it to him. It's mid-November, so the temperatures are in the upper fifties, but he's stripped down to his t-shirt and sweating like he just ran a half-marathon.

Perry grabs the bottle, twisting it open and draining it in a matter of seconds.

"Better?" I say, reaching for the empty bottle.

He nods. "There were cabbages all over the interstate," he says. "So I had Brody come pick me up, and we drove up 176 to get here, but there was a parade happening in Flat Rock and then an accident that stopped traffic, so I just got out and ran."

Oh, my heart. "How many miles?"

He glances at his phone. "Four-ish? I think? I tried to call you."

"I left my phone in my car."

His expression shifts. "So you thought I wasn't coming?"

Tears well in my eyes, and I look away. He's here now. That's all that matters.

"Lila, I love you." He takes a step forward. "I'm so sorry I put you through all this. That I freaked out. You were right about what you said. About me wanting to do it perfectly. But then I realized the thought of walking away from you—and from Jack—it hurt too much. Somehow that kid has worked his way into my heart almost as much as you have."

The words feel too good to be true.

"I don't really know how to be a dad," Perry continues. "And I can't promise I won't screw up. In fact, I should probably promise that I *will* screw it up. But I promise I'll do my best. I won't ever stop trying to be my best for you. And for Jack, too."

I launch myself into his arms, not even caring that he's sweat-damp and smelly. My lips find his as I cradle his face, and he tugs me closer, his hands pressed against my lower back. We kiss until a cheer erupts beside us, and we break apart to see Brody, Kate, Lennox, and Olivia hanging out of the windows of Brody's SUV as they cheer and clap.

"Somehow, it feels very appropriate that your family is a part of this moment," I say.

Perry chuckles. "They'll be a part of everything if we let them. Soccer games. School plays. Birthdays. Random holidays no one really celebrates."

I snuggle a little closer. "As long as we can close the door on our wedding night, I'm in."

"Our wedding night, huh?"

"Oh, come on. You just talked about being Jack's dad. Don't tell me you haven't thought about it."

"I thought about it that first day. When Jack asked if I could be his stairdad, something tugged in my heart. Like a part of me already sensed that's where we were headed."

"How poetic. You were seeing our future while I wanted to crawl under my car and disappear. I was so embarrassed."

Perry grins, so different from the grumpy, frowning man I first started working for. "I was enchanted," he says softly. "Still am."

I kiss him again—because honestly, after that line, how can I not?—not stopping until Jack is out of the car and tugging on our hands. Perry drops down and scoops him up so he's resting in the circle of our arms.

"Hey, Perry," Jack says like it's perfectly normal he's here with us, holding us like we're his family.

"Hey, kiddo," Perry says simply.

"I scored two goals. Did Mommy tell you? I was super-fast."

"I bet you were."

"Do you want to come and watch *Coco* with us tonight?"

Perry looks to me, and I nod my approval of Jack's impromptu plan.

"I'd love to. Think I could bring us a pizza?"

Jack's eyes go wide. "With extra cheese!"

Perry gives me a knowing look. "You have no idea how happy that answer makes me."

I laugh as he leans in to kiss me one more time.

"Hey," Olivia calls from the SUV. "I've got to nurse my kid before next Tuesday. Are you coming back with us?"

Perry holds up a finger, asking them to wait. "I'm going to go get my truck," he says to me. "And take a shower. Then I'll come back. Is that okay?"

I nod. "I would love that." I look at Jack. "*We* would love that."

He kisses the side of my head, then kisses the side of Jack's head before putting Jack down and backing away. "I'll see you tonight?"

I nod, not even attempting to curb my smile. "We'll be waiting."